WAR
IN
SPACE

By the same author:

THE FINAL DECADE

COUNTDOWN TO SPACE WAR
(with Bhupendra Jasani)

WAR IN SPACE

Christopher Lee

HAMISH HAMILTON
LONDON

First published in Great Britain 1986
by Hamish Hamilton Ltd
Garden House, 57–59 Long Acre, London WC2E 9JZ

British Library Cataloguing in Publication Data

Lee, Christopher, *1941–*
War in space.
1. Space warfare
I. Title
358.8 UG1530

ISBN 0-241-11591-4

Typeset by Rowland Phototypesetting Ltd,
Bury St Edmunds, Suffolk
Printed and bound in Great Britain by
Billings and Son, Worcester

CONTENTS

A one-legged pilgrim stood in the yard
with his mouth full of prophesies:
'Beware of terrible times . . . the earth
opening for a crowd of corpses.
Expect famine, earthquakes, plagues,
and heavens darkened by eclipses'

Anna Akhmatova, 'Slepnevo', 20 July, 1914

Headlong themselves they threw
Down from the verge of Heaven, eternal wrath
Burnt after them to the bottomless pit.

John Milton, 'Paradise Lost'.

Chapter 1

Overview

On a clear, blue day, look up and you will see for ever; millions of miles and lightyears of emptiness, until the limits of the imagination close across the greatest adventure of the twentieth century – space. What you may not see is any one of the 7,000 or so satellites and pieces of scientific debris orbiting at high speeds and at altitudes varying from little more than a hundred miles to many thousands. You will not see the Salyut space station manned by Soviet cosmonauts; the Intelligence-gathering craft just a few miles above the earth photographing in astonishing detail the military events in the U.S. and the U.S.S.R.; the discarded nuclear reactor of a Soviet space radar, the wake of a high orbiting oblong box that is watching and waiting for the first signs of a nuclear missile leaving its launch pad in the Soviet Union to attack the missile fields just outside Cheyenne in Wyoming, or the link that would allow the President of the United States to talk to his commanders throughout the world should that, or one of his missiles, ever be launched in anger. Space has become more than a frontier for scientists and technologists; it has become a crucial part of the East–West military balance.

Should the superpowers go to war, it would seem inevitable that war would begin in space. It would not end there. Worse still, it could be the catalyst for nuclear war on earth.

Today, almost every area of superpower military planning and execution relies heavily on space-based systems. Every aspect of warfare from strategic targeting of intercontinental nuclear missiles, down to covert operations by special forces such as Britain's S.A.S., or the Soviet Union's Spetsnaz, has an essential space link. Targets are surveyed, armies located, missiles counted and units are identified by low flying photo-reconnaissance satellites. (For example, Soviet satellites identified the elements of the British Falklands Task Force as they left harbour in 1982.[1]) Signals are intercepted by electronic Intelligence space craft known as ferrets. Nuclear submarines moving into missile firing positions check their exact locations by constellations of artificial navigation stars. A single soldier in the Falklands communicates with his base eight thousand miles away by tuning to a satellite loitering thousands of miles above the equator. A cruise missile is fed a route map of the journey from the Wiltshire countryside in England to a target outside Moscow; the map is from data supplied by a satellite. A Commander-in-Chief holds a four-way conversation with ground, sea and air units thousands of miles apart by bouncing his voice off a high orbiting satellite. At the height of a tense diplomatic incident the leaders of the Soviet Union and the United States attempt to soothe each other's fears by using the 'Hot Line', their signals going via satellite. Silently, the unblinking eye of a small space craft watches over the nuclear missile silos for the first sign that the 'Hot Line' reassurances have proved false.

Space is now dominated by the needs of the military. Space technology has promised to give the solution to so many of the traditional problems of the military commander that governments have had no option but to press onwards and upwards, until today it can be shown that about three-quarters of all satellites are used by the military. Space is now the eyes, ears and the voice of the modern military commander. Yet this is but the beginning.

Every day of the year, special aircraft fly zig-zag courses across the United States, others remain on standby in the Soviet Union. These are flying command posts. On board are generals who would hope to avoid the consequences of a surprise attack and be in a position to take over command of any war. Plans are now beyond the fantasy stage, for those same commanders to go into space, to be able to direct a battle if needs be from the vantage point provided by the new military environment even though they would be vulnerable to attack by new techniques developed by the superpowers. In America, a 'super shuttle' has been

[1] See Chapter 10.

designed that could take off like a conventional plane, fly to a high altitude and then, if necessary, boost itself into orbit – on board would be the Commander-in-Chief, the President.

Moreover, this spreading technology is moving towards the radical alteration of whole philosophies on how a nation might defend itself. The Americans and the Russians have both worked for some time on the idea of producing 'fast thinking' beam weapons to counter ballistic missiles. Whatever the rights and wrongs of the so-called Star Wars, Strategic Defence Initiative (it is not clear what the Russians have called their 'SDI' programme), it represents a belief that technology has advanced sufficiently to produce a limited, if not extensive, ballistic missile defence system. If it is possible to exploit that technology, then over a period of years strategic military thinking could shift from a potentially offensive nature to a purely defensive philosophy. (However this strategic debate concerns only the superpowers. When it comes to thinking about states outside the superpower blocs, then the U.S.A. and the U.S.S.R. must continue to base defence planning on traditionally offensive systems. Accordingly, in this respect alone, SDI cannot be seen as a farewell to offensive arms.) That is the thinking of many in Washington and a few in Moscow. It does not mean that ballistic missiles will disappear as some have suggested; it does mean that there will have to be more active consideration given to the principle that national security could be based upon thick castle walls and moats rather than on waves of bows and arrows. In other words: a move away from the present philosophy which states that as long as both superpowers remain vulnerable, then neither side is likely to attack because of the risk of unacceptable retaliation. The reason that some Americans, including the Reagan camp, believe this possible, is the advance in space technology.

The early thoughts about ballistic missile defence centred on the impossible task of trying to knock out *all* incoming missiles as they approached the target. Modern thinking is based on the idea that *many* missiles can be stopped shortly after they are launched. If that is to be so, then there has to be a system in space that can spot the missile as soon as it leaves the silo, decide if it is heading in a threatening direction, track it, take the decision to attack or not, line it up, confirm the decision to attack and then, if confirmed, attack. All this would have to be done in perhaps no more than 90 seconds and repeated possibly hundreds of times during that same 90-second period, as hundreds of missiles are launched in a war environment that would be degraded electronically with jammed and destroyed communications and command systems.

But because space technology has advanced so far, along with computer techniques and beam weapon research, many are convinced that it will be possible to satisfy the Reagan vision in some form or another. It must be true that even if America abandoned its ambitions for SDI then the Soviet Union might not. It must be true, also, that technological research will never be discarded. If a future American Administration rejected SDI, the research would continue in some other form because the essential techniques are not khaki-coloured, they are not entirely devoted to the military. The micro-technology, computer advances, data handling processes and directed energy programmes will go on because they are part of the evolution of science and technology research. This research is going to produce the systems, and the military are going to find it difficult to turn them away. We have long passed the time when new weaponry appeared only at the instigation of the military. Laboratories and research establishments decide military capabilities because they are more often in a position to tell the military that they have developed a system that can do such-and-such a job before the military is in a position to decide that they need such-and-such a job done.

Space development has been a curious mixture of the military and the laboratories working together. The commanders did not want new weapons. They wanted the scientists to improve existing military capabilities by putting them into space. The commander has always had reconnaissance, early warning, Intelligence gathering signals and navigation systems. The scientist has sent these systems into orbit so that they have improved accuracy and efficiency beyond the dreams of even the most inspired military leaders of just forty years ago. (It is possible, of course, that all this new technology in space and its support systems on earth will, in wartime, supply so much data that whole theatres of the war would come to a grinding, confusing halt.)

Not surprisingly, the advances in space technology have introduced a potential battleground that did not exist just thirty years ago. In its simplest imagined form, the Strategic Defence

Initiative would have beams directed from earth to space mirrors which would re-direct the energy at attacking missiles. That is something for the not too distant future. However, 'now' technology has produced weapons that have a single purpose: to destroy other space craft. As the military commander relies so much on and is so well equipped with reconnaissance, electronic Intelligence signals and early warning systems, then methods have had to be found to strike him deaf, dumb and blind.

Both the United States and the Soviet Union experimented with weapons to knock out satellites (Anti-satellite, ASAT) within a few years of the launching of the space age in the late 1950s. In the early days, the Americans abandoned the project, but the Russians went on to build a crude system which is now in service. Now the Americans are about to bring into operation a more versatile ASAT weapon. Both superpowers are developing new methods, including beam weapons, to destroy or render useless satellites in time of war, perhaps in time of tension. The concern here might be twofold: because of the ease with which satellites may be degraded (they do not have to be destroyed to lose their value) and because of their undoubted value, the temptation would be to strike at them before war began. This very act could sweep aside last-minute efforts to solve a crisis by diplomacy. Secondly, space is not the exclusive playground of the superpowers. There are signs that its military as well as its scientific advantages are increasingly recognised by non-superpowers. They too would be vulnerable to the nervousness of superpowers under stress. Many more countries are investing in satellite technology than is often imagined. China, France, Japan, Canada, Indonesia and the United Kingdom are but six countries deeply involved in space systems. Nevertheless the dominant factor today is the superpower involvement. Taking 1984 as a recent example of space launchings we see that more than a hundred military satellites were launched by the Soviet Union and the United States. 1984 was not an exceptional year.

Most of the launches were from the Soviet Union. Yet it would be wrong to assume that Moscow's military space policy is more aggressive than that of Washington. The larger number of Soviet space craft says more about the limitations of their programme than it does about their commitment, as we shall see. The commitment of both superpowers is absolute. Space has become the new high ground from which commanders might direct any future superpower conflict. However, what is happening in space today, although hidden conveniently from the human eye, is of enormous importance to everybody. We are all part of the military arms race in space; its consequences will touch us all in different ways. Man has travelled millions of miles during the past quarter of a century. As these pages are read, television sets in living rooms are receiving news pictures from satellites 22,300 miles up with the capability of providing 24 channels for viewers everywhere; telephone calls are relayed through satellites able to provide 30,000 telephone circuits a time; weather reports are coming from space; government communications are being intercepted by electronic Intelligence space craft; photographs of troop formations in Europe are being sent to earth for analysis, and men are designing and testing systems with which they believe the war of this world will one day start in space.

Space travel and its value to earthbound man has been recognised for centuries. The Chinese knew about rockets almost as soon as they knew about gunpowder. In sixteenth-century Bologna, the Ruggieri family incorporated in their family arms the word rocchetta – rocket. Rockets were used by the Russians during the late eighteenth century against the Turks. In 1857, Konstantin Tsiolkovskiy was born and, thirty years later, his thoughts on rocketry and space travel were paving the way for him to be the first space scientist. By the turn of the twentieth century, Tsiolkovskiy was publishing designs that suggested that man could really think seriously about reaching for the moon. In 1926, Robert Goddard in America launched the first liquid-fuelled rocket from the wintry flats of a farmstead. It was a 60 m.p.h. flight which lasted but 2½ seconds and represented 20 years' work.

Goddard's Smithsonian paper published in 1919 entitled 'A Method of Reaching Extreme Altitudes' was all but ignored, although it contained far-seeing thoughts that could have given the United States enormous advantages in the space race that was to come. Indeed it was only by accident that Goddard at last got some attention for his experiments, and then only because a test on some farm land resulted in the local Fire Department being called out because it was thought that there had been an air crash.

Meanwhile, in Russia, Konstantin Tsiolkovskiy had teamed up with an encouraged Sergei Korolev and Valentin Glushko and the two latter scientists went on to produce a rocket that was far more advanced than the German V-2 of World War II.

It is said that 300 million marks were spent building the V-2 site at Peenemünde. More than 5,000 technicians and scientists were called to the project which included the first supersonic wind tunnel. All the experiments were to lead to A4, the Fourth Aggregat or Assembly, which became known darkly as Vengeance Weapon Two, or V-2 – a 3,600 m.p.h. rocket with a range of 200 miles. At the end of World War II there was a scramble to capture blueprints, parts and scientists. The Russians had made Sergei Korolev the Chief Designer of Rockets and he and Valentin Glushko worked to improve the German designs for the liquid-propelled V-2s. By 1948, Korolev's team was able to build advanced missiles. The Americans too were determined to exploit the talent and technology of Peenemünde. The scientists went in behind the army to plunder the technical secrets. By 1952, the Americans had launched 63 V-2s from their desert test site in New Mexico.

And so the race went on; it was a romantic, almost MGM-scripted epic of individual success, technical frustrations, political intrigue and incompetence. But most of us did not really believe in space travel until 1957 when Sputnik 1 was launched by the Russians. Until then, space travel had for the most part been the area of science fiction writers. True, there were no creatures from outer space, but for the first time it was being demonstrated that man could enter this uncertain environment and survive. In the background, in 1957, the military thinkers were speculating that if they did not get into space, then they would not be able to guarantee man's survival on earth. The military planners in Moscow and Washington wanted to be the first to take to the new high ground. The Russians won.

Chapter 2

Sputnik Plus

When Sputnik 1 was launched, the Russians had very quickly done what the Americans had somewhat noisily promised to do – but had not. Both countries had promised the world that they were going to launch satellites. 1957 had not been plucked from the then still skies as some arbitrary date for the first space launches. That year had been designated International Geophysical Year and in 1955 the U.S.A. and the U.S.S.R. had declared that their major, certainly their spectacular, contribution to I.G.Y. would be the launching of small scientific satellites. What few in the West had imagined was that the Soviet programme would be ready before the much publicised American effort.

The Soviet Union had got on with the job and by being first had taken most of the world by surprise; that element of surprise was partly due to two particular reasons. The Soviet Union was in the 1950s regarded by most countries as a developing nation. It was a society of great social deprivation and economic shortcomings. It was a society that did not readily display great technological reputation. The United States, however, was relatively sound in the economic sense. It had, also, an enviable technological and scientific base. Certainly it was seen as a country with the greatest capability to launch a satellite. It saw itself as having the scientific lead over the Soviet Union and the majority of the world saw no reason to doubt America's confidence. The rocket programme running from Edwards Air Force Base only endorsed, to the uninitiated, this view of American expertise.

Secondly, the obvious difference in the societies of the superpowers encouraged observers to believe that America would be first. America was a very open society; the Soviet Union was ultra secretive. For all sorts of obvious reasons, including the budget bargaining that went on in Washington, the Americans called attention to their efforts. The space effort was one of promotions, badges, stickers and promises. The big space sell was convincing enough. The secret society that was the Soviet Union released few details of its programme. Furthermore there was a readiness in the West to doubt almost every claim and promise coming from Moscow. It is true also that in the West, and particularly in Washington, there was an astonishing lack of understanding of the Soviet Union. Departments, sections and officials supposedly concerned with Soviet affairs were quite ignorant of the Soviet Union, the Kremlin, its workings, even the language. This last point made it doubly difficult for those at the top to expect any reliable form of analysis of Soviet capability, never mind the even more complex task of understanding how the U.S.S.R. might intend to use this capability.

World reaction was that of wonder. To wake one morning to the tiny, almost cheeky, bleep of Sputnik way out in the cold and dark depths of space was indeed something at which one might wonder. To most people, space was the domain of the stars, the man-in-the-moon, fiction and imagination. Newspapers and radio reports throughout the world hailed the triumph. Soon, even the secretiveness of the Soviet Union was being left behind – or some of it. The Soviet papers and radio stations had of course made much of the event.

According to some Western experts, there had been a number of attempts to launch the Sputnik. There had been a series of failures before October 4, 1957. However, these assessments should be treated with some caution. The engineering for the space shot had little to do with the satellite. The skill was in the rocketry. The rocket used was based on the Soviet Union's first Intercontinental Ballistic Missile (ICBM) which had finished its initial flight trials in the summer of that year. It could therefore be assumed, perhaps, that Sputnik 1 was an early, rather than a delayed, success for the Russians. The rocket was big: 28 metres long and nearly 3 metres in diameter at its widest point. The rocket lasted for 57 days in space. However, the tiny satellite went on. It was a shiny sphere, just 0.58 metres in diameter, and weighed a mere 83.6 kilograms. Its orbit was quite eliptical reaching a height of 939 kilometres and swooping as low as 215.

A week after the launch it reached its second record. (Its first had been to be the first artificial earth satellite.) On October 11, Moscow radio reported that Sputnik 1 had been around the earth 100 times, covering 4,400,000 kilometres – and claimed the record.

It was at this stage that the Russians started to put out considerably more information. The Pulkovo Observatory had picked up the separate lines and traces of the rocket and the Observatory's director, Professor A. Mikhailov, stated something that most American military strategists feared most of all. The Professor said: 'It is important to point out that it has now been proved possible to launch into orbit not only a satellite, which is comparatively small in dimensions, but also such a huge body as the carrier-rocket.'

To Mikhailov, the importance of this was that in future it would be possible to launch bigger and various satellites. To the American Defense Department, it meant that the Soviet Union had acquired the capability to launch a nuclear warhead from the Soviet Union that could hit the U.S.A. There were those who believed also that it would not be long before the Soviet Union could be in position to put, instead of a sputnik, some form of nuclear bomb into orbit and bring that bomb back to earth when and where the Kremlin chose. In 1957 that was a fanciful idea, but within a few years the Soviet Union carried out such tests – although not with a 'live' weapon. Meanwhile Sputnik 1 continued to occupy major headlines, column inches and broadcasting hours and it was providing Soviet scientists with a very steep learning curve. After all, until Sputnik 1, nothing had been so high in such an alien environment.

For example, just six days after Sputnik 1's launch, the Russians noted that the satellite was being bombarded by what their scientists described as being micro-meteorites about the size of small specks of dust. These micro-meteorites were leaving tiny dents in the satellite, but they had not harmed it. It was important to find out when these specks bombarded the sputnik because it could be that they did not exist below a certain altitude. The scientists decided that the most effective way of knowing if there were micro-meteorites was to switch on microphones. They could then listen to the ping and rattle sounds of the bombardment. The crucial discovery was that between the high and low altitudes that Sputnik 1 was flying the satellite had not been hit by major meteors. The scientists wondered if it were possible that there were no *major* meteors in this area.

Professor Fedynsky, the leader of the group of Soviet meteor specialists, said, 'The satellite has not yet encountered major meteor bodies, a fact which enables us to calculate the probable distance between the destructive major meteor bodies in space and to predict with more accuracy than before conditions affecting the flight of artificial satellites and *rockets* through cosmic space . . .'

The excitement mounted in America and the Soviet Union as more information was added to the already laden learning curve. With this single space shot, many preconceptions were tumbling away. One Soviet professor of upper atmosphere physics, Valerian Krasovsky, observed within five days of the launch that the 'upper layers of the atmosphere were many times less dense than had been previously supposed'. Perhaps this would mean that the temperatures at these altitudes would be considerably lower. According to one former missile engineer in Washington, this sort of news had scientists wondering whether their missile calculations would have to be totally re-thought.

While much was being made of the new scientific data, the Russians did not neglect the propaganda value of the occasion – with some justification, as a Radio Moscow broadcast beamed in English to the West showed. 'That the Earth satellite is a victory for Soviet scientific thought is admitted by all the leading scientists and space travel experts in the world. The man-made moon flies on in space, upsetting the predictions of all the ill-starred prophets who claimed that Soviet science wouldn't cope with the task . . . of course there are some in the West who find this achievement of Soviet science not to their liking . . .'

Certainly there were those who echoed the concerns of many American strategists, but for different reasons. The American distress was caused largely by the thought that the U.S.S.R. might be gathering a military as well as prestigious advantage. There were those, however, who recognised even then that, although it would be impossible to stop the military intrusion, there was a very good case for some form of international control. The Russians sensed this as much as anybody and were quick to pick out a leader in Britain's *Yorkshire Post* (which they had assumed was politically to the right of centre) that highlighted the scientific and engineering achievement. Moscow accused the

United States of using the achievement to whip up what the Russians called 'atom war hysteria'. In one commentary, the Soviet Union said: 'Those quarters which are responsible for this hysteria are not loath to use the man-made moon too as justification for demanding new appropriations for the armaments drive . . . the launching of the Earth satellite is not a demonstration of military strength . . .'

Of course there was some element of truth in what the Russians said. There was a bigger demand for defence dollars as a result of Sputnik 1. But Sputnik 1 had only reinforced existing fears in the United States. Those worries had been building for some time, certainly since the Soviet Union successfully tested a nuclear warhead in 1949.

It must be remembered that there had been a series of underestimations by the West of Soviet capabilities, and not only those connected with space research. The first Soviet nuclear explosion in 1949 was well ahead of schedules predicted by many Western Intelligence analysts. The initial carrier for this new Soviet weapon was the TU4 bomber, a carbon copy of the United States B-29, called by its designer Andrei Tupolev 'a locally built Boeing product'. At this time, however, there was very little discussion in the Soviet press about nuclear weapons.

Then, in March 1953, Stalin died and many hours were spent in Washington trying to evaluate the changes that the new régime might apply to the Soviet armed forces. The concern was largely concentrated on the U.S.S.R.'s ability to carry the basic fission weapon (the 'atomic bomb') that the Russians had produced. Most estimates of its capability centred on the new generation of aircraft. Five months after Stalin's death, the Soviet Union successfully tested the next stage in nuclear weapons development, the fusion weapon – the hydrogen bomb. Again, this was 'ahead of schedule'. Many in high places in the Western Intelligence community concentrated on aircraft as the delivery vehicles for the hydrogen bomb. It was not until 1957 that it was generally realised that the Soviet strategists had applied their efforts to building a missile that could carry a warhead. Consequently, the most terrifying aspect of Soviet military power demonstrated in 1957 was the successful testing of a long range rocket, together with the Soviet claim on August 27, 1957 that it had an intercontinental rocket 'capable of reaching any point on the globe'.

The then American President, Dwight Eisenhower, made the point that the satellite was no threat to America although he was less sanguine about the rocket. In something of an understatement, Eisenhower said that 'the very fact that a rocket has been launched and penetrated the area it was planned to reach is in itself a great accomplishment'. Soviet radio broadcasts echoed this; one such example left little doubt about the rocket's significance: 'Today after the firing of the Sputnik it is perfectly clear that the Soviet Union possesses intercontinental ballistic rockets . . . this means a real change in methods of warfare, in military strategy and tactics . . .'

The Soviet engineers involved in the space programme presumably had few thoughts for American concerns. Instead, these scientists were planning for the future. It mattered little to them that the Americans were putting on a very public display of being left behind. In Moscow it was understood that their success might be short lived even though it was clear to the Americans that the Soviet Union was far from the space engineering dunce that many in Congress thought. There had been some exchanges of information, even personal contact between American and Soviet scientists, although this had not been publicised. The Russians had been quick to pick the brains of the Americans. A little-noticed article appeared in a Russian journal in 1957 which should have rung alarm bells in Washington. The journal, *Promyshlennaya i Ekonomicheskaya Gazeta*, was not widely read in Washington, perhaps it should have been.

The article in question gave a detailed assessment of the American rocket and satellite programme. It suggested that the Americans were behind in the space race, but nevertheless 'some aspects of U.S. rocket techniques are undoubtedly of some interest. For instance, the U.S. scientists practise the launching of experimental rockets from balloons, charged with helium and rising to a height of 20 km. The main advantage of this method lies in the cheapness of such experiments even though they have some negative aspects. Rockets launched in this manner have a large radius of diffusion and also require cumbersome means for transporting the helium.' The article then went on to discuss in some detail the measurements and sensors in the satellite that the Americans hoped to launch. Of particular interest to the Russians was the use of miniature systems such as transistors and American experiments with solar batteries. 'It is intended to launch the first experimental satellite in December but there is a basis for doubting whether this will come off as the U.S. scientists are meeting with difficulties with their carrier-rockets . . .' This fascinating insight into the Soviet assessment suggests that the Russians were more confident than might have been expected; that not only were they ahead of the Americans, they also knew more or less the state of American technology. Certainly the Soviet analysis and prophecies about American launching difficulties were extremely accurate, as we shall see.

American concerns might have been agitated by the obvious enthusiasm and confidence the normally secretive Soviet authorities were displaying. For example, while the Americans were trying still literally to get off the ground, the Russians were giving public seminars on how to do it.

And, within three weeks of Sputnik 1, there was a direct hint that the Russians were planning an even more spectacular space shot. In fact there were two clear signals to experienced Soviet-watchers who might have remembered that the Russians tend to drop hints of some action only when they are confident that they can carry it out and, often, only when they are about to.

The first indicator came on October 25, 1957 during one of the public seminars on rocketry and satellites. A Soviet professor said casually, 'The launching of still heavier satellites, now planned in the U.S.S.R., requires the construction of even more perfected rockets and the solution of new problems, one of the most important being the problem of how to make it possible for the satellite to descend intact to Earth . . . after that, living beings may travel as passengers . . .'

There was no mention of *human* beings, only *living* beings. Two days later there was a short report from Moscow on the work done at a laboratory run by Professor Alexei Pokrovsky. The professor's technicians were working on a dog called Kudryavka. According to them, Kudryavka had been fitted with a space suit, including a 'goldfish bowl' helmet, and blasted into the upper atmosphere (not space). Furthermore, the dog had been 'launched' on a number of occasions, always returning safely by parachute. On the same day, October 27, 1957, American diplomats might have been interested in a lecture given at the Moscow Polytechnical Museum by another scientist, Viktor Malkin. His subject for the lecture: Conditioning of Animals for Flights in Earth Satellites. The following week, on November 3,

1957, the bleep of Sputnik 1 gave way to the barking of Laika – Sputnik 2 was in space, this time with a passenger.

Sputnik 2 was launched from Tyuratam using the same type of rocket that had put Sputnik 1 into space. Whereas the first satellite had been a small ball, Sputnik 2, the first kennel in space, weighed 1,121 kg and reached a more elliptical orbit with a high point (apogee) of 1,660 km, almost twice that of Sputnik 1. The lecture notes, however, which had stressed the importance of recovering the capsule, apparently did not apply to this space shot. For seven days, Sputnik 2 sent back signals and then there was silence. The space craft is known to have decayed in space in April of the following year, presumably with Laika on board. But the Russians had proved to their satisfaction that a 'living being' could survive. Little notice at the time was given to the fact that Sputnik 2 was fitted with cameras. Later, reconnaissance analysis in Washington recognised the potential as well as the significance of this additional cargo.

In the United States, news of this second successful launch and flight did little to soothe the frustrations experienced in the American programme. Attempts to launch military rockets had met with little success. The main hope of a 'catch-up' launching focused on the U.S. Navy's Vanguard rocket. Two years earlier it had been decided that the Vanguard was the best rocket to carry America's satellite. Vanguard was not a military vehicle, but what is known as a sounding rocket, which, as its name implies, is a space probe rather than, say, a ballistic missile launcher used to boost a capsule into orbit. (The Soviet Union, having developed a military rocket that had the thrust and the capability of carrying a payload into ballistic orbit, chose to use this system from the outset.)

Watching the Soviet successes, people like Werner von Braun fumed at the bureaucratic indecisions of the Federal authorities. For example, had Washington been more far-sighted it would have been possible for America to have capitalised on the advantages that the German scientists had brought with them from Peenemünde. There had been designs to produce space-based bombers. One, in the 1950s, known as the Bomi Project, envisaged a space shuttle that could put a nuclear bomb-carrying aircraft into orbit and bring it back. The Bomi Project, under the direction of Dr Walter Dornberger, was only one of many such schemes. There was, however, an obvious reluctance in

Washington to get into any costly and escalatory programme. President Eisenhower was nervous of many of the seemingly far-fetched schemes that crossed his desk, and voiced his suspicion of a large number of ideas which he suspected of being nothing more than the industrial lobby promoting their own interests for commercial rather than patriotic reasons and with little scientific evidence to support them.

These doubts and suspicions had dogged the American space programme since the 1940s. At the end of the Second World War, there had been a general belief among the military that the future of Intelligence gathering, reconnaissance and communications would be linked with space exploration. Each of the branches of the armed forces had its champions, but inevitably they retained their single-Service jealousies and pride. Furthermore, the immediate post-war period witnessed great demands that defence spending should be scrutinised so that only essential projects went ahead.

The military in the United States had two aims for potential space programmes: to build long range ballistic missiles and to send satellites into space. For example, the Army Air Force had wanted to go ahead with long range missile building and to anticipate space-based defences against enemy missile attacks. Werner von Braun predicted that manned space flight would enable astronauts to act as space-based spies, watching enemy positions from hundreds of miles above the earth. The RAND group produced in 1946 a report entitled 'Preliminary Design of an Experimental World Circling Spaceship'.

The U.S. Navy tried to get the Army Air Force interested in a joint space venture, probably because the Navy recognised that such a project was so costly that only joint funding could make it possible.

Again inter-Service rivalry, especially the Army Air Force's fear that it would lose what it regarded as its rightful place as leader of any future space programme, made agreement almost impossible. In 1947, the restructuring of the American forces, with the creation of a United States Air Force, further complicated the chances of a single American space effort.

The U.S.A.F. made it clear that it would expect to have the major say in any space programme, mainly because the Air Force as its title suggested was in charge of 'air operations'. A further complication was the need by the Americans to develop missiles and long range jet planes. (The Russians did not have the same priority for long range bombers at that stage.) All this meant that funds that might have been available for a space programme were hived into other areas of expensive research.

Nevertheless, work went on in small stages and a series of important reports were commissioned and produced. Consequently, at the start of the 1950s, the Americans, in a programme known as Project Feedback, had identified the need and the possibilities of a new area of reconnaissance using satellites should they ever have the money to build them and the rockets to launch them. In spite of this example of foresight and the guarded enthusiasm of President Eisenhower (who as a writer of Service instructions during the 1930s had demonstrated his recognition for the need for advanced reconnaissance systems) a lack of co-ordination continued to damage the overall effort. Most people backed the idea of developing new reconnaissance systems although many believed that they should remain within the traditional ways of Intelligence gathering. The Lockheed aircraft company was building the U-2 high altitude 'spy' plane and there were quite a few people in the Department of Defense who believed that the U-2 was all that was needed and saw no reason to invest in costly and unproven satellite projects. As the experiences of the Second World War began to have less direct influence on those decision makers in Washington and as the technological studies appeared more feasible, so attitudes started to change. There remained the obvious rivalries and the problem that priorities were given to weapon systems rather than projects with uncertain values. But with the 1955 announcement from the White House that the United States would go into space during 1957, a committee was established to make the most important decision for that programme: which rocket to use. The committee chose the U.S. Navy's Vanguard project using the Viking rocket, which had the advantage of being the only contender that was not based on a missile system – it was a sounding rocket. It was a mistake. If the Army's Redstone rocket used by von Braun had been selected then it is quite possible that the Americans would have been ready to go into space before the 1957 deadline, or so von Braun believed.

Von Braun and his colleagues at the Redstone Arsenal in Alabama were convinced that America had no need to lag behind the Soviet Union. He certainly believed that an American satellite could have been in orbit by the mid-fifties. But it took the Sputnik successes to persuade the authorities in Washington to give von Braun the go-ahead for what were called the Explorer series; even so, the Navy's Vanguard rockets were to be first on the pad at Cape Canaveral in Florida.

There had been a successful test firing of a Vanguard rocket and there was a suggestion of great confidence when, just two months after Sputnik 1 and a month after Sputnik 2, America prepared to press the button on its space spectacular. On December 6, 1957, the countdown began. It was a countdown to humiliation. In full view of the world, Vanguard went up – but in a mass of flames. Officially it had lost its thrust after just two seconds. A second vehicle – or more accurately, Vanguard test vehicle 4 – was prepared for launching by the Navy, but this could not be ready for another two months. Instead, the Army came to the rescue. Von Braun's team had built a rocket based on the Redstone missile developed from the German V2. The system was called Jupiter. From this had come Juno. The combinations of stage launches had been available for some time and it is widely accepted that, if Washington had authorised the team to proceed with a launch programme, then the Americans might well have been able to put a satellite into space before the Russians.

The launch came late at night on January 31, 1958. The Jupiter rocket lifted off from Cape Canaveral with a small payload, the first in the Explorer series, a small cylinder just two metres long. America had a success. Not only was the launching straightforward, the probe made an important discovery. Scientists had long suspected the existence of a belt of strong radiation high above the earth. The orbit of Explorer 1 took the probe to a maximum height of 1,584 km. A team based at the State University of Iowa and led by Dr James Van Allen noted this radiation from some of the Explorer 1 data recorded by geiger counters on board. The signals were irregular, but when they were mated with signals received from two subsequent Explorer missions, then the belts of radiation were positively identified. Not surprisingly, they were named the Van Allen Belts.

The success of Explorer 1 was somewhat dampened five days later on February 5. The back-up for the failed Vanguard Test Vehicle was launched from the Cape. Lift-off went according to plan but almost immediately it went out of control and disintegrated about six kilometres into its flight. Exactly one month later, there was further disappointment for the Americans. The second Explorer was launched but the fourth stage of the Jupiter refused to burn and the mission failed to get into orbit. But at last there was success for the U.S. Navy's Vanguard project. On March 17 of that year, Vanguard went into orbit. It was to transmit data for six years, including details of what its instruments saw as a pear-shaped earth. During the same month, Explorer 3 was launched. It was another success and added to the information flowing back to Iowa State University about the radiation belts. There were hopes in Washington that, after the initial setbacks, the American space programme had 'lift-off'.

A month later, on April 28, the ill-fated Vanguard project launched its fifth test vehicle. This time it was the third stage of the rocket that failed. If that was not bad enough, in May the Russians came back with Sputnik 3. It was a copy-book launch from Tyuratam and the biggest of all the space craft. Sputnik 3 was conical with a base diameter of 1.73 metres and a height of 3.57 metres. It weighed 1,327 kg and was packed with instruments set to measure cosmic rays and the atmospheric pressures. Twelve days later, the U.S. Navy tried again. There was a trajectory problem and no orbit. The following month, there was a further attempt. The second stage of the rocket cut off too soon – and again Vanguard had failed. The particularly sad aspect of these failures was that the May and June attempts were the operational vehicles for satellites, whereas the earlier launches had been test vehicles. There was a further disappointment in September when the third Vanguard satellite launch vehicle (SLV3) did not produce the thrust needed to get into orbit.

But Vanguard was not the only damp squib that failed to fire the American space programme with enthusiasm. As we have seen, Explorer 1 and 3 had been successes. Explorer 4, the first space craft to come under the relatively new Advance Research Project Agency (ARPA), was launched on July 26 using the Jupiter launch vehicle. It went up from Cape Canaveral (often called the Eastern Test Range) and mapped radiation in October of that year. However, the United States Air Force was attempting something even more spectacular – a lunar probe. The first launch was called Thor-Able 1 after the name of the rocket. Launch date was set for August 17, 1958, sandwiched between

Explorer 4 and 5. Hopes were high after the good news about Explorer 4 but Thor-Able 1 had an immediate problem, and the first stage did not work. The Thor rocket was better known in military circles as the first of what are called Intermediate Range Ballistic Missiles, a term applied, for example, to the modern and more famous Pershing missile. At the time of this first lunar probe, the Thor in its missile form was already being based in the United Kingdom as part of the West's considerable reliance on the growing intermediate ballistic missile technology developed in the United States.

Although this particular Thor-Able was not a success, the project which became known as the Pioneer Series was to be spectacularly reliable. At this stage, however, the American failure rate had few compensations. The following week, August 24, in a rare display of space-based slapstick, Explorer 5 actually collided with itself when there was a malfunction in the upper stage and two sections which should have gone separate ways did not. In September there was a further Vanguard failure. Then, in October, the Thor-Able, by now renamed Pioneer 1, launched successfully towards the moon, sent back information for almost two days but did not reach the moon; and another project, Beacon 1, never achieved an orbit because its upper stages separated too early. In November, Pioneer 2 had rocket failure and failed to get to the moon. Then, in December, up went Pioneer 3. It looked good but, although it reached a distance of more than 100,000 km, it was not far enough for the moon shot. For the Americans, 1958 had seemed at the outset a year full of hope. Instead it had been one of considerable humiliation made all the worse by the national policy of wearing its space ambitions on its sleeve.

There had been one success apart from the Explorer, although it was short-lived. On December 18, the Advanced Research Project Agency used an Atlas rocket to put a small satellite called SCORE into orbit. SCORE was an acronym (Signal Communication by Orbiting Relay Equipment). It has been described as the first military communications satellite although it only operated for thirteen days and the definition is a little doubtful. SCORE could only send taped messages and it is remembered chiefly for the taped Christmas greeting from President Eisenhower that it beamed to earth that year. Nevertheless, the military community at the time certainly recognised the potential in that project and, equally, the need to develop a weapon system to destroy it should there ever be a war.

1959 opened with those same high hopes in Moscow and Washington and possibly a certain American nervousness as to what the Soviet scientists might do next. It was known that they were working on lunar probes, as were the Americans, and presumably on some form of manned flight. It was later noted that, apart from Sputnik 3 in May 1958, that year had not produced the space spectaculars which some had suggested might come from Moscow. Of the eighteen launchings, only Sputnik 3 had been from the U.S.S.R. On January 2, the Russians launched the first of their moon probes, Luna 1. Tyuratam was again the launching site. Luna 1 'missed' the moon, though it passed within 3,728 miles. The launch meant 'four-out-of-four' and suggested a stable vehicle with few, if any, teething troubles. Here, too, was an illustration of the great advantages in having a co-ordinated research programme although it should not be thought that this first Luna probe was born out of the Sputnik series. The three Sputnik satellites had been part of an entirely different project. Luna was probably a long-standing programme, perhaps conceived in the early 1950s. Luna 1's near miss was not the failure that some suggested. Much data was picked up by the Soviet scientists and they were already preparing for a second attempt in 1959 even as Luna 1 sailed past its target and headed into orbit round the sun, where it still remains.

Meanwhile the Americans were pressing on with only a modest amount of success. In February 1959 a Vanguard went into orbit but developed stability problems and had difficulty in transmitting usable data. On February 28 a new project was launched successfully and proved to be of particular significance for the military. Discoverer 1 was an ARPA programme and was launched not from Florida's Cape Canaveral but from what was officially called the Western Test Range. The W.T.R. is centred on Vandenberg Air Force Base. This was the first time that Vandenberg had been used.

Discoverer's function was two-fold: it was to test the concept that it was possible to bring back a space capsule under controlled conditions and, secondly, to see how difficult it would be to fly reconnaissance missions. The latter was of lesser importance than the former. Bringing back a space capsule had three obvious advantages eagerly sought by the Americans and the Soviet engineers – and especially by the military.

Having absolute and initially remote control over a capsule meant that one major obstacle to any manned flight programme could be removed. As the Russians had shown with Laika within weeks of the first lift-off, putting a man in space was relatively simple and quite possibly safe. Getting him back was another matter. If a capsule could be brought back without damage on re-entering the earth's atmosphere then not only could man return, but so too could, say, photographs. Finally, if it were possible to orbit a capsule and control its timing and point of re-entry then it would be possible to fit that capsule with, say, a nuclear weapon.

There were those in Washington who, even at that stage of space flight, believed that orbiting nuclear bombs were the weapons of the future and, of course, the ultimate threat. This concept was not confined to the Pentagon. The Soviet Union developed a system to echo American thinking. It was called FOBS, Fractional Orbital Bombardment System. The author was told in Moscow that, although the Soviet Union has never admitted to suggestions that it developed such a weapon, it could only be expected that the military would wish to consider all applications of orbital space flight. Certainly the Discoverer programme was to prove that putting a bomb in orbit and directing its re-entry to a relatively small area on earth was feasible.

Discoverer 2 was launched in April 1959. But first came another moon probe from Cape Canaveral. Pioneer 4 was launched from the Cape but passed by the moon. In fact it missed it by more than 37,000 miles and, like other systems, including the Russian attempts, went into orbit about the sun. Discoverer 2's orbit was a success and on the seventeenth pass the capsule was ejected. This was the first attempt at bringing back such a capsule. Re-entry was a less complete success inasmuch that everything fired more or less as it was supposed to do. More or less, however, was not enough and the capsule was never recovered; instead it was lost somewhere in the Arctic. However, it was very clear that, for the Americans, this programme had to be given top priority; and, from the end of February 1959 until February 1962, there were thirty-eight Discoverer launches by the Air Force.

The early attempts were not particularly satisfying. Of the first twelve launches the first did not have a capsule, five failed to go into orbit, two capsules never got as far as re-entry, and four capsules were ejected on either the fifteenth or the seventeenth orbits but were never recovered.

But, on August 10, 1960, thirteen became a lucky number for the U.S. Air Force. On that day a Thor-Agena rocket blasted off from Vandenberg. The missile-based Thor completed the first section of the flight, then the Agena took over, firing its engines and thrusting the whole package into a looping orbit that reached a height of 431 miles before swooping down to 157 miles above the earth. It was passing over the Pacific Ocean every 94 minutes. By using a system of gas nozzles, the space vehicle was turned completely about so that the conical 'nose' of the craft was facing the earth. Then on the seventeenth orbit the capsule part was ejected. The timing and ejection were spot on. Instead of skipping off the 'hard' atmosphere and spinning back into space as so easily could have happened, the capsule 'hit' the atmospheric re-entry point at the correct angle with all systems going. Once through, descent was moderate and at about nine and a half miles above the earth a parachute opened leaving the capsule clear to float down to the ocean. It was on target and as the capsule splashed down the U.S. Navy team was on hand for rescue. It was not only possible to bring back a capsule; it was now proven that it could be done with the accuracy needed to recover its cargo – human or otherwise – or to deliver a weapon.

Discoverer 13 was a test flight to the extent that the recovery techniques were imperfect. However, there also exists evidence in Washington to suggest that the August 10 flight included camera pods that were operated when Discoverer was over the Soviet Union. Which in turn suggests that Discoverer 13 was the first recovery for American space-based photo-reconnaissance Intelligence.

Eight days later, on August 18, the operation was repeated with Discoverer 14. This time, recovery was more spectacular and more important. Earlier in the year, the Russians had shot down an American Intelligence spy-plane, a U-2 piloted by Gary Powers. Powers had been flying over the Soviet Union photographing missile launch sites. Apart from the diplomatic incident the downing of the U-2 showed that aircraft reconnaissance was particularly vulnerable now that the Soviet surface to air missiles had the intercept range and accuracy necessary to provide a formidable anti-aircraft barrage. Furthermore, even though the Americans had flown these missions for four years, the Intelligence gathered was quite limited. If the right camera equipment could be developed, then a satellite with all the advantages of a better and broader view, could do a better job than aircraft when it came to spending long periods deep in Soviet territory.

It was true also that, with this further development of satellite reconnaissance, there was an added need for the Soviet Union at least to develop a system that could knock out not only U-2s, but satellites. Therefore, from the Soviet point of view, Discoverer made anti-satellite (ASAT) weapons essential.

Discoverer 14 was launched from Vandenberg. It photographed the Soviet launch site at Tyuratam. Capsule ejection and re-entry in the seventeenth orbit followed a similar pattern as Discoverer 13. The main and spectacular difference was the method of recovery. There was no splash down in the ocean. Instead an aircraft from Hawaii flew along the descent path of the capsule and caught it in mid-air by trailing snag lines to hook the parachute. This was the first mid-air 'catch' and it set a pattern attempted by the United States for some time.

This all happened between 1959 and 1960, but it was not the only space activity during this period. The Russians were continuing with their moon probes and on September 12, 1959 launched Luna 2. It will be remembered that, at the start of that year, Luna 1 had missed the moon by just under 4,000 miles and that the American Pioneer 4 passed within 37,000 miles or so. Luna 2 lifted off from Tyuratam and 34 hours later landed on the moon. Landed is perhaps too gentle a description. Luna 2 hit the moon. Within a month Luna 3 was ready for launch. It was a success but, instead of landing, Luna 3 went into a huge orbit that took the space craft around the earth's natural satellite. Luna 2 had been the first probe to land on the moon. Luna 3 was the first to photograph the far side. It did so using a television camera which allowed onboard transmission. For forty minutes Luna 3 filmed the 'dark' side of the moon and later sent back these pictures as the satellite's orbit brought it closer to earth. Once again the Soviet engineers, scientists and propaganda experts had chalked up a space first. The military analysts in

Washington noted the importance of being able to transmit television pictures of another country.

The Americans responded seven weeks later with a NASA space probe launched from Cape Canaveral. It hardly got off the ground let alone to the moon. The payload's protective shroud broke away after just forty-five seconds. At the same time, the United States Air Force was having problems with a little known space flight called MIDAS. As noticed earlier, the Americans were fully aware that the major element in the Soviet success story was the sound development of the rocket system and feared that those same rockets gave the Russians the capability of launching a nuclear attack on the United States. The MIDAS project started in 1960 was to guard against such an attack.

MIDAS stood for Missile Defense Alarm System. The American intention was that, by tasking a satellite system to watch Soviet missile fields, the West would double the warning time of a rocket attack. Until the MIDAS concept, the best warning time that could be imagined from ground-based radars was a maximum of fifteen minutes. MIDAS 1 failed because the second stage of the rocket would not break away. If the stages failed to separate, then the satellite could not be boosted into its orbit. Immediately work was brought forward on the next attempt. MIDAS 2 was launched on May 24, 1960, but the communications system failed even though the craft got into an initial orbit. These failures were particularly disheartening because the project could not work with only one satellite and therefore the chance of eventually achieving a true orbit for the system looked slim. The MIDAS plan called for at least twelve satellites fitted with infra-red sensors. These sensors were designed to pick out the heat from the missile gases as the rockets broke clear of their silos. (In simple terms this is the first element in the 'Star Wars' plan announced by President Reagan on March 23, 1983.)

The project was removed from the Cape to Vandenberg and a modified rocket introduced; and, with MIDAS 3, there came a successful launch. The space craft went into a near circular orbit about 3,500 kilometres above the earth and there it was due to remain for 100,000 years. This was in July 1961 and although the MIDAS series went on with moments of furious controversy from America's allies as well as the Soviet Union as we shall see, more spectacular things were going on in space, much to the Soviet Union's delight and to America's dismay.

1960 had started with a series of failures for the United States and silence from the Soviet Union. Between October 4, 1957 and the start of 1960 there had been 43 space shots. Thirty-seven of them had been American – most of them failures. But with this intensive activity and pressure to 'catch up' it may not be so surprising that the American success average was so low. The Americans were trying everything from simple satellite orbiting, to moon shots, to military reconnaissance, to recovery techniques. The first three months recorded even further failures for the U.S. Air Force and NASA. Then on All Fools Day NASA launched TIROS 1. TIROS stood for Television and Infra Red Observation System and it was recorded as being the first meteorological satellite. It encircled the globe and sent back thousands of photographs. Although it was described as a meteorological satellite, TIROS managed to photograph Soviet missile sites and airforce stations including apparently clear details of runways.

On May 15, 1960, the Russians, having been silent for seven months, sent up another Sputnik. On August 19, Sputnik 5 was launched from Tyuratam. Interestingly, the American Discoverer series had experimented with recovering capsules on the seventeenth orbits. Indeed, on the day before the Soviet launch, Discoverer 14's capsule had been caught in mid-air after the seventeenth orbit with reconnaissance pictures of Soviet launch sites on board. Sputnik 5, after the eighteenth orbit, was successfully brought back. On board were two dogs, Belka and Strelka (Squirrel and Pointer). On December 1, Sputnik 6 went aloft, but this time the recovery did not work and the animal passenger perished.

In America there was a certain uneasiness that the Russians were preparing for more than simple recovery techniques. The last two flights could be laying the way for a manned mission. The Americans were doing the same, but believed quite firmly that they would be the first to put a man into space. 1961 started busily enough – the Americans launched another early warning space craft, SAMOS 2, and the Russians launched another Sputnik which once it was in orbit launched Venera 1, the Soviet Union's first Venus probe. Then, in March 1961, there was a scurry of activity from Tyuratam. Two Sputniks (9 and 10) were launched with dogs on board. Chernushka and Zvezdochka were both brought back without mishap. In the United States, the American astronauts were making ready for the first manned space flight. It was not planned as an orbital flight around the earth, that was at that point thought to be too ambitious; nevertheless it was to be an attempt to stretch the distances of the manned rocket planes by shooting over the edge of the atmosphere into space like a super long range firework. America planned to be the first to put a man into space.

On April 12, 1961, Vostok 1 was launched from Tyuratam. On board was Major Yuri Gagarin.

Chapter 3

The Choice

By the time that the Americans were ready to go into the manned space flight business there were two obvious pressures among the many facing the architects of this adventure. Firstly, the Soviet Union had led the way towards manned flight and this appears to have been an enormous disappointment to Washington. At stake was the very reputation of the most powerful nation in the world, a nation justly proud of its technical and financial achievements; a nation yet to be cowed by defeat in Viet-Nam and disgrace in the office of the President. But these were cosmetic set-backs for the self-esteem of a nation which had to rely on the technological foundation of the emerging space industry. There was no dollar-technology wand that could wipe away for the Americans the international achievement of the Soviet Union in the autumn of 1957. Nor could the American space programme sprint to catch up within a few months. And so the scientific, political and diplomatic pride of America was bruised. The political and media pressure on the Administration 'to do something' was enormous. However, while the elements of pride and expectation fuelled the demands for action, the main concern of the military and those concerned with national security had more to do with fear.

Certainly the fear in the minds of many at the Department of Defense was justified by the strategic analysis set before them in 1957. The general public saw the launching of Sputnik 1 as an occasion. It was the spectacle that inspired the headlines throughout the Western world during those first few hours – man had gone into space. It mattered not that Man the Human was still on earth. Man the Achievement was there. It was all possible. It was easy at the time to conjure the fantasies of almost countless lifetimes, space was reachable; soon man himself (never woman herself) would fly beyond the atmospheres and, if he would, perhaps others from other galaxies could and would. It was almost as if the rational notions of space travel were being happily, deliriously, swept aside. If we could fly in space (did one *fly* in outer space?) then perhaps there was life on the planets. Could Martians be real – even if they were not green?

The second pressure was on the military world which had a somewhat different, a more sober view of the Soviet achievement, and it was one which would shadow American space programmes for many years. It must be remembered that the military saw Sputnik 1 as a military achievement at a time when the strategic pattern of superpower thinking was changing. Indeed, the whole term 'superpower' was being defined. Superpower had little to do with democratic achievements, nor with the accumulation of astonishing wealth and the application of that wealth to the progress of any one society. If this had been the case in the post-war years then the definition would have been less complicated and the distinction between the United States and the Soviet Union so great that the superpower status would never have crossed the Atlantic nor the Bering Strait. The overwhelming factor in defining the superiority of a power or a power bloc was the authority provided by nuclear weapons. The Soviet Union had by 1949 tested its own nuclear bomb; by 1953, the Soviets were capable of putting that weapon into service. But that was four years before Sputnik 1, so why should there be added panic in the hearts and minds of the strategic mathematicians in Washington whose job it was to work out the superpower equation? The answer was in two parts and very simple.

The technological achievement of the Russians suggested scientific and engineering advances beyond those estimated by the Western Intelligence committees. In other words, the Russians were much smarter than the Americans had imagined. Secondly and of greater importance was the launching of Sputnik 1 as an engineering achievement. Although the satellite was of obvious scientific and public interest, to the military the main concern was, as we have seen, that the Soviet Union had designed a rocket that was powerful enough to lift the satellite into outer space. The rocket was the focus of analysis, not the satellite, because the existence of such a powerful rocket meant that the Soviet Union had made the supreme leap in 1957. They not only had a nuclear bomb, they had a rocket that could carry that bomb into ballistic orbit and then to the United States.

The Americans were now threatened by a Soviet superiority in rocket engineering as well as a lead in space technology. To those with the vision, the strategic balance was having to be re-written. Immediately, the public, political and overall military view was that the United States had to catch up. The next stage of the space race was necessarily manned flight, even though the Americans had not yet managed the first stage. It is in this aspect that one can ponder the remarkable differences in the American and Soviet approaches to space flight and perhaps something of the character of those involved – an aspect that has to be understood if the wider implication of the superpower space race is to be judged.

In Washington, there was a conviction that, by putting a man into space, the Americans would be demonstrating their rightful technological superiority. In one sense, a manned flight would not make a great contribution to this ambition. Whoever was put into space would not have a great deal to do with the engineering, the science nor indeed the actual mission. He would not pilot the craft; he would be a guinea pig, wired for the interests of the medical scientists even though they were as yet uncertain as to the reasons for the experiments other than the obvious fact that they were moving into the unknown. In another sense, a manned mission was extraordinarily important, not because it promised to pierce yet another frontier, but because it signified confidence in its commitment. It was one thing to launch a 100-pound bleeping football into space; if that failed then it was back-to-the-drawing-board and try again. But to lose an astronaut would be hard to dismiss as scientific failure, mishap or carelessness. This would be the sort of national disaster that set back the political and financial funding of, say, airships, by fifty years. And, so, the need to be sure about manned flight was enormous, especially as there was the pressure that the Soviet Union might just win this race.

Understandably, the people less concerned and impressed with the Soviet Union achievement were those already engaged in advanced flight testing. It might be remembered that all this was happening in the late 1950s. The Second World War was not, as it is today, simply a memory, it was an event in the careers of America's top aviators. Senior pilots, that is active aviators and not those flying large mahogany desks in Washington, were experienced in the risk-taking that pushed operational flying to the very limits. There was an established élite of pilots with experience in the closing years of the Second World War or the Korean War. There was, too, an advanced test and research programme in which only the best of this élite took part. The programme had little to do with America's ambitions for space; it was the hair-raising world of high-performance flying, particularly the testing of high altitude jets and, above all, rocket planes.

When the news came that the Soviet Union had broken through and were now in space, there were many who saw this as nothing more than a logical progression from advanced high performance flying. Most of those who did see it this way were the down-the-line pilots. They were perhaps the modern gladiators; their lives were pitched at a level of calculated risk-taking rarely seen in peace-time forces. These men were flying a new generation of jet aeroplanes. Some of the flights were, to all appearances, straightforward. But the casualty rate both physically and mentally was high, and so those who survived were exceptional people.

Furthermore the 1950s were relatively early years in jet flying. There were new planes, new techniques and speed and altitude records to be broken that were not remotely possible when many of the pilots of this period had first put on uniform.

At the very edge of the frontier was the experimental flying in rocket planes and simple rockets with huge boosters to produce the enormous thrust needed to break into space. Most of this work was going on at Edwards Air Force Base and it was there that the advanced pilots worked day after day, month after month on achieving what was thought impossible the day before. To those men, pushing at the edges of speed and high altitudes, Sputnik 1 was not such a spectacular event.

Elsewhere, of course, the reaction verged on political and strategic panic. In Moscow, Nikita Krushchev chortled over America's confusion and perhaps nodded with much approval when his Chief Designer Sergei Korolev told him that this was but the beginning. The panic, the official desperation, was almost complete when America's own effort to go into space blew up before a fascinated nation, just two months after the first Soviet space flight, just one month after the second Soviet space flight and just two seconds after lift-off from the Eastern Test Range.

For the Americans the catch-up mentality took over and somewhat typically the ambition was to win straight through to the next stage of space flight.

The testing that had gone on at Edwards Air Force Base would take too long to get anywhere according to some influential desk men in Washington. The number one priority was to develop a system that would take man to the stars – astronauts were to be the flavour of the decade. Space in all its uncertainty was to be assaulted at breakneck speed – or so it was hoped. Even the National Advisory Committee for Aeronautics, NACA, the leading body in the race, took on new importance and a new title to reflect the urgency. NACA became NASA – the National Aeronautics and Space Administration. But what of the astronauts? These were the men who would restore the nation's pride were they not? The astronauts would make all that business about covered wagons and four score years worthwhile. Surely, the place to go was Edwards. Surely, the astronauts were going to be the ultimate in test pilots; they were going to drive America into space. To do that, the men chosen for the mission would have to be the leanest, fittest, steeliest-eyed, most intelligent, brightest and bravest of the legendary band of test pilots, what Tom Wolfe called the people with the Right Stuff. Well, not quite. A monkey would have done the job that NASA had in mind.

The test flights had been straight from the motion picture screen. Lean, tanned pilots in the slim flying suits that had attempted to replace the hand-tooled boots and stetson as symbols of unquestionable manhood; sleek, mean, powerful and roaring flying machines that were both faithful steeds and broncos to be tamed. The drama, and tragedy too, were there for some West Coast director to cut his television teeth. The rocket plane tests meant hanging the aircraft from the belly of a larger plane. When it had reached the right altitude, the test pilot climbed from the mother ship to the rocket plane and was literally cast off at about 25,000 feet. These early days of trying to break the sound barrier were, in pilot terms, far more stimulating than anything envisaged for Project Mercury, as the first American manned space flights were to be known.

The rocket tests went on. X-15 was an important project inasmuch that it represented space flight to the public image. It was not, but at that stage it hardly mattered that it did not. X-15 appeared twelve months after Sputnik 1 and, just as much as the technical achievement it promised, the rocket pilots represented the hero element in the national programme. Not even Sputniks nor the American Explorer rockets had heroes (although Sputnik 2 did have Laika the dog!). Until the seven astronauts for Project Mercury had been chosen, it had been left to people such as Chuck Yeager to stand up as, in his case, sound-barrier breakers. He was the true hero, something that America loved. An ordinary guy, joins the Services, becomes a combat hero, moves to flight testing, takes his rocking, buffeting craft to the edge of the world of sound and then goes one point further and into the stable environment beyond the barrier. To top it all, Yeager was a man who looked and sounded the part. So, surely, if all the hero worship was justified by the enormous achievements of the Yeagers and the Kincheloes of the conventional world of flying, think how much more was to be achieved by the first Magnificent Seven, the original astronauts in Project Mercury.

Indeed nothing was left to chance. The Seven – Scott Carpenter, John Glenn, Virgil Grisson, Deke Slayton, Alan Shepard, Gus Cooper and Wally Schirra – were presented at press conferences, signed up for minor fortunes by *Life Magazine*, offered super-executive homes at knock-down prices by real estate developers (to attract big spenders who wanted to live near astronauts), received huge discounts on fancy cars and generally were turned into the sort of nationally known figures associated with the more successful television soap operas. Yet, while all this was happening, they had not been anywhere! The news management of the Project was absolute. The astronauts could be exploited in a simply controlled manner. Articles about the men and their families were vetted, sanitised, re-touched and presented in a manner designed to make the nation feel good. The men were utter professionals. In some cases they did not like what was going on; however, the professionalism that had given them successful careers to that point was not about to let them and the nation down. These men were training to go into space in the most ambitious project designed by American scientists and engineers. They were astronauts, a new breed of hero; these were the men who would lead the victory parades that would surely follow when America regained her pride by becoming the first country to put a man into space.

By the spring of 1961, all was ready. There had been a series of humiliating set-backs such as test-rockets blowing up in front of invited audiences. But, by April, Alan Shepard, a naval commander on the Magnificent Seven team, was ready to go with the technology. There had been those (it seems like the whole of the American public) who had thought that John Glenn, the epitome of the hero, would be the first man in space. However, it was to be Alan Shepard; that is, it was *supposed* to have been.

On April 12, 1961, a rocket lifted off from Tyuratam and for about one hour Yuri Gagarin was in space. The Russians had achieved the unthinkable, they were the first to put a man into space *and* into orbit.

When Commander Shepard went into space the following month on May 5, he did not go into orbit. He reached an altitude of 116.5 miles and then splashed down in Freedom 7, his capsule. Virgil Grisson in Liberty Bell 7 had a similar flight in July. It was not until John Glenn and Friendship 7 were launched the following year, on February 20, 1962, that America could say that at last she had put a man into orbit around the earth. The difference between a simple venture into space and an orbital flight was enormous. Going into orbit meant that there was more control of the flight in the new environment.

The Soviet reaction to Commander Shepard's flight was a little muted at first. Many thought this was a calculated attempt to belittle the achievement. While there may have been something in this in the official Soviet mind, it should be remembered that until fairly recently, perhaps the early 1980s, the Soviet media have always been slow to react to any event beyond Russia's borders. In a society where the media are controlled by the ruling bureaucracy, and when that bureaucracy itself is cumbersome and utterly reliant on consensus, then snap news broadcasts and quickly written editorials are not to be found. Nevertheless, the Soviet reaction on the day was interesting.

There was a brief mention of Alan Shepard's flight during the four o'clock afternoon radio bulletin. It was brief and certainly not the main news of the day as far as the Russians were concerned. 'U.S. Press Agencies have just reported that a rocket with a man on board was launched from Cape Canaveral, Florida, today. The U.S. National Aeronautics and Space Administration reported that 15 minutes after the launching the capsule with Alan Shepard, the pilot, having separated itself from the rocket had come down in the Atlantic 302 miles from

Cape Canaveral. Shepard was picked up, together with the capsule and, as reported, now feels well. The rocket was launched vertically and reached a maximum altitude of 115 miles.'

When the next bulletin was broadcast, the news of Freedom 7 and Alan Shepard had for some reason disappeared from the news broadcast. It was back again in the evening. During the 7.30 p.m. news, Western diplomats monitored the Moscow Home Service. At first it seemed that the Russians were ignoring the first American in space. The first eleven news items were about the Soviet Union. Finally, two thirds of the way down a very long bulletin, came the item on America's space shot. It was very correct, but had a slight sting to it:

'. . . the launching was carried out vertically without putting the rocket into orbit . . .

'. . . the U.S.A. does not propose to put a man into orbit round the earth before next year . . .'

And, as a reminder that Shepard's voyage could not be compared with Gagarin's, the 8 o'clock news that same evening said:

'Our science correspondent describes this as a notable achievement by American scientists. It gives us reason to hope that in due course they will be able to put a manned spaceship into orbit around the Earth, *as the Soviet Union did recently*.'

The Americans were getting a pat on the head. By the following day, the Russians had settled down to an almost gleeful, but not spiteful, comparison of the Gagarin and Shepard flights: 'from the point of view of technical complexity and scientific value, it ranks below the flight of Yuri Gagarin . . .' The Soviet attitude was that of a nation who had won the first leg of a very long race. For the moment Gagarin had shown the way in spite of the achievements of Shepard and Grisson. It was not until the following year and John Glenn's flight that there was any public recognition at home and abroad that the Americans were catching up.

The interesting effect of this Glenn flight is that he far more than Shepard became the conquering hero. Shepard may have been the first in space, but Glenn was the first to orbit the earth. The significance of that may have been lost on the American public, but not on the publicists. After all, going round and round was *real* space flight! Furthermore, John Glenn was a perfect hero for God, Country and Family. And the cynic might say that being a hero at that stage was the main aim of the national machine that needed the dollars and political backing to continue the manned space programme and the largely military elements within it. But, in spite of their superb and supreme technical abilities, the Magnificent Seven did not have much to do when it came to getting the capsules into orbit and bringing them back. In fact, one astronaut, having splashed down, managed to start a mechanical process that led to his capsule sinking. The astronauts were encouraged to do as little as possible on the flights. How they reacted was faithfully recorded by an assortment of medical gadgetry wired to and secreted in almost every conceivable nook and cranny of the astronauts' expensive bodies. They were, in many senses, guinea pigs. However, guinea pigs and monkeys do not perform very well in the post-flight bonanzas and so, partly thanks to the Magnificent Seven, American space flight survived.

In the Soviet Union, the public disappointment and later triumphs were apparently seen with some amusement. One Russian who watched the start of this space race offered the opinion that there had been a certain element of surprise in Moscow. Because there had been a confident design bureau for decades investigating rocketry, there was every confidence in the Soviet promise to do exactly what it did – put a machine and then a man into space. But among the Soviet leadership there were certain doubts. They had not the confidence (sometimes over-confidence) displayed in the design bureau. The leadership did not exactly abound with qualified engineers and scientists able to make independent assessments of the forecasts and promises made by Soviet space engineers. Furthermore, the leadership in the Kremlin secretly feared the enormous dollar-technology of the Americans. When the Americans had said they were going into space, the tendency in the Kremlin was to believe them. What the Russians knew about American research suggested that the Americans had more than sufficient resources to back their claims. (This perception of the power of American technology continues to exist, which is one of the reasons that the Soviet Union made so much fuss about President Reagan's Star Wars plan.) And so, in the closing months of 1957, the Russians appeared to some to be quite confident of the American ability to catch up.

As far as can be known from open sources and a few private

conversations, the Soviet Union did not have the same problems with the selection of their early cosmonauts as the Americans did with theirs. Certainly there were no *Life Magazine* contracts although, in their own way of privilege and power, the original cosmonauts did very well, as indeed did those who followed the early teams. It has always been said that the first man in space was Yuri Gagarin. But there is a story, rarely if ever voiced in Moscow, that there was another, an earlier, launching, and an earlier cosmonaut. A late comer to the Soviet manned-flight team is said by some to have been a young man called Vladimir Ilyushin who was the son of the head of the plane design bureau that carried his name. The story goes that Ilyushin exploited his family position and used the time-honoured currency of the Soviet Union, *blat* – influence – to have himself promoted to lead pilot. The influence was said to have been great enough for the authorities to agree to the flight, and the young Ilyushin went into orbit at the beginning of April 1961. The flight is said to have been a technical success and the capsule recovered. However, it is said also that Vladimir Ilyushin suffered some sort of collapse which may even have been a stroke, perhaps during the strain of re-entry. Those who believe this story say that Ilyushin was taken to a private clinic where he lived for some time in a state of semi-paralysis.

The flight records in the West that are available for this period do not show any launching that would coincide with the alleged Ilyushin orbit. There was a suggestion in Moscow during 1982, that the launching of the Sputnik 10 space craft on March 25, 1961 could have contained a cosmonaut; in the author's opinion there is no evidence other than hearsay to support this. Sputnik 10 is considered to have carried a dog when it was launched from Tyuratam. Certainly the Soviet Union would not have wished to make public a failure at that stage, especially as it might have involved a member of such a prominent family. Some to whom the author has spoken have said that there was an earlier attempt to launch but that it did not actually take place. Others have suggested that the tale about Ilyushin is outrageous, while two independent observers volunteered the information that the story is true.

Such was the curiosity in Moscow about Ilyushin, that a well-placed official pointed out that, in January of that year, Ilyushin's leg had been in a plaster cast after an accident. The inference was that Ilyushin could not have been fit enough for a space flight by, say, March. Certainly there was a great deal of Soviet pressure to shake off the thought that Ilyushin could have been the first man to attempt to go into space.

Whatever the truth, it should be generally accepted that the first man in space was Yuri Gagarin, then a twenty-seven-year-old Air Force officer. Gagarin fitted perfectly the mould of the ideal Soviet success story. Should there ever have been a desire publicly to justify the philosophy of the Revolution, then Yuri Aleckseyevich was the example that would have been chosen. He even looked the part; to Western eyes he was the slightly stocky, blond, blue-eyed Russian with a permanent smile. Gagarin might have been taken down from one of those huge propaganda posters seen all over the Eastern bloc, he was indeed a text book product of Marxist-Leninism with a sad ending.

Yuri Aleckseyevich was truly a child of the masses. His parents were of peasant stock. Gagarin's father was a carpenter on a collective farm near the town of Gzhatsk when Yuri Aleckseyevich was born in 1934. Gzhatsk was in a region between Moscow and Smolensk that had seen its fair share of conflict during the previous seven centuries. There were tales of war that began with the Tatars and continued with the Lithuanians, the Poles, the Russians, the French and finally the Germans. Gagarin was bright and hard-working. However, he did not shine so much that he was snapped up as a future test pilot by the time he was sixteen. Indeed there is a suggestion that he had not even considered the idea of joining the armed forces as a career, although he knew that unless there was considerable *blat* he would have to go to the Army for three years as a conscripted soldier. Like a lot of young men, he sought a trade and was sent to a special trade school in Moscow. It was this, oddly, that started him on his journey into space. When Gagarin left the trade school in 1951, he was sent to one of the eight higher education institutes in the seventeenth-century city of Saratov on the Volga River. The school was an industrial college, it had nothing to do with the Services, but while Gagarin was there he joined a group learning to fly. And, just as Deke Slayton, Pete Conrad, Neil Armstrong and others had in the United States, he became hooked. Gagarin was in love with flying from the very first flight and, like some in the United States, he knew that flying would not only give him the freedom of the skies, it would be the way out from the expected, the predictable route that society was waiting for him to pick up in some industrial complex.

And so Gagarin was sent even further east, to the Air Force cadet school at Orenburg. He graduated in 1957 in time to see the Soviet Union launch the world's first space craft, Sputnik 1, in the October of that same year. If there was ever a year to graduate as a pilot with vision, then this was it. 1957 was a good year for morale-boosting in the Soviet Air Forces. Gagarin was only twenty-three and said to have been a natural pilot, and on his way to becoming a good one. It is said also that it was primarily Gagarin's ability and his outstanding skills as an aviator that resulted in his being transferred to the hallowed list of trainee cosmonauts. The Russians were looking first and foremost to the best pilots to be cosmonauts. Here was a contrast in approaches between the Russians and the Americans. The Americans did not think that they necessarily had to have the best pilots in the initial astronaut team of seven. If a man were good enough, then he would obviously be good at everything – including driving high performance aircraft, should that be his job. Certainly there were obvious examples among the Magnificent Seven that suggested clearly that NASA had not gone for the best pilots available. Driving a space capsule was not high on the list of tasks for astronauts. The Russians, however, did go for their top young pilots – until their first woman cosmonaut. The Americans wanted a prestigious payload who would ideally keep his hands to himself except in an absolute emergency that ground control could not handle by remote control. They wanted somebody who would be wired for every form of biological sensor while finding time to button crunch a few operational sequences. Even the switching and pressing could and would be monitored, especially if a sequence might be late or missed. The prime task was to put a man-sized payload into space and bring it back. The secondary task was to have a man in it.

There was, it will be remembered, a certain friction in the American camp once it was realised that there was no real need for an operational pilot and that, in the earliest designs, the pilot would not be able to see much anyway.

The Russians made a great point, that the man was important, and that the automatic and remote control technology needed back-up of the major skills of experienced pilots. When Gagarin went up in Vostok 1 he went as a pilot complete with manual controls and an ejection seat that had both been in the original design. When he came back, Gagarin was an international hero. It is said that the Americans were stunned. How could it be that the dollar-technology had once again failed to take them to first place? The Russians could only guess at the inner feelings of the Project Mercury team. Publicly the Soviet Union received international acclaim and more was to come with a succession of manned orbits. Those who followed Gagarin into space appeared to have been selected for cosmonaut training in 1960, or in one case identified in 1959, which was earlier than the American process. The Russian team was just as much of a mixed bunch as the Americans, the main difference being the emphasis on pilot training. The next man into space, German Titov, was younger than Gagarin. Titov was born in 1935 in Siberia, but he too graduated as a pilot on 1957. Andryan Grigorevich Nikolayev had been a forester before joining the Air Force in 1954 and then the cosmonaut training team at the same time as Gagarin. One of the older generation was the most senior of the original team, Colonel Pavel Popovich. He was born in the Ukraine, near Kiev, in 1930, although he was twenty-four before he joined the Air Force.

The military pilot pattern was broken in June 1963. Valentina Vladimirovna Tereshkova was born in 1937. She had been a keen parachutist and was to win many championships. It was her parachute training and achievements that caught the eye of the cosmonaut training organisation, and Tereshkova was signed on. It is said that Valentina Tereshkova was not the only woman on the team in 1963 and had not been picked for the flight of Vostok 6. She was the reserve, but got the flight. It is said also that the thoroughness of the Soviet space medicine system was not sophisticated enough to recognise that basic feminine characteristics might be affected by the rigours of launch, orbiting and re-entry. Tereshkova is thought to have gone through considerable discomfort during her 48 orbits. It is interesting that it was not until 1982 that the next woman went into space. She, too, was a Russian, Valentina Savitskaya, and part of her task was to carry out tests that would see more clearly the effects of space flight on a woman under controlled conditions, rather than the Tereshkova experience which appears to have been confined to something along the lines of 'How d'you feel?'

However, there was no lasting medical effect on the former girl from a cotton mill who became the first woman in space. Like her colleagues, she became part of the Soviet Union's élite.

It is interesting that, although there were no big *Life* deals, the Soviet cosmonauts did receive the same sort of heroic welcome that their American counterparts had experienced. In some cases they did much better than the American astronauts in simple material terms. There were parades, speeches, toasts, personal appearances, international visits, lectures and, of course, honours. Gagarin set the pattern when he became a Hero of the Soviet Union, and was given the medal of Pilot Cosmonaut of the Soviet Union and the Order of Lenin. By now it was not Major but Colonel Yuri Gagarin, and much later his home town of Gzhatsk was renamed in his memory, Gagarin. With this list of honours came the extras so important in Soviet life. Just as the relatively low-paid American astronauts had welcomed the magazine payments, and the special discounts, so Gagarin and his colleagues welcomed the special country homes, the dachas, the access to special stores where almost anything could be bought that was not available to the ordinary Russians, or even to other officers of their ranks. Gagarin, Titov and Tereshkova became deputies in the Soviet Parliament. Valentina Tereshkova, as seemed appropriate, became the President of the Soviet Women's Committee. Titov and Nikolayev became generals. Craters on the moon were named after them, statues appeared, streets bore their names.

And just as the Americans had stuck to their own characters, with the ambitious and determined such as John Glenn remaining ambitious and determined, so the Soviet cosmonauts stuck to theirs. Some went on, as they might have done anyway. Others enjoyed their special positions. The Russians were just as capable as the Americans of having their equivalent to a beer-call. There is talk of enormous parties, of excesses only to be enjoyed by those with influence and perhaps that special something that took them on the trail to cosmonaut training in the first place. Gagarin was no exception. He spent a great deal of time, it is said, entertaining and being entertained. He especially appreciated Air Force reunions and although he never went into space again he, like the American team, enjoyed the exhilaration of flying fast jets, which was not always easy to organise once away from operational duties. And that is how he died.

On March 27, 1968, just seven years after he went into space, Gagarin was flying with another pilot in a two-seater jet on what was described as a training flight. He crashed and both were killed. Gagarin's ashes were put into the wall of the Kremlin – an honour reserved for only the most special people in the Soviet system. And, to remember that first flight, April 12 has become Cosmonauts Day in the Soviet Union.

All this was but the beginning for both the United States and the Soviet Union. There is perhaps a temptation to over-emphasise the relative lack of importance of the astronaut and the cosmonaut in those early days of flight. Manned flight programmes may indeed have diverted resources from more basic military space projects, but if space was going to become anything but an alien environment, then man had to be sent there as soon as it was safe to do so. There were experiments that he could initiate and control, especially over a long period. It is true also that it was thought even during the 1940s that, at some later date, there would be small groups of people working in space. Certainly, by the 1960s, the military was convinced of the advantages of some space-based system. There was talk of space stations that could be used as observation platforms, just as von Braun had imagined after the Second World War. There was an idea of mounting a command and control centre in space. And why not? These were the thoughts of intelligent men and women whose job it was to recognise potential advantages for the security of their countries.

The pioneer astronauts and cosmonauts were more than the people who took the first places in space. Because they were successful in the public relations sense, so they made contributions to keeping public and political support for what were even then truly astronomically expensive programmes. This was particularly important as the military had no easy task in channelling funds into the space programme, which necessarily needed long-term commitment. But, from the beginnings in 1957, the progress of launchings continued to be marked by the heavy thumb-print of the military, and defence satellites, however well disguised, stood out like sore thumbs in the yearly lists of launchings.

Chapter 4

Platforms

For those who collect comparisons, averages and percentages, it is possible to produce impressive statistics of the use of defence-based satellites. For example, given that three quarters of all space launches have some military purpose, it could be shown that on average two satellites are sent into space every week with an easily identifiable defence-related task. Of course, such a statement is vulnerable to the charge of fiddling with statistics to prove a point. However the basic estimate that up to 75 per cent of space craft have some military use seems to survive most criticism and is rarely challenged by those who actually task and use the space programmes. To demonstrate the way in which satellites are used supports the general claim that the military has the majority shareholding in outer space.

There are eight readily identifiable types of military space craft. As might be imagined, satellite design varies from user to user, i.e. from country to country. Indeed, just as with more commercial flight programmes, technology is improving on capabilities and so one country may have more than one type of satellite in service doing the same job. The descriptions of these satellites tend to be unsatisfying to some because the elementary problem of Soviet secrecy means that technical descriptions and therefore capability assessment concentrate on American systems. Yet the functions of both American and Soviet satellites are more or less the same and so, with some caution, the descriptions that follow may be accepted for general purposes as common to all space craft in their categories. The eight types fall easily into an order of military importance: Photographic Reconnaissance Satellites; Electronic Reconnaissance; Ocean Surveillance; Communication; Early Warning; Navigation; Meteorologic, and Geodetic Satellites.

Photographic reconnaissance satellites were perhaps the most obvious development in the craft of defence Intelligence analysis once the superpower space programmes got under way during the late 1950s and early sixties. The ability to look down upon the enemy with relative safety had long been the ambition of all military commanders. Yet, at first, the raw Intelligence gathered by satellites provided no real advantages; after all, aircraft spy flights were long-established. Aircraft reconnaissance flights had featured as early as the First World War; photographic interpretation had developed to very high standards and to some extent this conventional form of Intelligence gathering was adequate for most commanders. Furthermore, aircraft retained two enormous advantages as reconnaissance platforms: they were (and remain) relatively cheap to operate compared to space craft and, they had (and have) enormous flexibility. An aircraft can be tasked at almost a moment's notice. It can be deployed almost anywhere in the world and it can return quickly with its pictures. Within hours of the sending of a spy plane, the photographic Intelligence can be on the analyst's desk. This flexibility was obvious in the earlier period of space flight. It could take days to get back photographs from a satellite. The problems were apparent, but not always appreciated in an age where technology had an increasing reputation for providing instantaneous solutions.

Although it was (and still is) physically possible to launch a satellite and bring it back once it had photographed its 'target', the costs, both fiscal and in terms of resources, were enormous. Consequently, it made some sense to leave a satellite 'up' for as long as possible; this could mean that pictures too remained aloft, although ways of recovering them before the satellite's return were quickly and simply found. Also, satellites had great restrictions on their orbits, and so it was not possible to gather information on every target, many of which might have been way beyond the space craft's flight path (or 'ground track' as satellite engineers say). There were difficulties also in recording what was possible to see as the satellite over-flew the territories of interest to the Intelligence analysts. A satellite in reasonably high reconnaissance orbits of, say, 300 or so kilometres could photograph wide areas. The cameras used were well able to cope. Getting more details of a particular area meant a sharper resolution from the satellite's equipment and ideally a lower altitude for the satellite. However, the lower a satellite flew, then in simple terms the shorter time it could remain in orbit, because the gravitational pull was greater in low altitudes. This meant that more effort, including a bigger energy supply, was needed to hold a satellite for long or, ideally, to be able to return it to a higher orbit. Accordingly, the thinking was that two satellites were needed: one for area reconnaissance and another for detailed reconnaissance. But there remained the problem of getting back good resolution pictures. In theory there was no great difficulty in transmitting pictures from a satellite to ground control. The task was to bring back those pictures in good quality. The surest way was to throw out a capsule of film that could be picked up and processed on earth.

The American programme experimented with capsule recovery for some considerable time. The first American satellite in the Discoverer series went into orbit at the end of February 1959. The orbit was a polar one, which would allow the satellite to photograph the world. But actually getting back the pictures did not come about for eighteen months. However, on August 18, 1960, when Discoverer 14 was launched, the Americans had at last achieved a reasonably reliable photographic reconnaissance programme although, as we shall see, the photographs were disappointing. Discoverer 14 is understood to have photographed the Soviet Union during a 27-hour schedule and then the film was ejected in a small capsule, which survived separation and re-entry and was picked up in mid-air using a very unspacelike technique. The Americans simply flew an aircraft trailing a huge web along the descent path of the capsule and endeavoured to catch it in the 'butterfly net'. On occasions when the system failed, a back-up meant that some capsules were picked up from the ocean, others were not. Some capsules failed to separate from the space craft and others went the 'wrong way' – up, not down. But, whatever the shortcomings of both the Soviet and American systems at this period in the very early 1960s, both superpowers recognised that it would not take very long for technology to iron out the initial difficulties.

The Americans were quick to establish a joint authority to handle this and existing forms of high altitude Intelligence gathering. The Intelligence Board in Washington set up

COMOR, the Committee on Overhead Reconnaissance. In 1961, and following an evaluation of the capsule recovery techniques tested in the Discoverer series, American Intelligence established the National Reconnaissance Office – still an extraordinarily secretive organisation and one of the few 'unlisted' American agencies. With the setting up of the N.R.O., overhead Intelligence gathering had truly come of age in organisational terms.

The Russians were having trouble with their technology. It was as if they knew what to do, but did not have the tools to do it. One consequence was that although they had got into space and had scared the Americans with their successes, the Soviet scientists now dropped behind in their programmes to build successful photo-reconnaissance. It appears that it was not until April 26, 1962 that the Soviet Union launched a reliable near earth photo-reconnaissance satellite, Kosmos 4. Kosmos 4 and subsequent Soviet space craft had short orbital lives. The authorities in Moscow decided that they had to be brought back for the films to be recovered. Often those flights were as short as a couple of days and never longer than about two weeks. (The reason that the Soviet programme is believed to have started with Kosmos 4 is partly because it is very difficult to see that any Russian system up to that point was capable of being dedicated to photographic Intelligence gathering. Once the programme was established, however, progress was reasonably simple to identify although there was no Soviet published analysis.)

The Kosmos photo-reconnaissance programme appears to have been divided into four groups – a characteristic initiated in April 1962 and continued to this day. This grouping meant considerable overlapping. For example, the first series continued until 1967 although the second started in 1963. The major differences were in size, equipment, flight times and orbital data, manoeuvrability and launch vehicles.

The first series tended to have flight times of no more than a week. The second series had, it is said, better camera equipment, a more or less consistent flight period of eight days, and used larger space craft. The third series was more elaborate still and probably had on board other sensors than mere cameras. This series established the twelve-day flight times used so often to illustrate the Soviet Union's preference for short flights. Although times on this series were extended by the 1980s, it was only by a few days. A further illustration of the overlapping is that the third series continues at the time of writing, even though the more elaborate fourth generation began in the autumn of 1975.

The latest generation of Soviet systems was immediately recognised as being considerably larger than anything seen before in the series. The first Kosmos cylindrical shape had measured 4.3 m long with a diameter of 1.83 m. The new series started with Kosmos 758 which was 7.5 m long and had a diameter of 2.6 m.[1] Considering that the technological advances since the first series must include miniaturisation of equipment and weight-saving materials, then the increased size might be said to indicate something of a considerable advance in on-board systems. The latest generation of Soviet systems is thought to be more manoeuvrable, thus introducing flexibility for those who task the craft for Intelligence-gathering. It is thought, too, that the satellite has a larger range of camera options and the ability to transmit high definition Intelligence to ground control as well as a multi-capsule system for ejecting film. It has been seen also that the new generation remain in orbit for much longer periods – another indication of the Soviet Union's ability to get back pictures without having to recover the space craft.

The Soviet Union maintains a continuous cover with low orbiting photo-reconnaissance craft. Taken as an example, Kosmos 1504 had a high point (apogee) of 307 km (191 miles) and a low point (perigee) in its orbit of 172 km (107 miles) when it was launched from Tyuratam in October 1983. But the satellites are not orbiting at similar altitudes. Kosmos 1499, launched a month earlier from Plesetsk, had an apogee of 415 km (258 miles) and a perigee of 356 km (221 miles). Satellites go into different orbits and angles of orbit (inclination) depending on their launch sites and their objectives. But what can Soviet photographic satellites really see?

As mentioned earlier, Soviet space craft had few problems counting and identifying ships of the Royal Navy task force as it prepared for the Falklands.[2] During those inspection flights, quite small modifications would have been apparent. A similar flight by Kosmos 1504 was able to monitor the American invasion

[1] RAE Table of Earth Satellites 1957–1982.

[2] See also Chapter 10.

of Grenada. At the end of the third week in October 1983, the Americans started to make diplomatic noises about the political situation in the Caribbean island of Grenada. There were some suggestions in Washington during the previous week that the United States was contemplating military action, even intervention. Although this was denied, the suggestions persisted. During this period, the Soviet Union launched its photo-reconnaissance satellite Kosmos 1504 from Tyuratam (October 14). On October 25 the American force invaded the island. It would appear that, although the Soviet Union had its photo-reconnaissance craft in operation, four days elapsed before it made a pass directly over Grenada.

During the week before the invasion, Kosmos 1504 was over the Caribbean monitoring U.S. Naval movements. There is no published evidence to suggest that the Soviet space craft was able to keep a constant watch on the events leading to invasion, nor are there any real indications that satellite observation was being relayed to Moscow with enough clarity to allow diplomatic intervention at, say, the United Nations. However, shortly after 0800 on October 29, Kosmos 1504 is known to have overflown Grenada, recording the deployment of U.S. troops, equipment and ships.

Kosmos 1504 was particularly interesting to satellite analysts. It was highly manoeuvrable, allowing ground control to position it with a modest amount of flexibility in an area that was of particular interest to the Soviet authorities. Furthermore, it would appear that Kosmos 1504 carried a series of high resolution cameras in its long cylindrical hull which would have recorded remarkable detail during its 53-day life span. Even the 53 days in space, while not unusual for American space craft, represented a relatively long period for Soviet photo-reconnaissance satellites, especially as top quality pictures are not so easy to transmit.

The problem of getting back pictures was a vexing one for the United States in the early days of photo-reconnaissance. Indeed, reconnaissance had tested the minds of Washington's defence thinkers for some years. It should be remembered that the idea of having military satellite reconnaissance is not something that evolved from the progress of the American and Soviet space programmes. From conversations the author has had with Soviet military experts it is clear that the advantages of satellite reconnaissance were recognised and developed in Moscow long before the first Sputnik.

As we have seen in Chapter 2, in the United States, the concept had been in official thinking for a quarter of a century before the first 'successful' photo-reconnaissance flight by a satellite. The RAND Corporation studies of space flight showed that Intelligence-gathering from outer space was quite feasible; these studies of the mid-1940s certainly had an impact on the Air Force. Further recommendations from RAND's Santa Monica bureau in the early 1950s endorsed this thinking. By 1954 Project Feedback, also a RAND study, urged the U.S. Air Force to enter the business of space-based Intelligence-gathering. The urgency was recognised but the technology was not at hand. The following year, both superpowers announced that by 1957 they would be launching small 'scientific satellites' to mark International Geophysical Year. Defence departments in both Moscow and Washington recognised that the term 'scientific satellite' would eventually cover a multitude of defence or defence-related programmes. And so, in the American capital, projects such as Pied Piper and Corona were conceived.

Pied Piper was an Air Force programme originally designed to build a satellite system that would gather pictures of the Soviet Union and send some of them back before the satellite came down. The C.I.A. put together a package, Corona, that was based on a spy-satellite flying by 1959. This satellite would eject a film capsule. Then followed the panic of the autumn of 1957 when the Russians beat the Americans into space. The National Security Council was less concerned with the loss of national prestige than it was with the military advantage that it believed the Soviet Union now had. Four months after Sputnik 1's launch, President Eisenhower – equipped with a military background that enabled him to believe the logic of the National Security Council's concern – was encouraging his Defense Department to get a reconnaissance satellite into space with all haste. By then, the Pied Piper programme (which was hardly a world leader) had been re-named Sentry. Sentry was part of a three-pronged programme which included the Discoverer flights and MIDAS (Missile Defense Alarm System).

An important aspect of the Discoverer series was that it included the Corona programme, and the sensitivity of Corona was based on its ability to test methods of recovering capsules of film rather than wait for the satellite to come back – if indeed that was a reliable possibility. But why should there have been this double dose of security? The reason was simple: there were many in Washington who believed that, if the true nature of the Discoverer/Corona programme became public, then the Soviet Union would perhaps take action to damage the satellites. Nobody could be sure if this was technically possible, but two factors were reasonably disturbing: nobody in Washington was willing to dismiss the thought that the Soviet Union was in space first and, unlikely though it might appear, could have the technology to manoeuvre a Sputnik into the path of a Discoverer; secondly, the Soviet Union had hinted that it was willing to go to extremes to protect its privacy. (It demonstrated this determination by shooting down Gary Powers in his U-2 spy plane.)

The C.I.A.'s Corona project was not particularly successful at first and certainly the U.S. Air Force knew that it had an opportunity to get its own programme into space. The Sentry project mentioned above had, by the end of the 1950s, become known as the Satellite and Missile Observation System – SAMOS. And so, when the Air Force launched SAMOS 1 in October 1960, it was with an expectation that it would have the only fully working photo-reconnaissance satellite. The majority of the thirty SAMOS launches between 1960 and 1963 were very successful in terms of satellite engineering. It is, however, as we shall see, difficult to support the claims that SAMOS was particularly good at photo-reconnaissance. The priority given to the project was established by the national security needs as seen in Washington. The President was convinced that the new high ground had to come under American command. SAMOS also had the advantage of Air Force backing at a time when the Air Force dominated the organisation of the N.R.O.

By the time SAMOS was running towards the end of its project life, the United States had established a new programme that was to be known as KH. Even in 1963, the KH satellites were clearly earmarked for a long career in gathering photographs of the Soviet Union. The KH series (often called Key Hole) were initially split into two types, reflecting the earliest recognition that, until there were vast improvements in technology, it would be necessary to have some satellites that would go after large area pictures and some that would be tasked to pick out details.

The first, KH-5, failed to get into orbit. Yet, by the time that the KH-5 series completed its programme in 1967, only four of the 46 area reconnaissance satellites had been classified as failures. It has been somewhat difficult to piece together the area and detail programmes, mainly because the United States naturally classified its military reconnaissance programmes; as far as the public was concerned, the KH programmes did not exist.

The KH-5 series looked at area targets. KH-6 looked for details. There were 36 close-look KH-6 satellites put into orbit in the four years starting in 1967. And it was with the dual role KH programmes that it was possible to get some idea of the needs and limitations of photo-reconnaissance satellites. For example, the KH-5 launchings carried more film and equipment than previous space shots; this was necessary as the satellites were expected to stay up for longer – on average for about three weeks or more. The close-look craft, the KH-6, stayed in orbit for less than a week. KH-6 flew in quite low orbits, often below 100 miles altitude, which meant presumably that they were subject to huge fuel problems as they fought the gravitational pull tempting them back to earth.

The problem of gravitation pull was illustrated in the next generation of detail satellites. The KH-8, which replaced the KH-6 in 1966, swept as low as 80 miles above the earth to take close-look pictures. However, the huge pull of gravity meant an obviously elliptical orbit was necessary; accordingly, KH-8 used a high point or apogee of about 250 miles. This high apogee reduced the drag on the satellite and allowed it to stay up for longer periods. Certainly, one of the characteristics of the KH-8 series was the longer life patterns. The KH-6 series had 'lived' for three weeks or so. The KH-8 satellites, commonly up for four months or more, were examples of satellites not necessarily having urgent tasks throughout their life span.

On February 28, 1981, the United States launched a KH-8. Most attention at this time centred on Poland where the Solidarity movement felt itself threatened by rumours of a Soviet invasion. The KH-8 is understood to have monitored the Soviet troop deployments in the Polish border region including the Zapad-81 troop exercises, together with the state of readiness of Soviet divisions based inside Poland.

For area surveillance, the less detailed picture, the KH-7 was the space craft first equipped with workable infra-red scanners.

This development would have overcome a basic problem of photo-reconnaissance in the earlier years: in the inability of satellites to 'see' at night. A further develoment for KH-7 was the introduction of an improved data link system which allowed reasonably rapid transmission of information to ground control. KH-7 was a considerable improvement on the Americans' existing area-surveillance system and, by the time KH-9 came along in 1971, it was logical that the new space-craft would have to be much larger in order to take on board the new technological advances, some of which had been developed for other space projects, such as the Manned Orbital Laboratory.

KH-9 became known as Big Bird – though it had a dull official title, Code 467. KH-8 was a cylindrical satellite about 4½ feet in diameter and perhaps 24 feet long. KH-9, or Big Bird, was twice as big and is thought to have weighed at least four times as much. Furthermore, this huge photo-reconnaissance craft is known to have stayed in orbit for as long as eight months at a time. Photographs were 'wired' back to earth or they could alternatively be sent back in the four capsules carried on Big Bird.

In spite of the innovations of the 1960s and '70s there had been for some time an obvious need for instant photo-reconnaissance. Both the Soviet Union and the United States had recognised that the ideal would be a 'perfect' television camera in the sky relaying instant pictures by night and day, through all kinds of weather, and through all kinds of camouflage techniques. The problem of weather, darkness and even camouflage were relatively simple to overcome; but 'real-time' transmissions of high quality pictures were not readily available. Certainly the need for this 'real-time' or instant photography was there for every military commander to see. The Middle East was just one area where both superpowers wanted to know what was going on twenty-four hours a day. That region also provided an example of the superpowers' desire to extend the military use of outer space to occasions, crises and targets beyond each other's borders.

At the time of writing it is believed that the United States has an advantage over the Soviet Union in real-time photography. That advantage was sent into orbit for the first time in 1976; it was known as KH-11 and more generally called Key Hole although officially listed as Code 1010. This space craft is 64 feet long but weighs considerably less than the Big Bird series, which says something about its role and the rapid development of miniaturised systems. But the most obvious, although not necessarily the most important, difference is the life of the KH-11. At a time when Soviet photo-reconnaissance satellites were orbiting for about 13 days, the KH-11 was up for 760 days, more than two years. The technical details of KH-11 are hard to come by, unless of course one happens to be a member of the K.G.B.'s technical analysis staff. Less than a year after KH-11's first launch in 1976, an obliging ex-C.I.A. officer sold the K.G.B. a copy of the space-craft's technical manual. Moscow may well think that the manual was a bargain – just $3,000 paid to the former C.I.A. employee. (The KH-11 is a C.I.A. satellite.) The extra aspect of KH-11 was its dual capability; this allowed it to act as a signals intelligence (SIGINT) satellite as well as a photographic craft. The SIGINT element, classified TOP SECRET UMBRA, had certain limitations which are now being corrected. These included the real-time transfer of information and the availability of the satellite. A new and as yet most secret project that could take over some of this work has been code-named AQUACADE. Its existence has never been publicly acknowledged, but it can be said that it could be launched from the American space shuttle. (If for no other reason, launching Aquacade from shuttle flights would reduce the Intelligence-gathering bill.)

So far, not even the K.G.B. is thought to have many details of the future generation of American photographic satellites. The next one will probably be launched in 1986. Officially, its development programme does not exist. It may be called KH-12. However, considering the development progress involved, the United States may be about to launch a new series. There are some in Washington who occasionally refer to a top secret project called the Ikon and it could be that this, coupled with Aquacade – which to some suggests ocean surveillance – is the next phase of photo-reconnaissance. Whatever it is called, the project will probably have an added night-sight capability, a better system of seeing through cloud and a method of instantly relaying higher quality pictures than those from KH-11, which are understood to be less successful than the technological advances available suggest. After all, the satellite engineering is of little value unless the Intelligence agencies can get their hands on the main purpose of the programmes – good, clear pictures. So, how do the pictures come back?

The space-based photographic industry has to be divided

into what might be called 'conventional' and 'unconventional' sensing. The ideal for a photo-reconnaissance satellite is to operate above clear skies, in daylight with targets bared to the lens of a super-sensitive camera. The problem is that ideal conditions for satellite photography rarely offer themselves.

The three most common types of air-reconnaissance cameras are strip cameras, panorama cameras and frame cameras. Strip cameras are very simple. For example they do not have shutters; instead light, i.e. the image, goes through a slit onto film that rolls on in time with the earth's movement. The major drawback of such a process is that the photographs do not produce a stereo-picture. This means that, say, a building's height cannot be measured, only estimated. The panorama camera, which relies on prism or lens rotation, often produces distorted images, but it could cover wide areas – hence its title. The last in the group, frame cameras, use either a single or multi-lens system. They produce tiny distortions only and they can be used for stereo measurement.

In its simplest form the technique of returning images is not difficult; in a one to ten league table of satellite problems, picture return probably rates no higher than one or two. (The quality of photography is further up the scale, as we shall see.) The pictures can come back using the capsule recovery technique described earlier. But a commander may not have time to wait for the next capsule drop and so the technique of onboard transmission had to be quickly developed – and anybody with a reasonable knowledge of commercial photography or a respect for polaroid-type systems will recognise that, in the basic system, the technique is obvious.

The film feeds through a short and long focal length system of double lenses. As the film is fed, it is automatically developed – and fixed. It then goes through a heater to dry and then it is spooled onto a scanner. The scanner is electronic. A beam is shone in horizontal lines across the negative. Because the photographed image has differing densities, the light beam penetrates the negative at differing intensities. This variation in the light beam is 'read' by a signal generator behind the film. The generator transmits signals that correspond to the intensity of the beam. The signals are picked up by a ground station and converted to the original form of intensity: thus the picture is reproduced on earth. There are evident drawbacks including loss of quality during transmissions and rebuilding the photographs, as well as inadequate originals.

There were perhaps three immediate problems facing the Soviet and American overhead Intelligence-gatherers from the very start: light, weather and platform. A reconnaissance satellite flies relatively low, fast and, allowing for rotation, may pass over the same spot only twice a day as it orbits the earth every 90 minutes or so during a far from perfectly smooth ride. Consequently, the pictures taken over the target have always needed to be ideal first time round. Secondly, some system was needed to steady the whole process. This was not too difficult, especially at the distances involved between lens and subject. But the other two problems – light and weather – were not so easy for the American and Soviet scientists to solve.

Most photographic equipment could work only in what is generally called the 'visible light' segment of the spectrum. (Satellite cameras found little use for flash attachments!) Consequently, simple photography meant that neither the American nor the Soviet satellites could photograph in the dark. The Americans had a further problem: weather. Northern Europe, and certainly the European and northern latitudes of the Soviet Union, have some of the consistently foulest weather in the world. For most of the year, there is considerable cloud cover above many important military sites. Even with modern techniques, it is by no means certain that American and Soviet satellites could monitor troop formations and strengths should there be a winter crisis on the Central European front.

However, techniques beyond simple photography were quickly developed or adapted for satellite use by both superpowers. To use sensors that did not depend on visible light meant working on infra-red systems. Basic infra-red photography got over the problem of darkness because, as its title explains, it works in the infra-red segment of the electromagnetic spectrum. Nevertheless it needed still to rely on being able to pick up a target's reflection – it needed to be able to 'see' the target and, although infra-red photography is blessed with cat's eyes, it is difficult to allow for cloud distortion.

An important aspect of infra-red photography is its use of colour. Colour infra-red film is peculiar in that it does not show objects in their natural colours – it uses 'false' colours. If a commander were to be shown a false-colour picture from an infra-red film he would find that all the tanks were blue and the leaves and grass were red. This property has very real advantages, especially when it is remembered that the film is depending on a subject reflecting its infra-red radiation. If, for example, a tank commander hides his squadron by covering them with cut bracken, this will perhaps prove adequate camouflage at first. But as the bracken dies it no longer has the same properties and therefore loses its radiant effect. Therefore the satellite's infra-red scan will not be fooled by the bracken because it will not be red but perhaps a bluish tint. Similarly, artificial camouflage netting will not show up red on the scan. A refinement of this form of photography allows systems to work in the outer ends of the infra-red electromagnetic spectrum, picking up heat traces of the subject.

The value of having a sensor that traces heat radiation is that temperature differences are revealing even when they would not be to the human touch. An infra-red sensor way out in space can pick up a parked tank from the heat given off by its engine. Perhaps that is simple to believe. What is harder to comprehend is the way in which that same sensor can tell how many aircraft have been standing in the formation even if they are hidden in a hangar, or even if they took off some minutes before the satellite passed over. The waiting aircraft will have left an almost imperceptible outline on the tarmac by radiating heat differences. It is common for Intelligence agencies to have photographs showing an empty runway, but at one end a clear outline of an aircraft. The outline is the heat shadow left behind and the satellite can pick it out.

A further advance in space photography has been the ability to combine the best techniques to produce one image. It is possible to use, say, combinations of mirrors and telescopes with luminous flux through lens multipliers. This multi-spectral scanning takes many pictures at once. Each picture is in a different region of the electromagnetic bands, the result being a more comprehensive look at the target. Furthermore, digital computer building has allowed military Intelligence scientists to break pictures into minute detail, to assign colours to certain portions and materials and then to rebuild the picture in such a way that key elements, that might otherwise have remained hidden, are revealed.

Nevertheless, to get the best results a satellite still needs stable and clear conditions. For example, a photo-reconnaissance satellite might be in what is known as sun-synchronous orbit – it moves in a north–south polar orbit in line with the sun so that each daily pass over the same spot is made when the sun is at the same angle, thus reducing the chances of confusion, e.g. shadow. All this assumes that the basic sensor can 'see' its target.

Even when the weather is clear, there remains the problem of resolution. Resolution is talked about a great deal in satellite reconnaissance studies; in layman's terms it is the 'sharpness of the picture'. It is possible to recognise resolution as the distance between two objects before they blob into one as far as the sensor is concerned. Therefore a good sensor will be able to distinguish very small objects, and it is then said that the sensor has a high resolution, i.e. the pictures are sharp. This is particularly important when satellites are used to pick fine details on an important Intelligence target. It is also one reason why satellites are so important on verifying arms control agreements. For example, a treaty might declare that one side is allowed only a certain size missile launcher (thereby restricting the types of missiles allowed under the treaty). The other side must have a satellite that is good enough to identify, examine and measure the launchers if it is to be happy that the treaty is being observed.

Furthermore, a high resolution satellite may be able to pick out, say, a submarine in harbour but it may not be able to satisfy the Intelligence analysts. Because of its obvious characteristics, a submarine could be identified as an object of some specific form by a sensor with quite a low resolution, perhaps 100 feet. But, before the Intelligence analyst could say what class of boat had been seen, he would need pictures of resolutions as high as six feet. To identify some new aerial or attachment on the submarine, the resolution would have to be less than one foot.

The Americans needed only resolutions of between three and five feet to pick out Soviet SS-20 sites. But resolutions of less than six inches were needed by the Technical Intelligence (TECHINT) branch for detailed analysis. In fact in 1983 and early 1984 the American Intelligence system failed at first to detect the potential deployment of SS X-25 missiles among sites originally identified by U.S. satellites as SS-20s; they picked out the sites, but not what they were to be used for. Consequently the American figures announced for SS-20s in Europe were misleading to the Western European members of NATO and the general public.

The Russians were not deploying SS-20s as fast as the Americans said they were. In fact, the general standards of military satellite photography has not always been as good as some have suggested.

There are those in the U.S.S.R. who have admitted that there were, especially in the early days, enormous deficiencies although their satellite targets in America were often in much clearer conditions than the American targets in the U.S.S.R. The famous SAMOS programme mentioned above is often said to have produced excellent results for American Intelligence. There is a series of recorded documents claiming that the SAMOS pictures of the early 1960s identified in some detail Soviet Intercontinental Ballistic Missile (I.C.B.M.) silos, Ballistic Missile Defence (B.M.D.) systems and much more. Yet, there has been no real evidence to support these claims, which is odd considering the important effect those pictures were said to have had on American missile policy. Indeed, there are some who might suspect that, although the SAMOS project proved the potential of this form of Intelligence-gathering, it failed to produce exceptional Intelligence.

By the 1980s there had been enormous improvements. Both superpowers had developed space-based radar imaging that went some way to getting over the problems presented by cloud cover. Synthetic Aperture Radar (SAR), for example, among other things allowed the sensor to look at its subject at an angle – essential for the analyst. There were also important advances in real-time picture transmission. The Soviet system is thought to be behind the Americans', but Washington's determination to have almost instant monitoring has led to faults in the overall system. One example considered by many in Washington was the lack of capsule return pictures. It is possible that the funds that went into building the onboard systems of the KH-11 paradoxically led to gaps in the American Intelligence network.

The KH-11 and developing systems boast a complete digital photo-reconnaissance system. The development programme allowed it to record an image and then, via another satellite, the satellite Data System relayed the pictures in digital form to ground control, probably inside 60 minutes. One result was that the capsule return systems used by the elder satellites were not improved nor were the number of satellites increased – the funds were in the more 'modern' system. However, it could be argued that the digital system does not provide the high resolution pictures of, say, the KH-8 and KH-9. None of this should detract from the capability of the KH-11 which, apart from its obvious roles, is said to have been used to track an IRA arms smuggling ship across the Atlantic (although the constant monitoring reported is unlikely) and to have checked out America's first space shuttle when it was thought to have lost some of its heat protection tiles. KH-11 was used also to survey the escape route for the abortive American rescue attempt of U.S. hostages in Iran. The system has limitations. For example, the original satellite pictures for the American invasion of Grenada in 1983 did not get through the small amount of cloud cover.

When it is remembered that, on average, Eastern Europe can expect to be under clear skies for no more than 40 per cent of the year, then the importance of radar enhanced sensors is understood. And there are parts of the Soviet Union where clear days are much rarer than 40 per cent. Some important military areas can go all year without more than a few hours' glimpse of a blue sky. Furthermore, because techniques have been developed to see in the dark and through cloud, it should not be forgotten that, under both conditions, the quality of the pictures may be almost useless to the Intelligence analyst. While the existing and developing systems have recorded for both superpowers important advances in the other's military orders of battle there have been some important 'misses'.

It is difficult to get details of Soviet failures – although, as we have seen, conditions for Soviet photo-reconnaissance are considerably better when monitoring the United States where many strategic bases are in 'clear-weather' locations. The Americans have had two major misses during the 1980s. The failure to count the correct number of SS-20 missile launchers is one (spy satellites count launchers, not missiles). The second was more serious. The Soviet Union has built huge and vitally important defence radar systems at Pechova and at Abalakova. Yet, in spite of the advances in satellite monitoring, it took nearly two years for the Americans to 'find' the Pechova radar on their scans. Furthermore, it was not until the Abalakova radar had been under construction for more than a year that the American system photographed it. To add insult to injury, the radars were not 'found' by space Intelligence, it was not a satellite system that 'told' Washington about the radars. The Defense Department and the C.I.A. were told by an agent that 'something' was being built in those areas, and that it would be a good idea to get the satellite to have a look at that 'something'.

There are those, of course, who would not accept that photo-reconnaissance has many drawbacks. They point to the success of systems that can identify and count an army unit, that can look at such a slant angle that a side view of a ship is clear, at systems that can detect camouflaged weapons and hidden missile silos, and spot railway lines that have appeared within mere weeks and therefore indicate a new missile site or weapon test centre. All this is true. It is true also that photo-reconnaissance satellites, in spite of the billions of roubles and dollars being spent, are not the great success stories that many think. However, to the military commander, they are absolutely essential as part of his overall reliance on space. For a quarter of a century the space-based photo-reconnaissance satellite has attempted to improve the military efficiency and readiness of both superpowers. In spite of the understandable secrecy surrounding them much can, as we have seen, be deduced. The same cannot be said of perhaps the most secret of all the satellites – the electronic Intelligence gatherers.

Chapter 5

Elint

A friend in Washington once joked that he never talked about SIGINT because one could never know who might be listening. Knowing his job, I suspected it was he who would be listening. In Moscow, I was told that the ability of the U.S.S.R. to eavesdrop on her potential enemies as well as her friends was no less than that of the United States to do the same. There is little known publicly about this form of Intelligence gathering, especially when it is applied to space-based systems. The general description of these satellites comes under the broad description of electronic Intelligence gathering, ELINT. This is a sometimes confusing term in as much as most satellite systems rely on electronics for gathering information including photo-reconnaissance. However, the description may be judged appropriate because by and large these satellites are trying to 'capture' electronic emissions. They listen for electronic noises; their targets are radar and radio transmissions. Once the satellite senses the squeak of a radio broadcast, then it pounces. It is not surprising, therefore, that, in the jargon of the Intelligence world, some of these satellites have become known as ferrets.

Generally, these satellites are described as systems used to gather information about missile tests, radar 'signatures' and general radio traffic, altogether an important function of Intelligence. During a missile test, for example, there are numerous signals sent out by the rocket so that ground control can monitor different aspects of the trajectory; this is how the engineers can tell how their weapon will perform. The Russians pick up American signals from sites in Cuba and from specially fitted ships beneath the rocket's flight path. The Americans do the same with stations in such places as Turkey and a special missile tracking unit built recently by the United States in China. So important is the information from the rocket tests that the Soviet Union now has most, if not all, of its missile signals in code. This would appear to be an obvious precaution. The Western argument is that test data should not be encoded. The data should be in plain 'language' in order that the West can tell if the Soviet Union is breaking arms control agreements by developing missiles not allowed under existing treaty arrangements, indeed part of the American objection is that, by hiding signals, the Soviet Union is breaking treaties. Monitoring treaties allows also a reasonable amount of information for the Intelligence analysts to prepare weapon assessments for their own missile builders and for those engaged in anti-missile defences.

This was obvious to both superpowers some time ago and Moscow started to encode this information as soon as it found out that Washington had the power to analyse rocket tests. For many years the United States had believed herself to be well-covered to monitor these tests by using a series of ground stations, in particular one at Kabkan in Iran which came under the general codename TRACKSMAN. At the time of the Islamic Revolution in Iran, few outside an inner Intelligence sanctum in Washington realised that the removal of the Shah meant more than the demise of a trusted, if abandoned, ally. The most crucial monitoring post for Soviet missile tests was threatened. For a short while, the Kabkan post continued to operate. American Signals Intelligence (SIGINT) agents kept the receivers switched on in the hope that, if the location could be continued without too much embarrassment for the revolutionary leaders, then the new régime would regard the Americans as some form of insurance against the Soviet Union interfering in Iranian affairs. But the revolution caught up with SIGINT. Kabkan closed down.

It was the closure of Kabkan that forced the Americans to go to the Chinese for help. The Chinese had some interest in the American suggestion that a listening post be built as soon as possible. Once an ally of the Soviet Union, the Chinese were long since regarded as potential enemies by the Russians. The Chinese believed that the Soviet Union would not give a second thought to launching a missile attack on, say, Peking should there be a Third World War. The Chinese believed such a conflict to be probable rather than simply possible. Consequently the authorities in Peking were 'all ears' when American officials asked for base facilities, especially as it was easy for the Chinese to extract a promise that the American analysts would share the results of their eavesdropping. Consequently the little-known listening post was built in a distant part of Western China in the Xinjiang Ulghar region. The Xinjiang Ulghar base has not completely replaced the Iranian post, but it has provided a useful addition to space-based systems. Furthermore, there are indications that, some time in January 1985, the United States made suggestions that her ground system in China might be added to. It is possible also that, with the Chinese interest in the Soviet Union's military activities, the part of the 'rent' on the listening post side is an agreement that the United States should hand over copies of its Intelligence reports when they concern Soviet capabilities that may be considered a threat to the Chinese. Some of that information would be gathered by satellites monitoring telemetry signals from Soviet rocket tests. However, land-based monitoring systems are limited and so Telemetry Intelligence (TELINT) had to be boosted by space systems.

The Americans and Russians had long used satellites for signals monitoring, although the Soviet systems were considered to be less efficient. Moscow's recognition of what they considered to be an American lead was heightened by a launching on March 6, 1973. The space craft was given no name by the Americans. It had an 'international designator' of 1973, 13A, and nothing else. In fact, this was the first launching of a most important signals gathering satellite. It was called Rhyolite. There are no official details other than its 1973 13A designation; however, it is probably cylindrical, about one and a half metres in diameter and less than two metres long. It was put into an orbit some 22,200 miles above the earth. The satellite was then 'parked' in geosynchronous orbit over the Indian Ocean where its main job was to listen for the Soviet missile test signals. Three more Rhyolite satellites were launched (two in 1977 and one in 1978). For the first three or four years, it appeared that the Soviet Union either did not understand or did not believe the extent of the Rhyolite's capabilities. It was only with a remarkable breach of American security that the Russians learned the truth. They managed to get information from a spy working in the United

States.[1] He told them not only the purpose of Rhyolite but added in some detail its operational function, including the way the data was transmitted back to earth and analysed; and the accuracy of that information.

The accuracy was considerable although the amount of information was limited. The original satellites were hampered by the need to have more sensitive antennae, and this was particularly important if the space craft were to correctly gather the vital data at the early stage of a test flight. In Washington, the Pentagon wanted more information about the important boost phases of the rocket. The boost phase occurs immediately after lift off as the term suggests, and it is the point of boosting the rocket's pay load into orbit. Knowing what happens at this stage will allow rocket engineers to compute trajectories, ranges, payloads and even targets. One by-product of this analysis is some idea of defensive measures that might be taken. This is particularly important today considering the enthusiasm in the United States and the Soviet Union for a new era of anti-ballistic missile technology. For example, an essential element in President Reagan's so-called Star Wars plan has been the desire to be able to attack the missile in this boost phase, when it is most vulnerable and the chances of destroying its mission are the greatest.

In all, it can be seen that satellite interrogation of signals is of vital interest to both superpowers. But, inevitably, there is much more involved in the space-based electronic Intelligence gathering systems. Some of it is straightforward 'snooping', other parts involve inter-government co-operation (in the case of the West) that is politically embarrassing – or, in parliamentary terms, could be – if the details were fully learned. For example, the connection between American and British Signals Intelligence (SIGINT) is considered to be so secret that essential evidence in the so-called 'Belgrano Affair' was withheld from the British Parliament and therefore the public. It may well have been possible for a limited amount of the information passed to Britain by the United States to have satisfied many Parliamentary minds and thus saved Margaret Thatcher's government from continued

[1] See Robert Lindsey's *The Falcon and the Snowman*, Simon & Schuster, New York, 1979.

sniping in both Houses, from the media and during the course of the Ponting affair. Yet the decision to protect the link overrode all other considerations.

An example of this 'secrecy' is to be found in Yorkshire. America's National Security Agency selected the site for a Signals Intelligence base in 1966. It is to the west of Harrogate, known as Menwith Hill, built on what was farmland until the 1950s and officially owned by the British Defence Ministry. However, although the installation is supposed to be British-owned, the operational control comes from Fort Meade, Maryland, the Headquarters of America's National Security Agency. This does not mean that the United Kingdom has no part in the running of this Top Secret establishment. British signals Intelligence staff from G.C.H.Q. (Government Communications Headquarters) at Cheltenham are assigned to Menwith Hill.

The work of the Yorkshire site is an indicator of the way in which electronic Intelligence gathering has progressed during the past twenty years. Menwith Hill is a listening post. Its function is to intercept messages including diplomatic traffic in Western Europe as well as that in the Eastern bloc. New technologies took Menwith Hill into the space age. It not only uses satellites to pass on its Intelligence finds to NSA headquarters, it apparently acts as a down-line station for American Intelligence satellites including the Big Bird series. But, of course, the main interest is in the satellites themselves.

The superpowers started operating ELINT satellites in the early 1960s, within five years of the first space flights. These first flights were crude and did not work particularly well. The Americans were said to have launched their first test ferret in December 1961. (Another source dates the first flight at March 1962.[1]) The Soviet Union was far slower in entering this area of Intelligence gathering and, although certain space craft may have had the capability of eavesdropping as a second or third role, the designated Soviet ferrets appear to have come much later than the Americans'. Soviet ELINT gathering craft, such as the Kosmos 1441 launched on February 16, 1983, are all about the same size with the same orbital characteristics. Kosmos 1441, with a weight of 2,000 kg, is in a reasonably steady orbit, reaching

[1] Tom Karaas, *The New High Ground*, Simon & Schuster, New York, 1983.

a height of 640 ks and a low point of 629 ks. As with other space craft, statistics are hard to come by in the Soviet Union (the Americans are equally sensitive) but, looking at the more recent launch and orbital statistics of the Soviet system, it appears to be operating in such a way that one ELINT satellite is phased with another. Presumably, this phasing improves the cover. For example, during 1983, three Soviet ELINT satellites – Kosmos 1515, Kosmos 1470 and Kosmos 1455 – appeared to be working together. The suggestion is that the Soviet Union has a twenty-four-hour coverage of radio and radar transmissions. It would, for example, be possible for a satellite to monitor communications between the Defence Ministry in London and a commander in the South Atlantic or Hong Kong although this is not as simple as many have suggested. It is of course more exciting to think that an electronic monitoring satellite could pick up a private telephone conversation between, say, a Cabinet minister and his senior defence adviser in N.A.T.O. headquarters in Brussels. There is a deal of evidence which suggests that this is possible, although it should be remembered that land-based telephone and signals interception is hardly a modern craft.

The first American designs for ferret Intelligence satellites appeared at about the same time as both superpowers were fighting to be first in space – in the 1950s. Just as the Intelligence agencies recognised the territorial limitations of aircraft photo-reconnaissance, so the electronic eavesdroppers had problems, in spite of the extensive range of land-based listening posts. As we have seen was the case in Iran, the land posts cannot be anything but politically vulnerable, especially should there be changes in host governments. There was a realisation, too, that the technology of the 1950s and 1960s would soon be overtaken and any planning for future space-based systems would have to absorb the huge leaps in technology if full advantage were to be taken of the new environment. The immediate problem in the early days was political as well as technical. Technology costs money and this meant that any forecasts presented to the budget controllers in Washington or Moscow had to be endorsed by a confident definition of what could be achieved in space that was not already available on earth.

There has long been a body of opinion which has suggested that the Soviet military does not suffer the same budgetary control as its American counterpart. There is evidence that this is only partly true, however; some experts in Moscow have suggested to the author that the Soviet electronic Intelligence programmes had great difficulty in getting through the established bureaucracy. If this should seem unlikely, then it might be remembered that, although a huge amount of financial and scientific effort was being put into the Soviet programmes in the early 1960s, the technical shortcomings were evident to those with the task of making the final recommendations to the decision makers.

It was not until 1970 that the Soviet Union launched its first comprehensive ELINT satellite to monitor American radar and communications signals. This was Kosmos 389. A similar craft, Kosmos 405, was sent up on April 7, 1971 and a regular pattern of these electronic snoopers was established with as many as four a year being launched by the mid-1970s. Their function was simple: to read military signals from even the shortest burst of radio transmission or radar emission. The satellites were said to be able to intercept signals and divert them to ground stations for unscrambling and analysis. They had, especially in the early days, enormous problems in being in the right place at the right time. A relatively low orbiting satellite, as these were, did not and could not loiter over one radar area and wait for it to 'shine' its frequencies. Consequently, the Russians found a need to launch a number of craft in order to space them out in the hope of improving the coverage. The Russians needed also to send up satellites that could 'specialise'. One result was to have some ferrets looking after land-based systems, while others took on the infinitely more difficult task of monitoring naval radars. By the mid-1970s, the Soviet scientists had managed to overcome some of the problems in the latter task to produce a system for ocean surveillance.

For the Soviet military Intelligence gatherers, the 1970s were a boom decade. If we look at any short period at random then the extent of that activity is impressive. For example, in 1973 military reconnaissance ferret satellites from the Soviet Union were launched on January 11 (Kosmos 543), January 20 (Kosmos 544), January 24 (Kosmos 545), February 1 (Kosmos 549), March 1 (Kosmos 550), March 6 (Kosmos 551) – launched on the same day as the United States sent up its first operational Rhyolite – March 22 (Kosmos 552), April 19 (Kosmos 554), April 25 (Kosmos 555), May 5 (Kosmos 556). These last two may have been connected also with a Soviet experiment for operating its nuclear ballistic missile submarines under the Arctic ice.

The year continued with launches on May 18, May 23, May 25, June 6, June 10 (Kosmos 572 – a new type of reconnaissance satellite), June 21 (Kosmos 519), June 27 (Kosmos 576), July 25 (Kosmos 577), August 1 (Kosmos 578), August 21 (Kosmos 579), August 24 (Kosmos 581), August 28 (Kosmos 582), August 30 (Kosmos 583), September 6 (Kosmos 584), September 21 (Kosmos 587), October 3, 6, 10, 15, 16 (Kosmos 600, a reconnaissance craft, and Kosmos 601, an ELINT satellite), October 20, 27 and 29 (Kosmos 604), November 10, 20, 21, 27 and 28 (Kosmos 610 and 611, both ELINT satellites), December 13, 17 and 21.[1]

1973 was interesting for the Soviet coverage of the Yom Kippur war. The war started on October 6. In September, confrontation had seemed likely and, during the closing days of that month, Kosmos 587 had been launched, but recovered two days before the fighting started. When the war began, Kosmos 596 was in orbit. It was an unmanoeuvrable craft but produced apparently an overall view. As we have seen above, there followed a veritable space scramble to get a good view of the conflict by photographing the area and by listening to signals. However, it should be noticed that a large part of the electronic eavesdropping, carried out by both the Soviet Union and the United States, was executed from earth-based rather than space systems. For example, both superpowers maintained ships in the area that were fitted with complex arrays of antennae and crewed by specialists from Signals Intelligence. There was nothing new in this war-snooping exercise in the region. Similar operations had been mounted in 1967 during the June War – and for the Americans with disastrous results which emphasised the need for space-based electronic Intelligence gathering. For that reason it is worth devoting a few lines to the incident involving the *Liberty* – an American spy ship.

In the early 1960s, the American National Security Agency

[1] The dates and details above are for those who would like to examine more closely the pattern of these launchings. This could be done by obtaining a copy of the Royal Aircraft Establishment's Table of Earth Satellites for that year. While the table will not say what kind of satellites were being launched, it does show the launch dates and orbital details with an enviable accuracy much praised on both sides of the Atlantic.

recognised that, although future space technology would offer much, the Soviet Union had a great advantage in its fleet of AGIs – Auxiliaries General Intelligence, more commonly known as spy-trawlers. The department called G group had been established more or less to monitor the Third World. It had grown from the old ALLO (All Others) section that intercepted signals sent by the non-strategic countries. This was a major department employing thousands of specialists whose job it was (and still is) to analyse signals and pick out Intelligence of value to the United States. Accordingly, it was this organisation that established the signals intercept operations in converted wartime merchant ships. One of these ships was the *Liberty*.

As reconnaissance satellites peered down at the onset of war, the *Liberty* sailed into the Eastern Mediterranean just as the conflict started. On board, the Agency's Arab linguist tuned in. Unfortunately, in spite of the enormous leaps in technology and especially Intelligence gathering, instructions that the spy ship should stay well clear of the territorial waters of the combatants failed to reach the *Liberty*. On June 7, Israeli aircraft attacked the *Liberty*. Cannon shells and napalm ripped into the upper decks, the radars, monitoring antennae and hull. As the ship's company gathered the dead and the wounded, the air attack was followed by Israeli naval craft. A shell and torpedo attack took care of the superstructure and the Intelligence compartment in the hull. As a culmination, it is reported that Israeli gunboats then attacked the life rafts that were launched. The U.S. fleet in the area launched aircraft in the *Liberty*'s defence, but apparently, because the U.S. stand-by aircraft were armed only with nuclear weapons, little could be done immediately, until the Naval Air Force re-armed itself with 'conventional' weapons.

It is not the purpose of this description to discuss the rights and wrongs of the *Liberty* incident. It does, however, provide an insight into the importance that both sides in a potential or actual conflict would attach to each other's ability to gather signals Intelligence. The Israelis said at one stage that the *Liberty* was mistaken for an Egyptian transport vessel. This seems unlikely, and more credibility might be given to the suggestion that the Israelis knew that the *Liberty* could intercept plans for a later phase of the fighting concerning Syria. Whatever the reasoning, it might be deduced from this one example that the importance of signals Intelligence is so great that, in some future conflict, the need to take out electronic, photographic and communications satellites would be absolute in any commander's view.

Even at this period in space weapons development, it would have been possible for the Soviet Union and the United States to attempt some action against each other's satellites, albeit without any certainty of a successful 'hit'. As early as November 1963, a satellite that suggested advances in anti-satellite capability had been launched from the Soviet site at Tyuratam. The satellite was called Polyot. The name translates as 'flight', which suggested a greater freedom than earlier craft. Polyot was distinguished as the first satellite that was able to change course and angles of flight by having a comprehensive system of remotely controllable manoeuvring devices. Proving that satellites could be manoeuvred so extensively (even more than had been necessary for the first experiments in manned flight) added a great deal to the Soviet research programme for anti-satellite weapons.

Meanwhile it was not necessary for either superpower to be convinced of the need to exploit the use of space as an environment for electronic Intelligence gathering, although the June Arab–Israeli war endorsed the views of those who believed research should be accelerated. Two particular points had increased the need for ELINT satellites after that 1967 conflict. The vulnerability of having limited ground-based facilities in a region not entirely available to the Intelligence agencies became more obvious. It might be argued that the *Liberty* incident need never have happened if the ship had stood further off the coastline, or facilities in Cyprus or Crete had been established. Yet electronic Intelligence gatherers need flexibility. Secondly, the speed of the June War – all but over in less than a week – showed the need to respond quickly. Therefore on the grounds of the necessities of quick response and geophysical freedom, space became an imperative playground for the Intelligencers in Washington and Moscow.

Electronic spying from satellites has been held as an all-hearing science. In the 1960s and 1970s there were enormous limitations. Most of the intercepts of signals traffic were carried out by ground stations. This is the case in the 1980s, which explains the need for National Security Agency stations such as the Menwith Hill station. At Menwith, for example, the Americans and British listen to traffic sent from Western as well as Eastern Europe. Menwith intercepts cables including those despatched by large commercial organisations. This provides the NSA Headquarters analysts in Fort Meade, Maryland, and similar experts at G.C.H.Q., Cheltenham, with important commercial as well as strategic Intelligence. Such stations could easily intercept, say, commercial loading instructions that should indicate if any suspect cargoes were being shipped to the Soviet Union, especially by devious routes. It is not too difficult to monitor cables between certain capitals by having key words, shipping agents or companies on a 'trigger' list. Such a system may show that a suspect agency is moving a computer cargo from Paris to Stockholm, but the suspicion might be that the ultimate destination is Leningrad. Similar monitoring techniques from other ELINT and SIGINT stations could intercept telephone and cable conversations that would suggest that an apparently innocent cargo was an IRA weapons shipment; and after that the rendezvous point would be easy to pick up.

The need to eavesdrop is justified by most governments. This need may have doubtful credentials when it is considered that Western allies spy on each other, when commercial traffic is intercepted or when it is obvious that even usually innocent birthday greetings telegrams are sometimes read. This doubt is doubled perhaps when the listening agency is in the West. The Western ideal of freedom does have some limitations. The Soviet Union is in the same business, but then, to put it crudely, the Soviet system has projected an image that makes it difficult for many to believe that official snooping is anything but part of the Eastern bloc way of life. Satellite Intelligence gathering systems can and do take on some of this work. It is possible to pick up a telephone conversation between a member of the Soviet Central Committee and his colleague in another city. The Russians can and do intercept, say, a call from a Washington hotel room to an office in the United Nations building in New York. But the billions of dollars and roubles poured into the ELINT satellite programmes during the 1960s, 1970s and now the 1980s were encouraged for mainly straightforward military reasons.

The series that started with Kosmos 389 in 1970 showed that the Soviet plan was to set up a string of satellites at about 400 miles above the earth. Each satellite was able to monitor radar and radio transmissions for up to two years. As we have seen, by the time of the next Arab-Israeli war in 1973, the role of the ferret electronic Intelligence satellite was well established.

During that year the Soviet Union launched fourteen satellites to be used for electronic monitoring of some sort or another. Seven of the satellites were short-lived monitors, not strictly ferrets, nevertheless they were capable of picking up signals and testing ground systems to the full. The Soviet launchings were, by this time, beyond the experimental stage, with easily noticeable characteristics in the flight data.

Kosmos 655, launched on May 21, 1974, was typical of the series of Soviet ELINT ferrets. It was launched, not from the big Tyuratam site, but from Plesetsk reasonably near Moscow. It was boosted into space by a C-1 rocket which is about 105 feet tall and a little more than eight feet in diameter and which was developed as a satellite launcher from the SS-5 missile. Once in orbit, the ferret Kosmos 655 circled the earth every 95 minutes at an average height of around 330 miles. It functioned for less than two years, but stayed in space until it decayed towards the end of 1980. Its job was to listen to radio broadcasts transmitted by military headquarters and sub-units, particularly those of the Americans.

That same year, 1974, the Americans supplemented their ferret programme with a number of small satellites launched together using just one rocket, on April 10. They were in quite low orbit and had decayed by the end of July. In December, the Soviet Union put up a new type of ferret and one which was immediately added to the target list of some future anti-satellite weapon. Kosmos 699's function was to intercept radar signals from Western navies. Others followed: probably Kosmos 777 on October 29, 1975 and Kosmos 838 on July 2, 1976.

The pattern of these craft continues today in various forms. One purpose is to pick out radar signals and to pass back positions of ships to Soviet commanders who can, among other things, practise using this information for mock attacks on N.A.T.O. strike fleets – especially attacks on aircraft carriers. There are two obvious counters to these satellites. A fleet commander has an up-to-date timing of when a satellite is likely to be over his area, therefore he can switch off during that period. With further satellite development giving greater coverage, this practice of controlling radar emissions may have less value especially as it is not always desirable to be so restricted. Accordingly, the second way of avoiding the satellite's long range stethoscope is to attack it.

The Soviet intention to devise a system to monitor ships in every ocean became apparent during the second half of the 1960s. It had been obvious for some time that if radar worked well on earth, why not put it into space? A weakness in electronic Intelligence had long been its inability to know where the other side was deploying its warships. Air Forces tend to be based at the same airfields, are usually listed in some obtainable publication and are reasonably simple to observe. Large troop formations are cumbersome groups which tend to give away their positions. However, within certain limits, once a ship puts to sea, it can within reason be easily 'lost', especially if it runs without too many radio signals and does not need predictable refuellings and replenishments from oilers and stores ships. The Russians put radar in space during the closing days of 1967. On December 27, 1967, Kosmos 198 was launched as the Soviet Union's first RORSAT (Radar Ocean Reconnaissance Satellite). A satellite with a radar on board has one major problem: it needs a powerful energy supply to keep the radar going. The Soviet RORSATS used a nuclear generator with Uranium 235.

In Washington and elsewhere, there was some concern that the nuclear power-pack could become a major hazard should it re-enter the earth's atmosphere at the end of the satellite's useful life. The American concern was not simply a propaganda exercise. There was sound scientific reasoning to endorse the view that very little had to go wrong for the reactor fuel to return to earth. There was, too, an element of experience behind this American worry, although the full details of that experience have been kept far away from the public relations brief in Washington. On April 21, 1964, the United States Navy had launched a Thor-Able rocket from the military pad at California's Vandenberg Air Force Base, the Western Test Range. The payload was a simple Navy satellite with a nuclear energy supply pack. However, there was a serious malfunction and the satellite never got into orbit, and the nuclear fuel was scattered across the Indian Ocean. Consequently, the Americans kept a close watch on the Soviet RORSAT programme, believing that it was equally vulnerable to technical mishap.

The RORSAT did not have a monitoring life of much more than two months. The Soviet plan was to separate the nuclear reactor from the craft and boost it into a high orbit where it could stay more or less into eternity. (Even this idea has many flaws, not least of all the problem that space is not meant to be a nuclear dustbin and the reactor will remain active for millions of years.) It took ten years for the Soviet system to go wrong in a quite spectacular way. Kosmos 954 was a RORSAT, launched on September 18, 1977. It came to the end of its life but, when the Russians attempted to boost its reactor into a higher orbit, they failed. On January 24, 1978, the reactor re-entered the earth's atmosphere and scattered radio-active debris across a large part of Canada. The Soviet Union postponed any further nuclear-powered flights for some two years.

On April 29, 1980, another radar satellite was launched for ocean surveillance. Kosmos 1176 was sent up from the Tyuratam launch site. The new craft appeared to be slightly lighter than the Kosmos 954 (4,450 kg as opposed to Kosmos 954's 4,500 kg) and went into a much higher orbit. The function was similar and once again the power supply for the energy-demanding radar was nuclear fuel. This did not much please the United States. There were comments of disappointment that the Russians were again using a dangerous fuel without foolproof safeguards. The noises off from Washington must have had more to do with the satellite's military mission than with the use of nuclear energy in space; after all, putting such power supplies into space was not an exclusively Soviet practice. This, remember, was 1980. For some years the U.S. Navy has used nuclear power units, known as the SNAP (System for Nuclear Auxiliary Power) series, including the double generators in the NIMBUS Arctic and Antarctic surveillance programmes. Furthermore, American government scientists had reached the conclusion that, should the Department of Defense decide to put certain beam weapons into space, then in at least one project, X-RAY lasers, that too would mean a large nuclear system, even an explosion.

In Moscow, the priority given to ocean reconnaissance was considered to be well-founded. The technological resources were considerable because the identification, tracking and targeting of Western fleets were weak areas in Soviet military strategy. Just two years after the resumption of the nuclear RORSAT programme, the Soviet Union had a practical test. The target was the South Atlantic during a crucial period in Britain's war with Argentina. One ocean surveillance satellite, Kosmos 1405, had been launched on April 29, 1982. Although this was part of the overall South Atlantic operation, Kosmos 1405 was not the

RORSAT expected by Western Intelligence. American satellite reconnaissance, however, reported further activity at the Tyuratam launch site. On May 14, 1982, Kosmos 1345, a 1,500 kg radar ocean surveillance satellite, RORSAT, was launched into a relatively low orbit of between 248 and 265 miles. The Intelligence community, having predicted the launching, now looked for signs that Kosmos 1345 would have a twin. Two weeks later, on June 1, Kosmos 1372 was launched from Tyuratam. It is believed that these two RORSATs monitored the British task force and presumably the by then limited activity of the Argentine fleet. (The Argentine Navy had not ventured far from home after the sinking of the *General Belgrano* a month earlier.) There is no hard evidence to suggest that the Soviet authorities passed on any information from Kosmos 1345 and Kosmos 1372 to the Argentine authorities. It has been suggested that the Argentines were, however, informed through a third power, although it is difficult to see that any Soviet-supplied information could have reached South America in time to be of any real tactical value, which would have been the priority by that stage in the conflict.

It is not possible to assess from open sources how effective are the Soviet and American ocean surveillance systems. No doubt, given the ideal conditions of a calm sea and known position of, say, a carrier battle group, then RORSATs are powerful additions to the military reconnaissance function. Yet, ships do have the advantage of being able to hide in the oceans. Furthermore, some in the Intelligence gathering business have suggested to the author that these particular satellites do have problems in relaying clear images of ships moving in relatively choppy seas. For example, one Western assessment of Soviet RORSAT systems concluded that a sea state above Force 6–7 would be a good hiding place for even quite large ships. Force 6–7 is nothing more than a sea with 'white tops'. It is not a gale force. A deep swell or trough affords similar cover according to this assessment. At the same time advances are rapid in satellite detection. Certainly, within this decade, many of the present difficulties could well be removed.

Some of the Soviet modifications are thought to be in hand, as well as the apparently continuing uncertainty over the engineering for boosting the nuclear reactors to higher and 'safe' orbits. Yet during the autumn of 1982, another RORSAT was launched, Kosmos 1402 and the problem that had occurred with

Kosmos 954 was repeated. The attempts to boost the nuclear reactor failed. On January 23, 1983 one part re-entered the atmosphere over the Indian Ocean and, the following month, the nuclear core landed in the South Atlantic.

In spite of the limitations, the Soviet RORSAT and EORSAT (Electronic Intelligence Ocean Reconnaissance Satellite) systems are considered to be threats to N.A.T.O. navies. The EORSATs which listen for radio and radar transmissions are the most easy to counter, simply by switching off when the satellite is in the area. However, it has been decided by the Americans that both systems are legitimate targets and in time of crisis would be tracked and, if necessary, destroyed. Both the Soviet Union and the United States recognise the threat posed by electronic Intelligence satellites. This threat could be degraded by present ASAT (anti-satellite) systems, largely because the systems discussed in some detail so far are 'reachable'. Their orbits are low enough and predictable. This puts them in range of the simple systems of ASAT developed by both superpowers. However, the threat from space systems extends beyond those satellites discussed so far. The role of navigation, early warning, communication and even weather satellites is considered by many strategists to be threatening enough for consideration to be given to ways of destroying them. Yet it is often the case that these 'higher flying' satellites are dismissed as harmless, unlikely to be damaged and therefore not easily considered as 'real' military satellites. This is a short-sighted view of a major element in the space support systems of any Eastern-bloc or Western commander.

Chapter 6

High Fliers

In recent years, the general study of the military uses of space has often concentrated on the more obvious systems. There have been understandable reasons for the focus to be on reconnaissance and electronic Intelligence gatherers. The functions of these two systems are unambiguous and the results easily seen or imagined. Furthermore, just as enthusiasts drool over the performance statistics of fast jets, missiles and tanks in their studies of conventional warfare, so the Intelligence-based satellites have an air of glamour in the world of space. As ever, the 'sharp end' equipment overshadows the enormous value of the apparently mundane logistical and support elements. Who ever hears of a navigation beacon leading a glorious cavalry charge! Yet the function of the navigator in positioning his commander's force is of enormous importance. The meteorologist is of no use to his general if he should wrongly predict the weather and the signaller is of little value unless he can establish contact with all units. So it is with the modern commander's most important aids to his battle plans. Certainly, in the three areas of navigation, weather forecasting and communications, space engineers have provided the most enormous improvements in battle management.

It may be argued that to include these three systems in a survey of military uses of outer space is to stretch the credibility of that survey. After all, the tasks are quite innocent, even benign. Certainly there is a danger that any new space craft that could possibly have some military value will be pulled into the increasingly fashionable net of criticism for any space system. For example, the author attended a meeting where television transmissions via satellite were discussed. It was suggested that this was sinister because the satellite broadcasts system could be used in a period of international tension, and in wartime, to relay psychological warfare operations (Psy-ops). Of course this has been considered and there have been covert practical runs by some Western agencies. Yet it would be quite wrong immediately to include T.V. satellites in the list of direct military uses of space.

Equally, it would be wrong to suggest that the nightly T.V. weather-forecasting pictures provided by satellites are examples of military uses. Thirdly, the ordinary telephone-satellite link is no more a military operation than the Direct Broadcasting Satellite, the weather picture and the Navsat used by supertankers and yachtsmen. However, they all represent basic technologies needed and exploited by the military.

Communications have always been enormously influential in the ways of planning and executing wars and the deterrence factors of the military. Deterrence is very much an ingredient of the modern East–West jargon, yet the same term might have been used for centuries. Deterrence is in part the ability of one side to maintain large enough forces for the other side to believe that no worthwhile gain would be made by challenging those forces. Another part of deterrence is the opposition's belief that the deterrent force would and *could* be used to defend dearly-held principles. In other words, deterrence relies as much on the opposition's perception of its value as it does on its military capability. With the development of sophisticated reconnaissance systems, the chances are slim of disguising the military values of various systems. The modern equivalent of dummy archers atop besieged battlements are fewer and more impossible to maintain. Consequently, assessments of threats at all levels (local, widespread and eventual) are seen to be easier to obtain. However, just as the military had advanced from the days of dummy archers, so it has gathered about it the extraordinarily complicated paraphernalia of war. Having used sophisticated systems to establish threat levels, the modern commander is faced with the enormous task of implementing a response. That response will be, at the very least, as complicated as the threat. Response will range from do-nothing to all-out nuclear war. Even an almost innocuous change in the so-called threat level will prompt a wide range of response hardly imagined by the civilian bystander.

Suppose, for example, that during a period of particularly tense East–West relations two apparently low-key happenings are observed in the Eastern bloc by Western signals Intelligence. Let us imagine that the time is late August and the SIGINT reports that Soviet troops for the first time in years are not being released to help bring in the harvest. Imagine, also, that an intercepted signal suggests, but does not confirm, that Soviet embassies in Washington, Bonn and London have been instructed to incinerate all classified documents. Thirdly, an unconformed report suggests that the Soviet leader may have returned to Moscow a few days earlier than expected from his holiday dacha in the Crimea. Nobody is going to start crunching nuclear buttons on this evidence of war-preparation. However, the Indicators and Warning analysts in Western Intelligence would probably be bringing each detail to the attention of senior commanders and eventually to the Supreme Allied Commanders Atlantic and Europe, SACLANT and SACEUR. The removal of troops from the traditional harvesting duties could mean that ground units were being brought to a higher state of readiness. (Soviet forces are maintained in three stages of readiness. A, B and C. Only Category A units are near a war footing, the others have to be brought up to standard by influxes of equipment and manpower.)

The early return of the Soviet leader is not so unusual, but in general it may be easily seen as a sign of him taking personal charge. The burning of documents would be in some circumstances seen as an indication that the embassy was to be evacuated, or precautions taken in case it should be overrun; document-burning is a classic war-indicator. Continuing with this reasonably low-key set of Indicators and Warning, it is possible to imagine what might be the military response in the West. Remembering that the scenario is placed in August, the response would be extremely sensitive. A great part of N.A.T.O. goes on leave in August, so much so that many units shut down altogether. Therefore a sudden and widespread recalling of officers and men could aggravate the situation and even lead to a direct response because of either side miscalculating the intentions of the other. However, orders would have to go out to bring in certain groups of personnel, to make sure that essential equipment was brought up to a higher state of readiness and that established supply lines were free of physical and bureaucratic obstructions. Ammunition, fuel and spare stocks would have to be double-checked and arrangements made to correct any deficiencies. Reserves of equipment and manpower would have to be located although not necessarily activated. Checks on merchant shipping needed for transporting men and materials would be carried out as quickly as possible. Units that needed to be would be discreetly pre-positioned. Surveillance systems would be put on a higher work-rate and the analysis of their labours given maximum priority. And the results of all the readiness checks, analyses, preparations so quietly obtained would have to be passed along an enormous system of military, diplomatic and political conduits. The information could start at such extreme points as reconnaissance satellites in space, listening posts in China, South-East Asia, Norway, West Germany and Turkey, airborne patrols operating north of the Greenland/Iceland/Faroes Gap, a single observer at the entrance to the Bosphorus, and then proceed to such apparently mundane points as army transport stores or a Special Branch and Internal Security report on activities of known agitators and suspected subversives.

These are but a few of the responses to cautionary reports on a warm August afternoon.[1] But all those reports would be moved through the communications complex in the form of separate signals. Each one of those signals has to get through to the right desk at the right time so that it can go into the melting pot of analysis kept brewing in every modern commander's back room. Furthermore, the signals spectrum is even more confusing when it is remembered that, just as every signal is important, every attempt has to be made by the enemy to intercept each signal. A simple communication may appear insignificant; when it is put with other received or intercepted data then the commander will have better control and his enemy more time to make and amend his own plans. From this brief, imaginary and perhaps simplistic view of the use of signals, it may be accepted that one of the biggest problems facing a modern battle planner is the Command, Control, Communication and Intelligence (C^3I) system. Military systems have become so complex that in many instances they have become unacceptably cumbersome. Often,

[1] For a more developed war scenario, see page 147.

only the general or admiral at quite a high level has the necessary information about the enemy and the intentions of his Supreme Commander. Therefore his prime function is to maintain contact with the state of his own forces so that he can manipulate them in accordance with the overall battle plan – which may need changing by the hour. Improved battle systems and weapons have demanded (but not always received) improved Command, Control and Communications. Satellites have gone a long way in helping solve the basic problem, so much so that about seventy per cent of all long-distance military signals now go via space-based systems.

The first communications satellite (Comsat) was launched little more than a year after Sputnik 1. However, it was the American and not the Soviet space effort that achieved this development. Under the direction of ARPA, Advanced Research Project Agency, SCORE was launched on December 18, 1958 from Cape Canaveral. It was a great success although its ambitions were modest. SCORE was not a comsat as we know them today. It did nothing more than relay taped messages stored on board before launching.

Yet for the thirteen days of useful life, SCORE showed the value of satellites as relay stations and the technical opportunities available, considering that the engineering problems were by no means difficult for the emerging technologies of the late 1950s and early 1960s. In Washington, military space exploration had long been a matter of some political interest, an interest which, as we have seen, pre-dated the first flights. Some would suggest that comsats were victims of this political intrigue. Certainly there were those who felt that comsats should be relegated below the more obvious aims of the space programme: to establish military authority over the Soviet effort and to channel resources into a manned flight. SCORE decayed on January 21, 1959 and it was not until October 4, 1960 that the Americans launched successfully their next comsat, Courier. An attempt had been made during the previous August to launch a Courier satellite, but the booster exploded less than three minutes after lift-off from the Cape. The October launch of Courier made it into an orbit about 1,000 kilometres above the earth. This satellite was notable because, for the first time, a space craft was being used solely as a 'repeater'. It could catch signals and then repeat them for ground terminals.

A single satellite cannot be expected to cope with the twenty-four-hour world-wide cover needed by the military which has a potentially higher classified workload than civilian systems. Single satellite systems were, however, launched for commercial reasons, including the first amateur or 'ham' radio satellite, OSCAR 1, in 1961. In July 1962 TELSTAR, a commercial comsat was sent up from Cape Canaveral. But although there had been individual military experiments, including those dealing with the special needs of submarines to operate on V.L.F. (Very Low Frequency) bands, it was not until 1966 that the Americans launched their first stage of a mini-constellation of communication satellites. On June 16 of that year a Titan III rocket lifted off from Cape Canaveral with eight satellites on board. One of them, described as GGTS (Gravity Gradient Test Satellite), was put into orbit with little comment. The other seven were part of the U.S. Air Force's IDCSP, Initial Defense Communication Satellite Programme, which subsequently came to be known as Initial Defense Satellite Communication System (IDSCS). Even later, the term 'Initial' was dropped and DSCS was pronounced as DISCUS.

The IDSCS satellites were put into orbits at altitudes of around 34,000 kilometres. By 1968, a constellation of 26 small satellites formed what was then the most comprehensive military communications link ever devised. It connected military stations throughout the world, transmitting signals and reconnaissance pictures. The programme had its setbacks, including a disaster in August 1966. This launch should have carried the second batch of satellites into orbit. Instead, the Titan III rocket malfunctioned and all eight craft were lost. Even as the programme was being put into position, work was going ahead to replace it. The original lifespan of IDSCS was estimated at less than two years. Some elements continued to function for five times as long, but by 1971 DSCS (the system was renamed with this flight) stage II was ready for launching. On November 3, two fat cylindrical satellites, 3.92 m tall and 2.75 m in diameter, were launched from the Cape into almost perfectly circular orbits, more than 35,700 km high. They were the first of sixteen satellites in America's new military communications complex. Again, there were failures to get into orbit, but by the end of 1978 the whole system was working, with four DSCS II satellites operational at any one time.

In October 1982 the next phase, DSCS III satellites, began launching. The different groups have been interrelated. It is said that, at any one time, four satellites are operating to give more or less global cover. Should the satellites work as advertised it is possible for commanders to talk to each other in 'secure' voice. The satellites have systems that allow them to be tuned into every major command unit and to set up anti-jamming circuits to protect tactical and strategic commanders. The importance of having such a system may be illustrated by the fact that DSCS III is part of the communication through which would go the American Emergency Action Message. This message would carry the President's orders to 'go nuclear' on either SHF or UHF bands. The Emergency Action Message is broadcast in a number of ways other than satellite communications. The system has to be able to cope with a much degraded environment that might be expected in wartime. For example, an American aircraft is on constant patrol over the sea to be ready to keep in touch with nuclear missile submarines by trailing a long antenna which allows the aircraft to send the Emergency Action Message via V.L.F. (Very Low Frequency). The U.S. Strategic Air Command has some of its Minuteman missiles fitted, not with nuclear warheads, but with recorded messages. In emergencies when all systems had failed, the Minuteman could be launched and beam down the fire order to its brother missiles waiting in their silos. Equally, the Minuteman could carry a cease-fire order. However the reliance on survivable satellite systems is enormous and much of the wartime plan for the Emergency Action Message includes re-broadcasting on the Air Force and Navy satellites. The E.A.M. would be re-broadcast on what is known as AFSATCOM (Air Force Satellite Communications) and FLTSATCOM (Fleet Satellite Communications).

When it was launched, FLTSATCOM was the perfect illustration of how all the conflicting elements in the military communication chain could be brought within one system. The operational requirement was for four 'on-stream' space craft. Each satellite was hexagonal and squat, measuring 1.27 m high and 2.3 m in width. Poking from the middle of the hexagonal 'drum' was a short antenna. On one side of the 'drum' an arm extended at an upward angle. On the end of this arm and pointing vertically was an offset spiral antenna. The whole structure, from the top of this mast to the base of the hexagon, measured 6.6 m.

The first of these satellites, FLTSATCOM 1, was launched on February 9, 1978. It went into orbit nearly 36,000 km high and was positioned at 100 degrees westerly longitude, westward of the Galapagos Islands. Three further FLTSATCOM were orbited by October 1980: one over the Atlantic north-east of Cape Sao Rogue, another over the Indian Ocean south of the Maldive Islands, and the fourth over the Pacific north of Nauru Island.

These systems link the National Command – the highest-ranking politician or military man surviving through the various stages of war – to commands over hundreds of ships and submarines, thousands of aircraft and missile units, each with a nuclear mission. Through these systems, the United States covers almost all its nuclear forces. However, special satellites under the innocuously-named SDS (Satellite Data System) cover the polar regions. SDS is Top Secret and carries Intelligence pictures as well as commands and reports. Some nuclear forces would use the polar routes to attack the Soviet Union (missile-firing submarines have exercised beneath the polar cap) and, as the normal satellites in synchronous orbits cannot reach the polar units, then in wartime special satellites would be launched.

The complex of communications reaches all levels. Some systems have channels for nuclear missile submarines; others feed the Top Secret WWMCCS (World Wide Military Command and Control System) which links 26 U.S. Military Command Headquarters; some are used to communicate with individual platoons, while others 'store-dump' messages to be picked up by units, planes or submarines at predetermined moments. (It was this store-dumping system that may have led to the initial confusion about the instructions for the British submarine *Conqueror*, to attack the Argentine cruiser, *General Belgrano*.) Some satellites now allow messages to be jumped from satellite to satellite, so avoiding enemy interception.

The American system has now been established to work at all these levels and to link them. For example, TACSATs, Tactical Communication Satellites, have been built in such a way that it is possible to link land, sea and air units to the same communications, an essential function in the case of combined operations. Quite soon even the more up-to-date systems will have to be replaced with more secure and versatile units. One such

American project is MILSTAR (Military Strategic-Tactical and Relay). The concept is for groups of MILSTARs to be at operational altitudes over the Atlantic, Pacific and Indian Oceans. They will provide a most secure two-way traffic between ships, planes, submarines, ground units and supreme commanders. In space, also, will be back-up satellites and spares, orbiting high out of the way of anti-satellite systems. Some of these reinforcements may be parked up to 200,000 km in altitude. They could be called down when needed, perhaps a reminder that man has adapted with some agility to the new high ground. MILSTAR is not that far in the future; it could be fully operational towards the end of the 1980s.

Once again Soviet detail is harder to come by although it has been thought for some time that the Soviet Union operated similar systems to those of the Americans and N.A.T.O. Initially it would appear that the Soviet Union did not recognise the need for totally separate satellite systems. This would suggest that, as the military had priority on all levels of new equipment, then purely commercial and domestic use took second place. During the first few years of Soviet space exploration, programmes were centred on preparations for manned flights and some planetary expeditions. The first communication satellites were launched in 1965: Molniya I, in April of that year, and Molniya IB in October. The third, Molniya IC and fourth, Molniya ID were launched during 1966. Molniya IE went up during May 1967 and in October 1967 Molniya IF and IG were launched. The Soviet Union appeared to be building its own communications constellation under the codename ORBITA. The eighth was launched on April 21, 1968, maintaining a pattern of spring and autumn launches from Tyuratam. This pattern was broken with the ninth satellite in July 1968, but returned with the tenth in October. By this time some of the early craft were coming to the end of their lives and were being replaced in the chain.

In 1969, also, plans were agreed in Moscow to provide comsat launchings from an alternative site, Plesetsk. The same AZ-E rocket was used, but the thirteenth Molniya was launched from Plesetsk and not from Tyuratam on February 19, 1970. There was later speculation that the Plesetsk launchings suggested that the military had absolute control and use of the Plesetsk-launched craft. However, it should be allowed that there did seem to be a general policy that nearly all comsats in the different

Molniya series should be launched from the same site, which was now ready. In fact since 1970 only a handful of communication satellites have been put up from anywhere but Plesetsk. This would suggest that logistical reasons have as much a part to play as military control. Reasonably, it should not be forgotten that the eventual control of all space programmes comes from the Department of Space, a little-known section referred to, in the inner workings of Moscow, as YKOS (pronounced OO-KOS). This department is controlled by the military.

What would seem likely is that the military had priority over all comsats and that the Molniya series carried both commercial and civilian traffic. There was a steady launch pattern which suggested that the Molniya Mk I (which continued during the lifetime of later models), Mk II and III were dual purpose. On average there were eight launchings a year during the 1970s. Then, in 1980, the pattern changed with the introduction of systems that appeared to be dedicated to the military. For some years the planners in Admiral Sergei Gorshkov's navy had been making a case for their own satellite system. The Soviet Navy had expanded and its nuclear role and operational deployments had grown on a global basis. As with any other military system, growth and sophistication had brought with it problems of Command, Control and Communication. On February 11, 1980 Kosmos 1156, 1157, 1158, 1159, 1160, 1161, 1162 and 1163 were launched: eight satellites from Plesetsk in almost circular orbit between 1,396 and 1,541 kilometres about the globe. There was every indication that the Soviet Navy now had its own satcom system. And there was more to come. In December 1980 there was a further launch from Plesetsk of eight satellites into similar orbits. The following year, still further launches suggested that the Soviet forces now had the equivalent to the Western TACOM (Tactical Communication System). Using satellites, the Soviet high command could establish a relatively safe system of talking to ships, aircraft and shore bases through the same network. Although the Molniya programmes have continued, much attention has been given by the military to improvements to these constellations of eight satellites being launched every few months. The military appears to need arrays of more than 30 satellites in order to maintain its own world-wide military command and control system. (One consequence of this demand is the extraordinary amount of Soviet space junk – to add to the

American debris – because the operational life of the satellites is no more than between eighteen months and two years and the satellites do not burn up at the end of that working life.)

The communications system for the Soviet Union is completed by satellites such as Kosmos 1420 which have lifetimes of less than a year. Furthermore the military has access to dual purpose communication systems such as the Gorizont series, Raduga and Ekran satellites – although these are primarily for civilian use. If at first glance comsats appeared insignificant, then so might have navigation and weather satellites, yet the importance of these two systems is considerable. Communication satellites are vital to the military because they provided exclusive communications that can carry highly confidential traffic to extraordinarily confidential subscribers with the minimum risk of a break in security, considerable protection against collapses in the system and minimum chances of traffic not getting through because of jamming.

Navigation and weather systems in space are as important and to some extent for the same reasons. As satellites appeared in the late 1950s, ships, submarines and aircraft were getting used to new navigation systems. For years the navigator on the ship's bridge had sailed his vessel thousands of miles every year by the simple use of a vernier sextant, a chronometer, the stars at night, the sun for a noon-day fix, and a sharp horizon. When the weather had failed him, then Dead Reckoning (D.R.) arithmetic had allowed him to estimate his position until clouds cleared enough for a star sight. Some refinements such as the introduction of the micrometer sextant made life easier, but did not necessarily improve the accuracy of the fix. In the 1950s navigation was getting more electronic aids, including the superb Decca Navigator. These systems relied on a series of land-based beacons producing a web of radio beams that gave a ship its position to a degree of accuracy envied by the old salt navigator jealously guarding his sextant, stubby pencil and star sight skills. Satellite navigation brought more than accuracy to the ship's bridge and aircraft's flight deck. The main problem of relying on shore-based beacons was that in wartime there could be no guarantee of the beacon's safety. For most of the time the navigation systems would be perfectly good, but satellites offered a range of technology that could not be ignored. Furthermore, warships and aircraft have peculiar needs such as the necessity of often maintaining anonymity; receiving satellite positioning helped avoid too many beam receptions and reduced the electronic activity. In another area, submarines do not care to spend much time on the surface where they are vulnerable. The advantages of surfacing a navigation aerial to pick up a quick fix are obvious. Furthermore, the need for the most accurate positioning system is evident when it is remembered that, say, a ballistic missile-firing submarine needs to know exactly where it is before firing and then correcting its weapon.

Finally, satellite navigation has offered accurate positioning to a much wider range of military units. For example, carrying the minimum of equipment, a four-man mortar platoon can fix its position in the middle of the night to within a few yards. Small units can be more independent and their commanders more assured with the knowledge that, even through the muddle and fog of war, at least it is possible to know where they are.

Such is the advance in satellite navigation that it will probably replace most if not all positioning systems within a few years. In everyday civilian terms, for example, it will be possible that, by the end of the 1980s, car manufacturers will be offering dashboard satellite receivers as optional extras. By 1990, it will be possible to sit in a 'lost' car and get a position which is more accurate than the road map. It will be possible to feed in a destination's co-ordinate and drive there on a beam. After all, that would be nothing more than an enormously simplified version of the guidance system used by a cruise missile.

The first attempt to launch a navigation satellite, NAVSAT, was from the American site at Cape Canaveral. That was on September 17, 1959, just two years after the first artificial satellite, Sputnik 1, and only the thirty-sixth attempt at a space shot. It was called Transit 1A. The third stage of the rocket malfunctioned and, as with so many American space attempts during that time, it failed. (Out of the 36 space shots at that stage, only four had been by the Soviet Union, therefore the American failure rate was almost bound to appear wretched.) However on April 13, seven months after the first attempt, Transit 1B was successfully launched. American scientists now had something to work on. The pressure on the scientists was considerable, more so on those in the United States than those in the U.S.S.R. By the early 1960s, the Soviet merchant and armed fleets had not achieved the global dimensions that were to worry Western strategists in the 1970s. Although Admiral Gorshkov's fleet was building, and including the early forms of a nuclear missile submarine force, it did not have the dimensions, complexities and commitments of the U.S. Fleet. For the Americans and later for the British, satellite technology coincided with the emergence of what was to be the third leg of the so-called Strategic Triad, the ballistic missile submarine. The Transit Navsat was directly connected to this development, especially the Polaris submarine.

Polaris, perhaps more than any other submarine or indeed surface ship, needed to maintain the absolute secrecy of her position and to be able to fix that position in any weather condition. The need to develop an all-weather navigation system beyond the existing electronic aids was therefore essential, especially as Polaris could expect to operate in the North Atlantic – an area of the oceans not well known for its clear skies and sharp horizons at all times of the year.

Transit therefore became the essential navigation system for the strategic missile submarine fleet and it was extended into other areas. Commercial shipping was able to tune into Transit or NNSS (Navy Navigation Satellite System) as it became known, ships' masters were getting positions from space that were so accurate that it is doubtful whether they were able to mark them on the charts with such precision. Although Transit had maintained its precise function, the American Air Force had decided that it wanted an even more accurate and secure system. Transit and its developments have a role still and some are being stored in space. Presumably this would allow the system to have ready back-up units in time of war. However, the satellites orbit at about 1,000 km altitude and so would be vulnerable to attack. Furthermore, in time of tension it is better not to sharpen a period of crisis by the launching of anything but essential satellites; also, essential satellites would make such demands on launch facilities that it is better to store space craft as part of the old military precaution of pre-positioning.

The result of scientific improvements and added demands by the military is an American system called NAVSTAR (Navigation System using Timing and Ranging). NAVSTAR, sometimes known as GPS (Global Positioning System), is an enormous constellation of satellites. The satellites are located in small blocks around the globe in 20,000 km orbits. On board the satellites are small atomic clocks so accurate that they are not expected to lose or gain more than one second in 36,000 years.

The signals that go from the mini-constellations include precise times and distances (ranges) from the earth. These signals are picked up by the receivers on board ships, submarines, planes, missiles, jeeps or a soldier's back-pack. The precision of the information is translated automatically into a series of calculations that gives the receiver's location relative to the batch of satellites. This provides a fix accurate to a few metres. Consequently, vessels, aircraft and ground forces can update positions with astounding accuracy, missiles can automatically correct courses and thereby improve their own accuracy while in flight; and all this can be done in relatively secure conditions. The forces have only to receive the signals, they do not have to interrogate the satellites for the information.

There are a few drawbacks. The cost of maintaining the system is high – the American procurement executive thinks in billions of dollars. Secondly, there have been Intelligence reports in Washington suggesting that the Soviet Union is tuning into the NAVSTAR system for its own use. Some of the NAVSTAR functions could not be interrogated unless the Soviet Union had the correct codes and receiver units. Neither drawback should be regarded as insurmountable by the Soviet Union. Its own version of NAVSTAR is called GLONASS. The present system is thought to have ambitions for a constellation of navsats somewhat smaller than the American system. It could be that it has indeed been designed to take advantage of the advanced American technology. The irony of modern space science is that it cannot be beyond the powers of competing nations to capitalise on each other's expertise. It is possible also, according to talks that the author has had with Soviet experts, that a second system is to be developed. That system may have a purely military function and be a supplement to GLONASS which the Russians have suggested is primarily designed for use by aircraft.

Finally, both the Soviet Union and the United States have developed a further system of satellites that is of use to all arms of the forces: weather satellites. The defence departments need weather details that are removed from simple domestic use. A tactical commander wants to know the conditions in which his forces may have to fight at any given moment. The commander's concern is not entirely for the comfort of his troops. A tank commander understands how heavy rains may turn the tide of an armoured thrust. Logistics officers need to know what conditions may affect reinforcements and lines of ammunition, stores, supplies and casualties. A theatre commander will perhaps make his final choice about the use of chemical weapons only when he has studied weather reports. (Chemical agents can perform quite differently in dry weather with light winds than, say, in rain and strong winds.)

Furthermore, the weather forecasts and conditions extend beyond the battlefield. Wind speeds, atmospheric pressures and moisture content might well influence the performance of something as apparently impassive as an intercontinental ballistic missile (ICBM). Both superpowers have long recognised the need to have uncluttered access to weather predictions and tracking. METSATS (Meteorological Satellites) were among the first to be used by the military on both sides. The Americans have a series of satellites known as the Defense Meteorological Satellite Programme, DMSP. The Soviet system appears under full military control with information being used for civilian purposes as a secondary function.

Whatever the priorities of these and other satellites, it is clear that various estimates are true that between 70 and 75 per cent of satellites have either direct military functions or strong indirect values to the military; and there are some that have not been examined in these pages. Taken at random they make interesting reading. For example, one of the last satellites to be launched in 1983 was Kosmos 1518; it was an Early Warning Satellite. Kosmos 1518 was blasted into space from Plesetsk on December 28. It was sent on station in a highly elliptical orbit, reaching an altitude of 39,787 km before swooping to just 590 km. It replaced Kosmos 1341 and it too was due to be replaced towards the end of 1985. Kosmos 1518 was one of a series of Early Warning systems. Some are contained in other satellites as a secondary role, others have that single function.

The job of Early Warning is arguably a perfectly peaceful assignment. In many ways, a number of military space systems have peaceful roles. Even spy-satellites contribute to stability and therefore peace by making sure that neither side is surprised at the development programmes of the other. Yet in war, or the period leading up to it, it is quite possible that all these systems, Early Warning, Electronic Warning, Photo-Reconnaissance,

Electronic Intelligence Gathering, Communications, Navigation and even weather satellites will be deemed hostile. They may be seen as an advantage to the enemy and a threat to the other side. Therefore, the sometimes-stabilising systems will be vulnerable to attack. Already, there have been cases where the Soviet Union has tested lasers on some of the U.S. polar region comsats, according to American and European sources (the latter will possibly have received their information about these laser experiments from the Americans). However, from what we have seen in this and the preceding chapter it is clear that today's commander relies on satellites as his eyes, ears and mouthpiece. Consequently both sides are developing major systems designed to strike the other's commanders blind, deaf and dumb in wartime.

Chapter 7

ASAT

No sooner had the superpowers launched into space by the late 1950s, than they started to prepare active plans to destroy each other's satellites. The new and exciting environment was heralded as a great scientific opportunity for man – and so it has proved to be. However, even before the launch of the first Sputnik, both sides realised that space would be dominated by military and not civilian considerations. Indeed there were those, certainly in Washington, who were thinking of the possibilities of anti-satellite weapons long before the first satellites were launched. Certainly within two months after Sputnik 1 was sent up, the U.S. Army had produced a recommendation that anti-satellite systems should be developed urgently. However, the American Administration under Eisenhower seemed at first reluctant to get into an ASAT race.

This reservation aside, it was not surprising that, within a few years of Sputnik 1's launch, both superpowers had tested Anti-Satellite Systems. Whatever the original reservation, it was soon recognised that satellites posed a real threat to national security.

During the early 1950s both superpowers suspected that future space craft would be vulnerable to attack. Studies such as Project Feedback in the United States and a similar study in the Soviet Union had made good cases for reconnaissance satellites. Many working on those projects must have understood that if they were to come to anything it would be because they were potentially efficient and therefore vulnerable to attack. The problem was how to design systems that could stop satellites working without necessarily degrading other space craft. In 1958, for example, the Americans had carried out high altitude explosions of nuclear weapons, partly to judge the effects of the radiation. Four years later, a nuclear test in space in the American Fishbowl series, degraded an American navigation satellite and a British space craft recording ionospheric data. It was clear from the start of the anti-satellite programmes that the use of nuclear warheads would have to be discarded.

The Americans ran test programmes for all three Services under a project called Space Intercept, or SPIN for short. This indicated once again that, although independent research programmes could produce startling innovations, there was also a sense that resources were being wasted. This independence of the Services had been a feature of the U.S. space programme from the very early days. One of the first programmes was run by the U.S. Air Force, beginning in 1958 under a project codenamed Bold Orion. The idea was not unlike the programmes in development today. Missiles were fired from converted B-47 bombers. These tests were quite difficult. They could not be carried out against a satellite when it was at its highest and slowest point. The missile could not reach that far into space, the aiming point was somewhere close to the lowest point of the target's orbit; this is the point where the satellite is hardest to hit, although well in range, because it is at its top speed (rather like a big dipper at the fairground). The B-47 programme never achieved a great deal; there was a certain success in that one test flight passed within a few miles of its target, an Explorer satellite. But shortly after this series, it would appear that the general Air Force opinion was that ASATs should be ground launched as missiles, rather than air launched from planes.

A lot of the testing relied on rocket-launched systems rather than the B-47 method of launching in flight. One U.S. Air Force project, begun in 1959 and code named SAINT for Satellite Inspection Technique, was perhaps the first attempt by the Americans to develop ASATs.[1] It relied on the Atlas-Agena B rockets for lift off. These rockets had already been used to launch highly secret military satellites which lent a certain irony to the

[1] SAINT was part of the anti satellite development, but as the name suggests, its prime task would have been to inspect Soviet satellites. SENTRY might have been a better name considering its 'Who goes there?' role.

thought that they were now to be used to destroy satellites. However, this was another project with little to show for the enormous effort and cost and foundered in 1962 partly because the Air Force simply could not afford to carry on. Other tests were made using rockets launched from the Pacific Ocean, including a U.S. Army test under Program 505.

Program 505 was based on a missile called the Nike Zeus. It was important because it demonstrated the idea that the technology for anti-satellite weapons and anti-missile weapons were often very smilar. The 1980s jargon for anti-missile weaponry is SDI or Star Wars technology and so having appreciated the similarities in technology, it is easier to understand that one reason why the Soviet Union was so against President Reagan's SDI programme, was that it would produce advanced anti-satellite systems as well.

The first ASAT test for the Nike Zeus missile took place in December 1962 and the second in February 1963. These tests were simple: the missile was aimed at a fixed point in space and apparently successfully reached the 'target'. The tests that followed had varying degrees of success. But by the August of 1963, the rocket was declared operational as a fully fledged ASAT system, even though there were doubts about its true capability. Those doubts together with continuing inter-Service rivalry, encouraged the development of another ASAT system, known as Thor or Program 437 by the U.S. Air Force.

Work on Program 437 had been going on for some time, long before the Army Nike Zeus was in service. Bureaucratic infighting and the need to revamp basic infrastructure programmes to support the project, meant that the Thor was not in operational service until June 1964. More than a dozen test launches took place between 1964 and 1970 during which Program 437 was largely successful within the obvious limitations of the system.

In September 1964, President Johnson announced that the United States had two operational ASAT systems. These were the Thor and the Nike Zeus. The two obvious limitations were to be found in the systems' warheads and launch facilities. The warheads were nuclear weapons. Apart from their effects on enemy satellites, they had the same ability to damage friendly satellites. Secondly, because they were fired from fixed ground positions, the ASAT missiles had to wait for targets to pass over their regions instead of having the flexibility to hunt them – a problem with the existing Soviet system.

Meanwhile the Navy, not to be left behind in the ASAT race had been testing a programme known as Early Spring – a title which had more to do with military quick reactions than it did with any seasonal expectations. The concept was attractive to many who wanted the idea of 'mobile' ASAT missiles to become standard policy. The Navy decided to match a small missile to the Polaris rocket, the warhead carrier used by strategic submarines. Another project known as Skipper had a similar idea of using missiles launched from ships and submarines. Not unexpectedly, the Command and Control systems were difficult to work out and the only really feasible Navy plan came in the form of air-launched rockets from Phantom jets. Although this project was never endorsed by the American government, it once again pointed to the system that would eventually be accepted as cheap, accurate and flexible. Meanwhile, it was appearing that the Air Force would take the lead in ASAT development.

The Air Force believed that the threat to America's security came from two sources in space: conventional military satellites, e.g. reconnaissance craft; and Soviet satellites carrying bombs – the much-vaunted fractional orbital bombardment systems.

So for four years during the 1960s the Air Force ran a series of tests under a programme called Squanto Terror. During this time, the 1967 Outer Space Treaty was agreed. It banned nuclear weapons in Outer Space. To conform to the spirit, if not the letter, of the agreement, the Americans might have cancelled their Squanto Terror system. However, the basic system was kept until 1975.

By the mid-1970s, the United States had abandoned its Anti-Satellite programmes; there were a number of sound reasons for doing this. The perceived threat from Soviet satellites and possible space-based weapons was not considered high enough to spend the vast sums and resources needed to maintain and modernise the system. Further, the ASAT weapons themselves were not very impressive. They had limited ranges and could not go out and seek with any assurance even the low-orbiting Soviet craft. The U.S. systems had to wait until the Soviet satellites came within quite close range. Also, there was too much acceptance of the idea that the most effective warhead would be one giving a low-yield nuclear explosion. This presented a number of obvious problems, not least of all the fact mentioned above: that exploding a nuclear weapon in space might do extensive damage to American as well as enemy satellites. Apart from destroying them, the electromagnetic pulses from the nuclear warhead would also knock out American signals. The run-down of the American programme did not signal lack of interest. The technology was changing and so was the perception of the threat. United States ASAT policy was twin-tracked. It wanted its scientists to research and develop a more efficient weapon, not prone to the same range restrictions and with the capability of using a warhead that would not, unlike a nuclear charge, cause self-inflicted wounds. The second part of this twin-track approach was for the United States to see if there was a way of outlawing such weapons by international agreement. As we shall see later, there were treaties whose clauses brought into question such systems, but there was sufficient ambiguity to make research and development a matter of military precaution. Furthermore, there was no sign that the Soviet Union was willing to abandon its own development programme. There had been a lull of five years in the Soviet test programme, but this resumed in 1976. At about that time, the American programme was stepped up and the present system brought about.

Very simply, the Americans favour a missile that can be fired from a modern jet – in principle, it is not that much different from the original plans to use rockets fired from converted B-47 bombers. The latest project is known as ALMHV, Air Launched Miniature Homing Vehicle.

The system is based on a two-stage rocket, 18 feet long and under 2 feet in diameter. It is conventionally cigar-shaped with a blunt nose and four tail fins, and hangs beneath an F-15 interceptor. This is the twin-tailed McDonnell Douglas jet which for a long time many have believed to be one of the, if not the, most sophisticated fighters ever built. The aircraft takes off and receives flight and intercept details from ground control. It would climb to, say, 50,000 feet and then release the rocket. On the rocket is the all-important Miniature Homing Vehicle – the brains of the system. It is a 12″ by 13″ cylinder. Inside are eight infra-red telescopes that pick up the target satellite. Packed closely to these telescopes are a laser-gyroscope and a mini-computer. Combined, they make the final adjustments for the attack. When the rocket is launched from the F-15 it picks up a speed of 30,000 miles an hour. The rocket then boosts the MHV into an attacking position and the closing speed would be sufficient for the MHV to destroy the satellite simply by hitting it. So, no warheads are needed and, at the moment, no treaties broken. (Treaties with clauses protecting reconnaissance satellites – or 'national technical means' of verification, would be broken should a satellite be attacked. But by then most treaties would be of academic interest.)

There have been a number of test flights of the American system. The first booster flight took place in January 1984. This was important as a first flight test, but it involved only the rocket and the aircraft release. The Miniature Homing Vehicle was not attached and no target was struck. There will be about ten test flights in this final series. These tests include attacks on obsolete or obsolescent satellites. The first test carried out in 1985 was described as a success. Assuming there are few technical problems, then the United States Air Force could have two squadrons of anti-satellite weapons fully operational by the end of 1987. There is, of course, a further assumption that no treaty banning such weapons is agreed with the Soviet Union by that date.

The Soviet Union already has an ASAT weapon which U.S. Intelligence claims is fully operational. The existing system appears to have been first tested in 1968, although there is some evidence to suggest that Soviet engineers had developed an anti-satellite missile as early as 1962, five years after the first Sputnik was launched. If this is so, then there is little to suggest that it was ever put into production. At about this time, the then leader of the Soviet Union, Nikita Krushchev, is said to have told the Americans that Moscow had developed a rocket that was so good it could 'hit a fly in space'. There are many reasons to doubt Krushchev's bragging, but there were those in Washington who took him seriously, because they accepted that the Soviet Union could indeed be in a technically advanced state to produce such a missile. What is certain is that the Soviet programme appeared for all to see in 1968. It ran until December 1971 and then 'rested' until February 1976. The first period looks as if it was more successful than the second. The basic principle was, however, the same. Whereas the United States relied on an ASAT weapon fired from an aircraft, the Soviet scientists put all their hopes on a conventionally-launched satellite: hence, the often-used term, 'hunter-killer satellite', applies more to the Soviet than to the American system.

The Soviet interceptor satellite is quite small, about 6 metres long. It weighs between 1,500 and 2,000 kilograms, which is about the size of a Russian communications satellite or a reconnaissance craft. It is more than likely to be launched into space by a version of an SS-9 rocket, a modified intercontinental ballistic missile, from the Tyuratam site. There is no sure way of identifying the weapon from normally published data in the Soviet Union, nor at the United Nations where basic launch details are lodged. However, it would appear that 20 interceptor tests have been carried out since 1968. The success rate has not been high. Of the 20 tests, nine have apparently succeeded. The first Soviet ASAT test was carried out on October 20, 1968. Kosmos 249 was launched from Tyuratam, the 91st of 117 satellites launched that year by the superpowers. There was no indication from the Soviet Union what might be the nature of the craft. All that was known were the basic details: it had an inclination of 62.4 degrees (which was not very significant), a low point of 520 kilometres and a high point in its orbit of 2,096 kilometres. It manoeuvred in what might have been a 'strike' position after two orbits but, according to Western analysis, the test was not successful. (The launcher used on that first test was the F-1-m rocket. The same model has been used in all tests and these have sometimes been in addition to a complete ASAT deployment.) Twelve days after the first test, Kosmos 252, a second ASAT satellite was launched. This was recorded as a success. But neither test at this stage used a target. The launches were from Tyuratam, the only base of the F-1-m or SS-9 as it is more commonly known. Two years later, there were two more launchings during October. As with the 1968 tests, it appeared that the Soviet Union was practising manoeuvring the hunter-killer satellites; then, in 1971, there were three tests (February, April and December) and the series stopped. The tests started again in 1976, this time using techniques to cut the intercept time from two orbits to one. However, not many of the 13 intercepts

(1976, 1977, 1978, 1980, 1981 and 1982) have been particularly successful.[1]

A normal Soviet test and therefore, it is thought, an intended operational procedure involves two satellites. A target satellite is put up from the Plesetsk launch site. Perhaps ten or twelve days later the 'hunter-killer' is launched from Tyuratam and takes probably two orbits to get into a position where its track crosses that of its prey. The hunter then uses either an active radar (i.e. it sends out a signal rather than just listening for the target) or a less obtrusive system of optical sensor. Tests so far indicate that the Russians would intend to either collide with or blow up the target, although no complete test has been carried out. Success or failure is measured by the hunter-killer being in a position to destroy or degrade the target before it can take evading action.

To many Intelligence analysts, the most spectacular Soviet test took place in June 1982. On June 6, Kosmos 1375 was launched from Plesetsk. It was one of eight launches from that site that month. The others were easily identified as military communications, photo-reconnaissance, navigation and early warning satellites. This was towards the end of the Falklands War and one hypothesis is that the Soviet Union was using the conflict as a war scenario. Kosmos 1375 was quite different from what the mass of Intelligence gatherers expected at that time. It weighed about 2,000 kilograms and went into a peculiar orbit with its highest point at 1,010 kilometres and its lowest at 980 kilometres. Twelve days later Kosmos 1379, a hunter-killer satellite, was launched from Tyuratam. After two revolutions it came close to Kosmos 1375. There is a body of opinion that suggests that this test was a failure. The evidence is not conclusive. Certainly, others suggest that it was successful because it manoeuvred enough to degrade if not destroy the target, Kosmos 1375. The importance of this test goes beyond that argument because the operation appears to have been part of a major Soviet strategic nuclear wargame, whether or not it was using the Falklands War as a scenario. The ASAT test coincided with exercise firings of strategic, theatre (including SS-20s) and submarine-launched ballistic nuclear missiles. This would

[1] See Garwin *et al.*, *Scientific American*, June 1982.

suggest to Western analysts the possibility that for the first time the Soviet Union was testing and demonstrating its ability to include space as another theatre of war.

Yet it would be too simple to cite Soviet anti-satellite weapons as a major element in Moscow's own quest for Star Wars technology. ASAT weaponry is quite apart from that research and is in its infancy. In all, neither the Soviet nor the American systems could expect to cope with the potential range of targets. Certainly there are major drawbacks to the Soviet system as it exists.

Firstly, the Soviet ASAT programme makes it a very obvious weapon. At the moment it is launched only from Tyuratam. This means that a launch could be monitored and, because it is confined to one launch process from one area, it suffers huge targeting difficulties. Because the Soviet system could be quickly identified, it would need to take major anti-jamming precautions. The satellite may take two orbits to meet its target, therefore the ASAT weapon would itself be vulnerable to enemy attack for about three hours before it made contact.

Another drawback is the need to use the SS-9, or something similar, to boost the weapon into orbit. This means that the Soviet forces would have few options (if indeed more than one) for launch sites. And, because the existing booster rockets are liquid-fuelled (as opposed to solid fuel rockets), they need long pre-flight preparations, which suggests that there could be no guarantee that the ASAT weapon would be launched in sufficient time or numbers to meet the target. This is especially important when one remembers the operational restrictions forced on the Soviet Union by its geography. A satellite can only be hunted and destroyed when it flies more or less over the launch site region. Because the Soviet system is launched from static sites, then the Soviet ASAT commands would have to wait for the target satellite to overfly. This in turn means that the commander could have few chances a day – perhaps as few as two – to make a successful strike. A final restriction is that the Soviet system would need a much bigger boost procedure if it were to stand a chance of hitting the American early warning and communication satellites.

There are many estimates that suggest that the existing Soviet ASAT system would need as much as ten days to take out an American satellite system. Even then this would only be the near-earth orbiting space craft and, although they are most important, they represent only a part of the overall reliance by the military on space in time of tension and war. As noted elsewhere, up to 80 per cent of Western military signals go by satellite. The ASAT system described above could not get at the signal systems. It may be, though, that the United States would not have so many problems as the Soviet Union.

The American F-15-flown ASAT weapon has yet to complete its test programme. However, there are already advantages to be seen over the Soviet system. The American plan is to have two squadrons of F-15s fitted with ASAT missiles operational by late 1987. One squadron will be in the Eastern United States at Langley Air Force Base in Virginia. The second unit is scheduled for McCloud AFB in Washington State in the Western United States. But the military advantage of the F-15 system is its size and therefore mobility. Unlike the Soviet system which is confined to one or perhaps two fixed launch sites in the U.S.S.R., the F-15s could be deployed anywhere in the world where there is a friendly air base. Furthermore, by using aircraft carriers and air-to-air refuelling (the carriers could fly-off the air tankers), the range of the F-15 force could be extended beyond anything the Soviet Union could hope for. Whereas it could take a complete week for the Soviet system to destroy the low-orbiting American satellites, the U.S. has the potential to knock out the Russian space craft in a matter of hours.

It must be remembered also that, although high-orbiting craft are considered beyond the range of ASAT weapons, many of the Soviet satellites have elliptical orbits which dip within range of the F-15 missiles. If, however, the United States is to take advantage of the Soviet vulnerability it has to think in terms of overseas bases.

For example, a Soviet satellite with a highly elliptical orbit is most vulnerable at the lowest point of its orbit. This could place the satellite somewhere over the Antarctic. Consequently, the American strategic planners, in informal discussions with some of the Allies, have apparently considered the prospect of basing ASAT weapons on the British-owned islands of Diego Garcia in the Indian Ocean, Ascension Island in the Atlantic, and in Australia. This last base could, according to those who have studied the prospect in the Pentagon and the State Department, prove to be the most difficult. The difficulty would be political rather than military, depending as it will for some time upon the political complexion of Australian politics.

When the same question was raised by the author concerning British politics, the general opinion in Washington was that, in spite of the anti-nuclear stance adopted by the British Labour Party, no problems were envisaged over Diego Garcia and Ascension Island. Moreover, the Falkland Islands with their extended runway and ideal geographical location have been added to the list of desirable real estate for the American ASAT system. Some pressure might be applied to America's Allies for ASAT-basing facilities when the United States is able to show without doubt that the Soviet Union has made a further leap in anti-satellite deployment. This could happen within a few years, perhaps no more than one or two from the time of writing. There have been reports among some Intelligence circles, that the Soviet Union is developing an ASAT weapon which is very similar to the American F-15 unit. It is said to be based on a MiG fighter airframe and has had one test flight with a shortened version of a potential ASAT missile carried along the main fuselage line. Again, at the time of writing, no test firings have been observed.

There is a so-far unconsidered element of potential space targeting. Most, if not all, public attention is focused on the superpowers. Yet, it should not be forgotten that other countries are getting into space-based systems, and those countries include China. Indeed, some have suggested that the main element of the Soviet programme is geared towards Chinese rather than American satellites.[1] This may be a consideration in Soviet thinking but it would not explain the early Soviet test flights.

A deal of attention is paid to the so-called 'hunter-killer' satellites. There are other possibilities. The most obvious way to destroy a satellite's value is to shut down the earth-based terminal. A well-organised sabotage team could knock out the basic flow of information by blowing up the satellite's ground terminal. However, in time of tension, terminals would be well protected and it is interesting to note that space technology is on the way to giving satellites more autonomy. For example, the basic communication pattern has been for a satellite to send and receive through one or two ground stations. Advanced switched

[1] See Garwin *et al.*, *Scientific American*, June 1984.

systems allow satellite signals to hop from once space craft to another. Consequently those signals become more protected than ever before. Therefore they become a greater priority for a direct attack. Again this need not be from the direct ascent system favoured by the Americans, nor from the Soviet co-orbital hunter-killer satellite described above.

There is a real possibility that space mines could be deployed at almost any altitude, thereby threatening all kinds of satellites. The space mine could be launched and then switched off, perhaps with the public excuse that it has malfunctioned. When needed, it could be switched on, manoeuvred closer to its target and then either exploded or brought onto a collision course. The space craft could even be booby-trapped in case the opposition manoeuvred another satellite to inspect it, or tried to 'hook' it, as we have seen is possible using simple techniques on board the American space shuttle. Today's technology suggests that it would be difficult for one country to hide a space mine. Because of what is known as onboard housekeeping, a satellite needs to be 'woken up' every so often to check that all continues to function and to make minor adjustments. At the same time, technology is sufficiently advanced to overcome that problem, if indeed it is one, as critics of space mining have suggested. There really is no need to hide a mine. It is possible to create some uncertainty as to its real role. Further, in an environment where ASAT systems are becoming a fact of military life, the space mine could become an 'acceptable' obstacle just as tank divisions are on earth today.

There is a further weapon system under research and in some cases development that could threaten satellites in the near future. The same technology, that is aimed at providing prototype Strategic Defence Initiative beam weapons, is capable of producing enhanced energy systems to destroy or degrade satellites. There is, in 1985, an advanced programme that would produce a chemical laser and a targeting unit, that, in theory at least, could take out the low-orbiting satellites deployed by the Soviet Union. It is thought that Soviet engineers are working on a similar project. There is after all little technical difficulty in directing, say, a laser beam at a satellite.

As we have seen, anti-satellite weapons are in their infancy. This is in spite of the effort that has gone into their development. So, would they work and might they be worth the effort of the superpowers and eventually other space nations? Both the Soviet and American systems would appear to be able to threaten the low-orbiting important satellites – including the reconnaissance vehicles. Furthermore, technological advances suggest that the upper regions might too be vulnerable in the not too distant future. Certainly space mines could have an important role in this. Looking through the test programmes of apparently innocent space launches by both superpowers, it is possible to find 'unexplained' satellites. Some of them have some of the characteristics that might be associated with space mines.

Closer to earth, the main difference between the reconnaissance satellites of the superpowers has been the time in orbit. The Soviet Union has tended to have short-stay satellites, whereas the Americans have kept theirs in orbit for months. Consequently, it has been simple to assume that, although the Soviet ASAT system has geographical disadvantages, it would have fewer targets because there would be fewer American satellites in near-earth orbit. Similarly, although the United States might one day have a more versatile ASAT system with its mobile F-15s, there would be correspondingly more targets. But there are signs that the Soviet Union is moving towards longer flights for its reconnaissance craft. It must be assumed that the capability to launch at shorter intervals is being retained in spite of hard-pressed launch facilities. Equally, it may be that the U.S. would have to think about launching more satellites in time of tension to assure survivability, and the shuttle could be ideal for this, although it too would be liable to attack.

There are in development various sophisticated devices to electronically protect satellites. These include anti-jamming devices and extreme sensors that trigger on board alarms which alert the satellite's guidance system to outmanoeuvre an intruder. However, it is accepted generally that the most obvious antidote to an ASAT assault might be a large satellite replacement system. Whatever the answer, it is worth considering the ultimate consequence of a successful ASAT assault. But, before doing so, the view of a former American Defense Secretary should be allowed. His was no casual appointment. Dr Brown's career in defence planning and thinking has been particularly impressive. For twenty-one crucial years (between 1960 and 1981) he was the Director of the Lawrence Livermore Laboratory (the nuclear weapons laboratory), Director of Defense Research and Engineering at the Pentagon, Secretary of the Air Force, President of the California Institute of Technology and Defense Secretary. Talking about arms control Dr Brown says, '. . . one side's ability to launch a few dozen, or even a few, anti-satellite weapons could have a devastating effect on the other side's Intelligence and communications capabilities. That makes verification a great problem. A few dozen undetected I.C.B.M.s would not change the strategic balance between the United States and the Soviet Union in any meaningful way, but successful use of a dozen ASAT weapons could change the balance of space support capabilities enormously . . . it is worth trying to inhibit actions against satellites in situations short of war. (In war any such agreement would go by the board.) One way of doing this would be an agreed declaration that an attack on a satellite would be seen as a belligerent act. That might have the effect of slowing down an unproductive and potentially dangerous trend towards space wars.'[1]

However, that trend to move towards a capability to fight a 'space war' seems to be well under way. In the middle-1960s, when scientists and strategists talked about anti-ballistic missile defences and the chances of using space-based systems to defend the United States, there was a general impression that this was Buck Rogers talk. The technology wasn't there and it wasn't about to be.

When, in 1983, the subject came up once more, and this time with Presidential backing, the suggestion was that, although the technology still wasn't there, there was just the possibility that it could be coaxed from the scientific cupboard. In truth, there were enough people around to believe that Star Wars was this time a possibility. There were even those misguided enough to hope that technology could take the threat of conflict hundreds of miles into the sky away from an increasingly nervous earthbound population more and more convinced that nuclear war is likely rather than just possible. And so, when President Reagan made his 1983 Star Wars speech, there were plenty of people willing to listen – even if secretly they believed that Buck Rogers rules still applied.

[1] *Thinking About National Security*, Harold Brown, Westview Press, 1983.

Chapter 8

SDI

President Reagan's Star War speech may have sparked public interest in what the Pentagon prefers to call the Strategic Defence Initiative, but for many in the United States and the Soviet Union there was nothing new in his concept. Both countries had been carrying out quite major research into the possibilities of beam weaponry and updating the existing and somewhat crude anti-ballistic missile technology. Certainly, the concept of knocking out in-coming ballistic missiles had been around for twenty years.

The President focused public attention on something many scientists and military men had worked on and promoted for some time. However, the significance of that March 23 speech may be that it gave Presidential blessing to the research, brought more of the various research programmes under one banner, and of course made it easier for those programmes to get collectively the dollars they needed to carry on (although some individual laboratories suffered because allocations were more closely scrutinised). At the same time there was an extensive lobby of informed and still influential retired military men determined that its concept of future military space systems should not be overlooked. People like General George Keegan were convinced that the Soviet Union had devoted enormous financial and technical resources in order to develop beam weapons. As head of Air Force Intelligence, Keegan had access to satellite photographic and signals Intelligence to back his beliefs. Certainly the Intelligence arriving in Washington during the late 1970s suggested that some forms of experiment were going on in the Soviet Union that appeared to be using energy as a potential weapon system. In other words, there was evidence that concentrated energy could be just a generation away from providing the death rays of the comic strips. Equally, there were those who could not accept the analysis that the Soviet Union was pressing ahead with the development of rays and beams and was on the verge of producing a weapon.

Most believed that research and development were far from producing a practical weapon. Others saw the hypotheses put forward by General Keegan and others as nothing more than an attempt to get excessive funds for American programmes. The general, however, picked up considerable support even though he was at the same time criticised as being something of an outrageous, or outraged, hawk. But he was not alone. The United States did not have the 'now' technology to provide beam weapons nor did it have a clear policy which would show how these systems, if they existed, might be used. But, even before President Reagan made his Star Wars speech, General Keegan's fears were being supported by an increasing number of people in the Pentagon.

It was about this time that another retired general, Daniel O. Graham, gave more publicity to a project that was to become completely in line with President Reagan's vision and appeal to the Administration's emerging philosophy of defence – the idea that defensive weaponry could become more important than offensive weaponry.

In fact, it should be remembered that the President had put his Star Wars thoughts forward, not as an instant solution, but as something that might be possible – one day. What he actually said on March 23, 1983 was this:

'Let me share with you a vision of the future which offers hope. It is that we embark on a program to counter the awesome Soviet missile threat with measures that are defensive. What if free people could live secure in the knowledge that their security did not rest upon the threat of instant U.S. retaliation to deter a Soviet attack; that we could intercept and destroy strategic ballistic missiles before they reached our own soil or that of our allies . . . My fellow Americans, tonight we are launching an effort which holds the promise of changing the course of human history. *There will be risks, and results take time* [author's itals]. But, with your support, I believe we can do it.'

The speech had a great deal going for it. Until that point, certainly in Europe, there had been a fear that every time the

President talked of ways of countering Soviet military threats, real or imagined, it was in the form of building bigger and better missiles. The Reagan Administration came into office on a ticket that promised to 'make America strong again'. The new team talked of a new mood. It 'hit the decks running'. Echoing the gallant nineteenth-century duke, people might have declared that such a Presidential team might not frighten Moscow but it certainly frightened much of Western Europe. But here was talk, indeed a vision, of a totally *defensive* system; one which could make the world a safer place in which to live *and* keep America strong. No matter how far-fetched, for many it was an attractive thought.

Lieutenant General Daniel O. Graham, and his group High Frontier Inc., had already voiced what he called a new strategy for national survival under the title 'We Must Defend America'. General Graham had served with the American army in World War II, Korea and Viet-Nam. He was, when he retired in 1976, the Director of the Defense Intelligence Agency and his concern for the future was centred on this decade, the 1980s. He appeared frustrated by the Carter Administration's attitude to defence and naturally enormously concerned with the Soviet intervention in Afghanistan (he saw it as invasion rather than intervention). He was fearful of the way of East–West relations. Most of all, he bemoaned the American failure in the past to understand what the Soviet Union's technological advance rate would achieve in a very short space of time. He suffered with many others America's humiliation during the spring of 1980 when Eagle Claw, the mission to rescue the Iranian hostages, collapsed in the desert. Naturally enough, as a military adviser to Ronald Reagan, he was relieved when Reagan was sworn in as a president determined to recreate the United States as a tower of Western strength. The general's concern for America and his version went further: the High Frontier group's plan for a space-based defence system was not simply a fantastic rummage through the boxes of new technologies littering Federal laboratories and industrial workshops. It covered everything from laser beams to machine guns.

To understand the origins of the Star Wars debate one should explore General Graham's original concepts, *because however discredited they might have become, they influenced Reagan's senior advisers*. Graham and his colleagues claimed that the need for the High Frontier programme was partly because the technology was either available or would be, and therefore it had to be exploited. The philosophy of the group was perhaps clear from the general's own concern: 'Many American intellectuals and politicians today are echoing the plaints of intellectuals and politicians in pre-World War II Britain: "Peace in our time, no matter the price."

'One need not be a historian to realise the disturbing similarities between pre-war Britain and America today. In the face of an even more powerful totalitarian state with even more clearly stated goals of world domination, American politicians and intellectuals pursue the same arguments and policies which tempted the aggressor to strike Britain in 1939.'

Certainly, then, there can be no doubting General Graham's motives. He believes that there exists in the Soviet Union a very real threat to Western peace. Equally certainly, the general recognises that the present American military machine is not capable of deterring war indefinitely. Furthermore he, along with many of his opponents, thinks that the West believes still that the concept of both sides having so many missiles that they would be scared to use them (a shorthand explanation of Mutual Assured Destruction) will prevent war. There have been attempts to change or disguise this philosophy although few of them have been convincing. Strategists have talked of introducing new balances in arms control and force structures. Graham is impatient with the theorists; his impatience is reflected in his adherence to Bismarck's 'Righteous indignation is no substitute for a good course of action'.

The High Frontier 'good course of action', according to Graham, 'is a comprehensive, new U.S. national strategy; it addresses not only our security problems, but also economic, political and moral issues facing the nation.' If adopted, High Frontier would accomplish the following:

- Replace the failed and morally suspect doctrine of Mutual Assured Destruction (MAD) with a strategy of Assured Survival;
- Effectively close the 'window of vulnerability' by denying the Soviets [sic] a nuclear first strike capability – without deploying one more U.S. nuclear weapon;
- Create a reliable effective deterrent to nuclear war by defend-

ing the United States and the Free World rather than by threatening a suicidal punitive strike at Soviet civilians;
- Create an immediate surge in the high-technology sector of the U.S. economy by opening and securing space for private enterprise;
- Provide positive and challenging goals for American youth and a restored image of U.S. success and leadership abroad;
- Do all of the above at costs to the taxpayer below all other available alternatives to meet the Soviet threat;
- And do so with or without Soviet co-operation.

General Graham agrees that these are heady claims for his concepts. Certainly some of the phraseology suggests that the High Frontier programme has little to offer in practicable solutions although quite a lot in patriotic slogans. However, although they suffered criticism and ridicule from the informed as well as the ever-present sceptics, High Frontier programmes were modest compared with some that were being voiced in official circles after President Reagan's speech.

The High Frontier concept sees a two-stage space-borne system. The first is known as GBMD I or Global Ballistic Missile Defence I. It was claimed as a simple project, relatively cheap and technically feasible within five or six years of being accepted. GBMD I is based on a maximum of 432 satellites with a lifespan of some five years orbiting 300 miles above the earth.

Now, satellites by themselves will not provide a defence against missiles. What High Frontier put together in the early '80s was a plan for the satellites, all 432 of them, to be carrying small missiles. Each satellite could have up to forty missiles – a sort of space-based rocket launcher. Consequently, the organisation's strategists soon started referring to the satellites as 'trucks'. Each truck would have its own computer brain controlling a sensor for locating attacking ballistic missiles, an electronic eye to track them and a communications package. (Even at this point in the Graham scenario it is easy to see why so many have found it fanciful.)

It would be up to the computer to decide which target to go for. Once that has been decided it would fire a missile or even a group of them to some point in space where it has calculated that the Soviet ballistic rocket will be at some given time. High Frontier's team worked on a missile design that could correct its own position just before attacking and then would ram the incoming enemy. The force of the two colliding at enormous speeds in space would be enough to destroy both of them. But, just in case there was a near miss, the Global Missile Defence System I also carried good old-fashioned 'buckshot' which would throw out a 25-foot cloud. That too would be enough to destroy the ballistic missile.

But this 'thinking' satellite truck would have to be protected from itself. After all, anything so self-contained might shoot down peaceful satellite tests, even manned scientific flights on their way into orbit.

And so the project envisaged a three-tier system of control. The first allowed the trucks in space to do nothing more than pass on information. Even a positive identification of a missile lift off would have to be sent back to ground control. This would be a peacetime role. It would be no different from the control exercised over all the existing strategic systems where a ballistic missile launch is likely to be nothing more than a test flight.

The next stage of control would be during some period of East–West tension where war was considered a probability but where the diplomatic machine was attempting to prevent confrontation. Then, the High Frontier plan would allow the satellites to go onto a semi-automatic alert. This might mean that the United States had decided upon a level of acceptable damage before retaliating. Perhaps a ballistic missile attack against an ally such as Japan or one of the European countries. (This is not so unlikely as might be imagined. The author has had several conversations in Washington, all of which have suggested that there are scenarios – especially under a more liberal Administration – where such attacks would be 'regrettable but acceptable'.)

On semi-automatic control, the trucks would allow a limited number of missiles through and then move onto fully automatic response.

In time of extreme tension the system would be almost independent. High Frontier uses the Cuban Missile Crisis of 1962 as an example of the GBMD being placed on full alert. It would, says General Graham, 'fire autonomously on every missile rising from hostile geography'. And, according to the general, hostile territory could mean countries other than the Soviet bloc. He is only too aware that, with the growing proliferation of advanced technologies, it can be only a matter of time before a Third World nation with perhaps an unstable leader decides to fire a nuclear missile during some regional conflict. The target could just as easily be one of the superpowers. Consequently, there are those who see a Global Ballistic Missile Defense system as having some world-wide policing task and not simply acting as an East–West deterrent. Those who find GBMD I attractive do so because it has immediate defence and industrial possibilities and because it is imaginative. At the same time its supporters see it as but a first step. GBMD II is in the hands of the model-makers.

The basic system, GBMD I, according to High Frontier, could be capable of destroying between fifty and eighty per cent of a Soviet missile attack. High Frontier's ambitions are such that fifty to eighty per cent kill rates are not sufficient. So GBMD II is considered to be the follow-on technology. It is seen as the system that can reinforce GBMD I by improving sensors, so giving the trucks more time to spot, track and then attack enemy ballistic missiles anywhere in their flight. The technology to do that is emerging, but slowly. High Frontier sees the problem as being one of contrasting temperatures. A missile in its early stages of flight is very hot. When it first gets into space, which is very cold, the missile 'glows' – its heat contrasts with the coldness of space. Consequently the missile presents an obvious target. But, as it travels through space, it cools and therefore is not such an easy target for the sensors on the small rockets in the High Frontier trucks. The trick is to develop a sensor which is able to keep track when the missile is at its most obscure. That, at least, is the problem as seen by General Graham and his colleagues. If the complex and highly technical GBMD is seen as the two layers of space-based defence, the High Frontier's third layer is far less technical although many may find it just as incredible and equally unlikely.

The system is based on a rapid firing gun, rather like the old Gatling. High Frontier says that it has examined the results of a General Electric 30 mm gun and that a pair of them firing at an incoming warhead would be almost a hundred per cent sure of destroying it. There are those who doubt this; there are those who have thoroughly examined the High Frontier programme and found it ambitious, lacking in technical explanation and quite unlikely. The Reagan Administration has never officially endorsed the technical claims of High Frontier. However its contribution to the debate of strategic defence has been recognised by President Reagan. On June 3, 1983 he wrote to General Graham to express this recognition. He said, among other things, 'You – and all those who have made the High Frontier project *a reality* [author's itals] – have rendered our country an invaluable service for which all future generations will be grateful . . .'

Whatever the true value of High Frontier as a defensive concept it certainly added to the debate in the United States, suggesting that a space-based missile defence system should be worked on.

The reason for spending so much time on the High Frontier programme has been to demonstrate the extent of that debate among reasonably influential military men and defence analysts which was going on well before the 'Star Wars' speech was scripted. Many would dismiss the High Frontier ideas as a series of space-based fictions that could never work, would never be funded and would never find a place in informed strategic discussions. Nevertheless the High Frontier project did manage to attract the attention of a large, impressionable, if not informed, audience and is perhaps indicative of the concerns among many that the old concepts of Mutually Assured Destruction were no longer acceptable. Those same concerns were relevant to the reasoning behind the Reagan SDI programme partly, but vigorously, promoted by some of his closest advisers including the man who was to become the President's National Security Adviser, Robert McFarlane.

Twelve months after President Reagan's Star Wars speech, the Department of Defense announced an appointment that was seen as an earnest attempt to co-ordinate the Reagan programme. In March 1984, Defense Secretary Caspar Weinberger called in Lieutenant General James Abrahamson to become director of the Strategic Defense Office at the Pentagon.

General Abrahamson had been the Associate Administrator of the National Aeronautics and Space Administration (NASA) for Space Flight. Anybody who had doubted the military interest in the Shuttle programme had only to look at General Abrahamson's record to have those doubts removed. For the previous two and a half years he had personally supervised ten Space Shuttle missions. The general, a graduate of the Massachusetts Institute of Technology, was chosen, said Secretary Weinberger, as somebody with 'the intellect and the vision to direct a highly technical program critical to the national security'.

Certainly General Abrahamson's appointment signalled the Administration's official belief that SDI could work. Indeed Weinberger said at the time that two teams of experts had been given the job of answering two essential questions. The first: do defensive technologies provide a real promise as a means of ending the threat of ballistic missiles? The second followed on from the first: would a world in which such technologies were deployed be safer and more stable than the world faced in 1984? The answer to both questions according to Weinberger was, Yes.

Six weeks after his appointment, the general went before America's legislators to state his case and support Mr Weinberger's confidence. He appeared before the subcommittee on defense of the House Appropriations Committee – a very proper thing for any director to do should he wish to justify his appointment and later press his claims for billions of dollars. Just how many billions of dollars the President's speech kicked into circulation is not readily understood. The initial part of the programme considered about twenty-five, that is twenty-five thousand million dollars. But that was seen as nothing more than the starting figure. It was the estimate for finding out if the vision of March 23, 1983 could be made to work. As a concept it was thought to be worth pursuing, and that once started the technology would emerge at just the right moment so that nobody would be brave enough to scrap the idea.

General Abrahamson saw a four-phase programme. The first has started; it covers a basic 4 or 5 year research programme. Logically some of the research programmes will move at different speeds according to their complexities, advances in various laboratories and techniques. It could be, for example, that general research for a space craft to carry, say, the necessary computers and reflectors for a ground-based laser system could be completed within a couple of years. But the laser research may take eight or ten years. By the time it is finished, satellite launch techniques may have changed or basic ballistic missile defence systems may have advanced, so making existing research obsolescent. But at some point, possibly by 1990, all the research will be expected to be in place for the next stage, full-scale engineering development. At this point it would be up to the President then in office to ask Congress for funds to go ahead with this development phase.

If the decision is taken and the funds are forthcoming, then development engineers would start to build prototypes of the defensive systems and carry out tests to see if the theory of the research supports the original concept. By this time, however, it is likely also that the concept itself would have undergone considerable revision.

Supposing then that the testing and development are successful; it is at this point that the first claim for the system will be scrutinised. The important claim for the Strategic Defence Initiative is not entirely that it will work in time of war. The real importance of the proposal is that it will be so impressive in its deployment stage that it will act as a comprehensive ballistic missile deterrent and that it will encourage the Soviet Union to reach an agreement with the United States that would result in a significant reduction in the numbers of these ballistic missiles.

Here, though, is an extra thought: it is very likely that the Soviet Union is developing, or will have by the middle to late 1990s developed, similar technology or, more likely, workable counter-measures. Stalemate? Not necessarily, but a reminder that, at this stage at least, the United States is thinking in rather outdated terms when it comes to arms control. Presumably by the mid-1990s arms control will have the numbers of missiles and warheads as a secondary consideration. The main function of bi-lateral agreements will be a more sophisticated way of preventing weapons being used, not simply the numbers of weapons that might be deployed in war. Nevertheless there is considerable merit in the thought behind this third stage of the SDI programme that the envisaged system will make ballistic missiles significantly less effective; although few believe that SDI could do anything but defend a few missile sites – certainly not cities. Even this assumes that by the 1990s ballistic missiles will not have gadgets that will counter the technology of the SDI; or that the Soviet Union simply builds more missiles to overwhelm the defences.

However should all the hopes of President Reagan also be those of the White House of say 1995 or so, then the fourth stage of the 1983 SDI dream would be put into action: the deployment of what Washington calls a highly effective multi-phased defensive system. What, then, is it supposed to do? (apart from breaking existing arms control agreements.[1])

General Abrahamson's concept may be taken in seven groups: the Initial concept, the Technologies, Beam Weapons, Missiles, Battle Management, Support Systems, and the cost of it all.

There is little point in coming up with some sensational-sounding scheme unless there is a clear understanding of the threat. To understand what the SDI would attempt to do, it is worth considering what a ballistic missile does and how it flies.

The traditional view of an intercontinental ballistic missile is a tall cigar-shaped rocket, pointed at the top end and blunt at the other. Nothing much has happened in missile design to change that picture. What some forget is that, although the whole lifts off, very little is designed to reach the target. In crude terms, only the tiny piece at the sharp end is lethal. That is the 'bus'. The 'bus' contains the warheads – assuming there is more than one. The whole missile from lift-off to landing goes through four phases, or stages. Stage one is the so-called boost stage; this is the main thrust of getting the rocket off the ground and into space. Once the main engines have boosted the missile into space and onto a trajectory, they have no value and so they break away. It is this second stage when the bus, containing the warheads, separates from the engines. The bus opens to let out the warheads. In the bigger intercontinental missiles there may be as many as 14 warheads in each bus. They can fly on separate trajectories in space; this is the third stage of the missile flight. In the third stage, the warheads are outside, or beyond, the earth's atmosphere. The final stage, the fourth, is when the warheads start their approach to the targets. They re-enter the earth's atmosphere at what strategists appropriately call the terminal phase of the flight.

The problems are obvious for the military engineers and scientists charged with making SDI work. A Strategic Defence system must be able to destroy a ballistic missile in all its four stages. Ideally, the attack on a missile should be made as soon as it is fired during the boost stage. The closer it gets, the more chance the missile has of getting through and the greater the agility needed by the defensive system. Further, it is clear that one

[1] See Chapters 12 & 13.

system will not work for every stage of the operation. To illustrate this point it might be remembered that a landmine planted ten miles from a defended position may be the ideal defence against an armoured personnel carrier full of soldiers when it is ten miles away. A hand-held missile may be the best defence when the vehicle is just two miles away. If the soldiers get through and burst into the compound, then a short-range sub-machine gun may be the best defence. Imagine, then, the complications for the Strategic Defence design team; the task is to develop the most complicated-ever defence system and one which is governed by the three traditional needs of the sniper: Target Identification, Tracking and Killing – and all three have to be right first time round.

As might be imagined, there is an American acronym for this process contained in the first phase of the SDI research programme. It is SATKA – Surveillance, Acquisition, Tracking and Kill Assessment. SATKA envisages a system that will probably incorporate space-based technology. It would keep the Soviet missile sites under constant surveillance. At the first sign of activity, certainly launch processes, then the surveillance system would report this to its ground control, while at the same time going automatically into the next stage, Acquisition. The system would be expected to pick up the missile as it was launched. There would not have to be any reference to ground control to do this. But the decision to take on the missile would have to come from the battle commanders.

General Abrahamson's grasp of the technical difficulties is essential to the direction of the programme. His job is to do more than be a token director. The general's background as a technologist in the Air Force and with the Shuttle missions allows him to make personal assessments of the claims and counterclaims put forward for the technical development and research phases. His concern is neatly summed up in evidence he gave in Washington shortly after his appointment during 1983.

'The goal of this program is to develop and demonstrate the capabilities needed to detect, track and discriminate objects in all phases of the missile trajectory. The technology developed under this program is quite complex and any eventual system must operate reliably even in the presence of disturbances caused by nuclear weapons effects or direct enemy attack . . .'

His point about discriminating objects is one example of the confusion likely during war, or that period of tension between the superpowers that could lead to war. A detection system should be able to tell the difference between a test rocket and a hostile missile launch. It should be able to pick out the decoy – an unarmed missile that might be fired to pull away the defence system from the real threat. It is not enough for a space-based gadget to see a rocket lift off, and to assume that it is a missile and therefore to automatically react. Nor is it sufficient to rely on getting a contact as soon as the rocket has been launched. The system may miss the launch. What happens then is even more important. The SDI relies on the observation platform picking up the target throughout any stage of the flight. A rocket has its own radar signature. It has a radar 'shape'. It will give off an infra-red glow during the flight. That glow will be different during the various stages of the flight. A simplified illustration would show that, for example, a hot rocket subject to all the drag and vibration of travelling through the earth's atmosphere will glow brightly as it enters the coldness of outer space. It will be as prominent as a red-hot poker against a cold background. But, as the rocket cools, so it will blend with the cold background and so its infra-red signature will change.

It can be seen that a new area of technology has to be explored because old-fashioned sensors that worked well in near-earth and ground conditions will not be good enough for the varied conditions to be found in space. General Abrahamson's programme includes, therefore, research into low-temperature sensors that can pick up the subtle differences. Radars which might not work effectively may have to be replaced by systems using laser techniques. His intention is that this first phase of research must be shown to be feasible by the end of this decade. To maintain the credibility of the SDI concept there will probably have to be four key demonstrations. One will show that it is possible to detect a rocket while it is still in its boost stage and then track it. Another is to develop long-wave length infra-red sensors that can pick out attacking missiles in mid-course flight. The next demonstration could well include the need to spot and track the missiles should they get through the net waiting to catch them on lift-off and then while they are in outer space. When they re-enter the earth's atmosphere the missiles are in the final stage of attack. They are minutes, perhaps seconds, away from targets. The technical means of identifying, tracking and then destroying would have to be infallible. It is a tall order. That is why the Abrahamson programme admitted that until this research stage was completed nobody really knew whether the whole thing would work in spite of the enthusiasms of the Administration.

Having identified and then tracked the incoming missiles, the Strategic Defence system would need to have super-efficient weapons to destroy or divert the missiles. Those weapons could be divided under the headings, Kinetic Energy Weapons or Directed Energy Weapons. Directed Energy Weapons include beams, the so-called death rays of science fiction. But, under the SDI programme, there is nothing fictional about the four areas of research covering what can truly be accepted as death rays, but as Abrahamson pointed out shortly after taking on the SDI project, the targets are missiles – not humans.

There are four basic concepts: ground-based lasers, nuclear-driven directed energy weapons, space-based lasers and space-based particle beams.

A laser is best described by spelling out its acronym: Light Amplification by the Stimulated Emission of Radiation. Laser beams work through the electromagnetic radiation spectrum and show up as equal wavelengths. To take advantage of this, the task is to produce a power source that will repeatedly 'energise' atoms and molecules. The atoms will throw out radiation including light for a brief moment before returning to their original state. If, however, they can be captured and agitated as soon as they are in this energised state, the atoms will continue to throw out a beam of energy, light, which is then recognised as the laser. Lasers are common in industry and even in the entertainment business – coloured lights of extraordinary intensity. What the military scientists are attempting to do is harness laser beams of very high intensities and direct them over great distances. This is far removed from the industrial applications. Twenty kilowatt lasers are used in industry, but a beam weapon would need higher energy lasers measured in hundreds of kilowatts or even thousands. (The laser tests against the U.S. Shuttle, in June 1985, used a low energy – 4 kW – laser.)

Experiments to find the right laser for the right job have been carried out for some years in both the Soviet Union and the United States. Two advanced projects have concentrated on gamma-ray lasers (inevitably called grasers) and X-rays. Tests on X-ray lasers have used small nuclear explosions to supply the energy. This has led many to believe that the nuclear-powered X-ray laser is the next generation of nuclear weapons. The obvious follow-up to this is the deployment of such systems in outer space; this concerns international lawyers who point out that such deployment would violate international agreements designed to keep space free from any form of nuclear weaponry.

For those who believe that the beam weapon idea really is to remain safely among the sci-fi pages for years to come, it is worth noting that General Abrahamson's scientists believe they are almost ready to decide which 'power-pack' is best for such systems. Furthermore, proper weapon testing could begin by the end of this decade.

As a result of deeper and more sensible examination of the problems in producing weapons to fulfil the military ambitions in space, a series of systems is starting to appear in model and test-bench form. They include the thermal lasers that could burn through the shell of a warhead, or the rocket while in its boost phase. Some lasers could be used to produce shock-waves that would disrupt the guidance mechanisms in the attacking missile. Electronics could be melted by particle beam systems.

Particle beam weapons are being developed both in the United States and, apparently, in the Soviet Union. In simple terms they are streams of sub-atomic particles that have been energised. Another weapon on the drawing boards is the space-based rail gun. The designs that have emerged show a small satellite with its own power supply, surveillance system and a long gun barrel from which projectiles would be fired every second. In some cases the designs have gone from drawing boards to workshops.

The American Air Force is said to see such weapons, known officially as hyper-velocity electromagnetic rail guns, as more than anti-ballistic missile systems. The Air Force would consider putting rail guns in space to act as sentries standing watch over American satellites. Research is advancing and more than eight companies and universities have teams working on multi-million dollar programmes. For example, the Westinghouse project has been tested in the laboratory and their gun has been fired, using projectiles travelling at more than four kilometres a second.

The spotlight of the American SDI has concentrated on the astonishing possibilities of the weapons. Since the Star Wars speech of President Reagan, thoughts have centred on whether or not the world could really be coming towards the age of death rays, beams and battle stations. But perhaps the most important aspect of SDI, although too often forgotten, is the means of keeping all this weaponry under control. The systems needed to make space sentries work correctly are as confounding as the development programmes on the weapons. The Americans call this research project Systems Analyses and Battle Management. It is here that the newest-of-jargon BM/C^3 (pronounced Bee-Em-See Cubed and standing for Battle Management Command, Control and Communications) takes over. Equally exotic is the SDI's description of the programme:

'The Battle Management Command, Control and Communications technology project will develop the technologies necessary to allow eventual implementation of a highly responsive, ultra reliable, survivable, endurable and cost effective BM/C^3 system for a low-leakage defense system. This BM/C^3 system is expected to be quite complex and must operate reliably even in the presence of disturbances caused by nuclear effects or direct enemy attacks . . .'

The reference to 'low leakage' means that it has to be good. It has to be able to take on and account for an enormous fusillade of missiles. The system must be leak-proof. In Washington they talk about the need to guard against a leaky SDI umbrella. A further reminder of the problems faced by generals in wartime is contained in the reference to 'disturbances'. One effect of a nuclear explosion is a phenomenon called EMP, Electro Magnetic Pulse. EMP interrupts communications; it is a form of super-interference with signals. Without perfect signals, the performance of dazzling weapons is dulled. The SDI project scientists are now working on what they call a 'sanity check'. Simply put, this is a study designed to show whether or not a weapons system is capable of doing what the President and his advisers say that it should do. General Abrahamson has put it this way:

'We have to be sure that we can turn on the system when it is needed and turn it off when it is not. Just as importantly, the system must not be regarded as a paper tiger by the Soviets [sic] if it is to serve as an effective deterrent to nuclear war.'

The demonstrations by test firing systems, most under laboratory conditions in the early periods of research, will indeed be crucial if anybody – not just the Soviet Union – is to be impressed

In another world . . . American astronaut Robert L. Stewart floats away from Space Shuttle, Challenger. Twenty years earlier, on March 18, 1965, the Soviet cosmonaut, Alexei Leonov, became the first man to walk in space – or, as it is officially known, took part in 'extra-vehicular activity'. NASA Picture

Proving that the big brothers are indeed watching each other: in 1984 an American reconnaissance satellite took this picture of a Soviet Black Sea shipyard. The image was enhanced by a computer and the result was a very detailed picture of a new Soviet nuclear-powered aircraft carrier, interestingly being built in two sections. This picture shows the front half.

Where it all began for manned flight. The launch pad at Tyuratam from where Yuri Gagarin was blasted into space, in April 1961.

A Soviet mini-shuttle being recovered after a splash-down. There are suggestions from some analysts that the craft may be used as an experimental reconnaissance craft, probably with a two-man crew.

Los Angeles as seen from a satellite using quite ordinary synthetic aperture radar (SAR).

An American Boeing 707 converted to a flying test-bed for laser beam operations. The beam is fired from the hump on top of the main body of the aircraft. US Air Force Picture.

An artist's impression of the American Navstar, a navigational satellite with impressive accuracy as part of a constellation of 18 satellites in the so-called Global Positioning System.

The American Challenger being rolled out to launch pad 39A. To give some idea of the size, and therefore the engineering and boost needed to get it into orbit, note the small group of people on the left of the top platform. The enormous cost and inconvenience of launching has resulted in engineers working on the next phase of re-usable space craft: a conventional take-off shuttle. It would take off as an aircraft, fly to an enormous altitude before boosting itself into orbit. In some future war, such a space craft could carry the President to overseas operations. However, it would be vulnerable to techniques developed for anti-satellite attacks. NASA Picture.

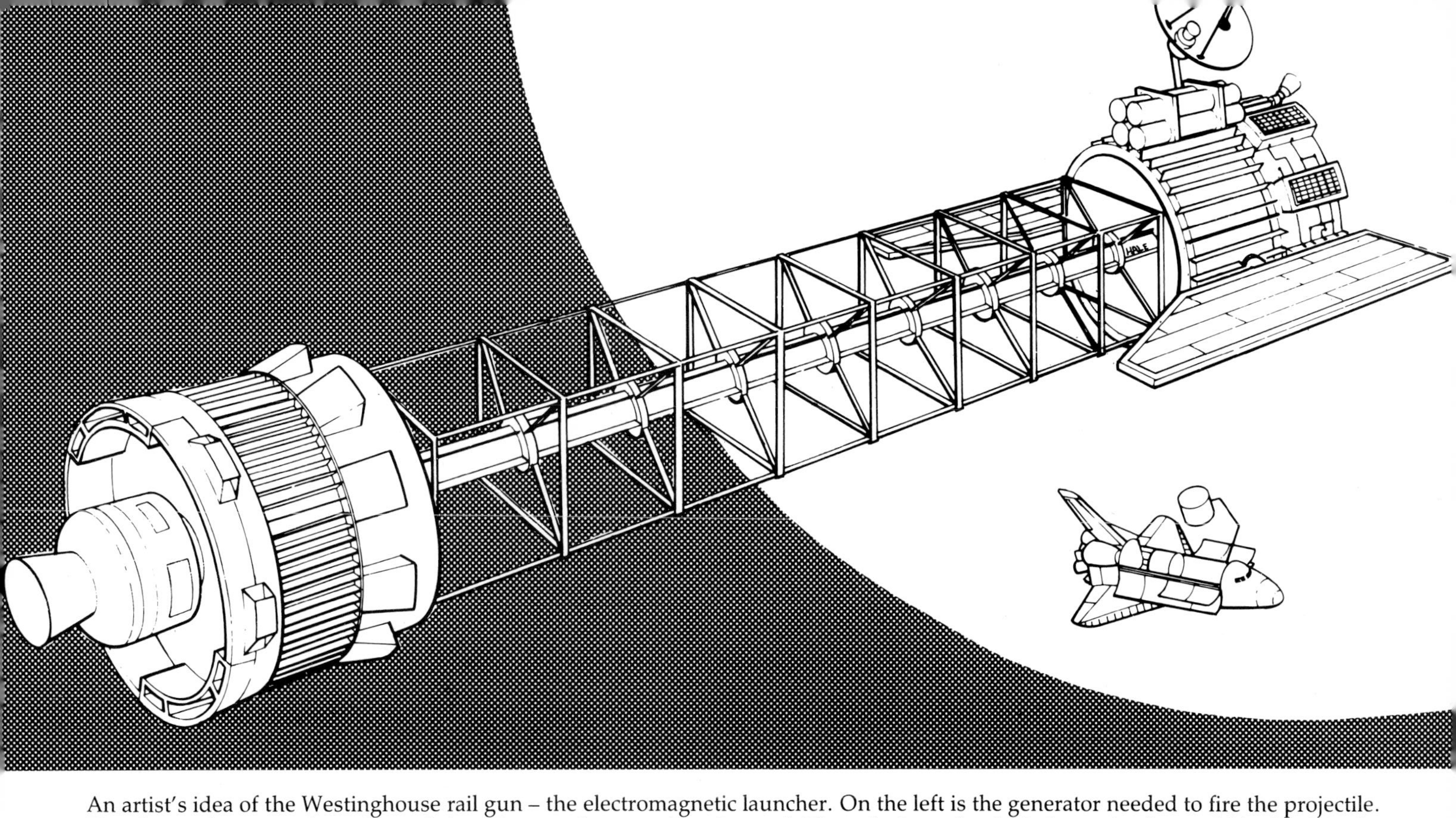

An artist's idea of the Westinghouse rail gun – the electromagnetic launcher. On the left is the generator needed to fire the projectile. The electrical system, the radar and the solar panels are at the other end. The rail, through which the projectile would be fired, is the tube through the centre of the box section.
Westinghouse Drawing

The American F–15 Eagle jet carries beneath it an anti-satellite missile. Note the squadron insignia on the jet's tail: an aircraft attacking an orbiting satellite. There has been some serious thought that, in the future, arrangements would have to be made to deploy such aircraft as far south as Australia and the Falkland Islands to complete the coverage of the ASAT squadrons. US Air Force Picture.

Artist's impression of the ASAT missile after being launched from the American F–15 Eagle jet. US Air Force Drawing.

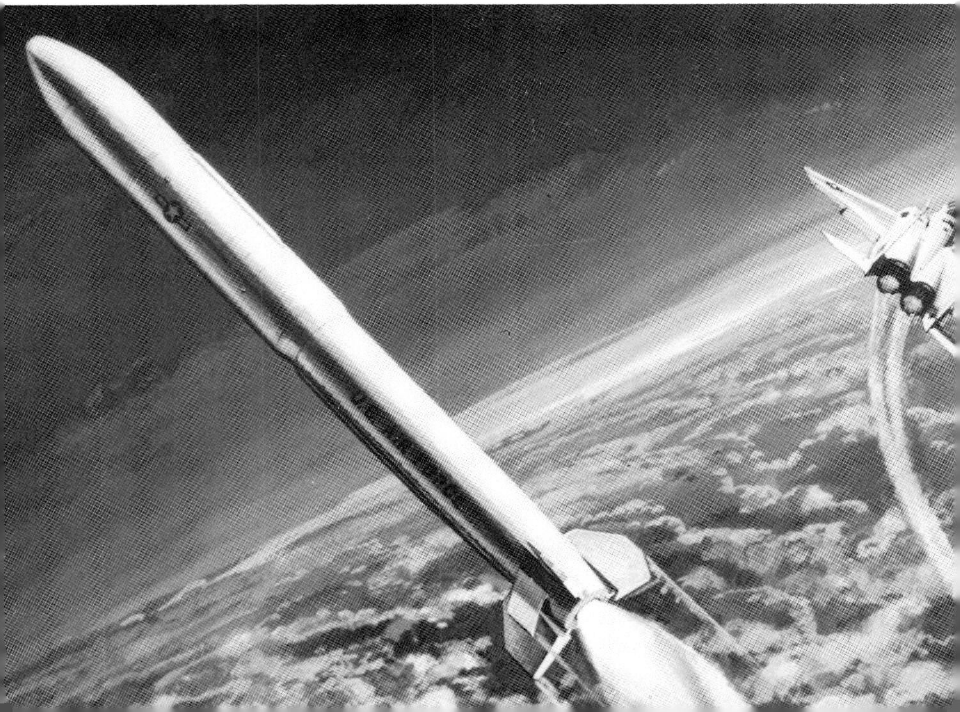

enough to regard SDI as a credible concept, never mind a potentially major deterrent. As can be seen from the brief outline above, the problems are enormous. The ideal system provides layers of defences. If the first layer failed to catch all the incoming missiles, then the second or third layers would be expected to mop up the nuclear missile 'leaks'.

The essential element in the system would be in that first stage, during the first five minutes or so of the rocket's boost flight. However the chances are that, within the five-minute 'window', the first two minutes would be taken up by identifying the target, tracking and deciding whether or not to attack.

An added complication is that the system has to be designed for an ultimate attack, that is one which might have two thousand missiles or warheads. Taking out one warhead at any of its stages of flight is difficult enough, but imagine the numbers of different sensors and weapons there would have to be in space to handle 2,000 targets. (And what if 2,000 and *one* missiles were launched!) Even simple problems obvious to every infantry officer are contained in this type of scenario. For example, what would happen if a number of sensors and sub-systems all concentrated on the same target? It might well be destroyed, but others would get through unchallenged.

All these systems are a long way from 'flying'. Yet it should be remembered that while it is reasonable to be cynical about some of the claims and ambitions, it is reasonable to recognise that modern computer technologies and advanced processes allow many problems to be solved far more quickly than could have been the case, say, ten years ago.

*

The initial reaction, even in the Pentagon, to the President's 1983 speech was, to say the least, cautious. Others have opposed the SDI programme on simpler grounds; it will, they say, quite clearly lead to an abrogation by the United States of the Outer Space Treaty and of the Anti Ballistic Missile Treaty signed by the U.S. and the U.S.S.R. Although many Administration officials have tried to deny this last charge, Caspar Weinberger, who was Defense Secretary when the Star Wars speech was made, has tacitly accepted that the ABM Treaty is likely to suffer. This treaty has restrictions on testing and deployment of some of the technology envisaged within the Strategic Defence Initiative. When General Abrahamson was appointed in March 1984, Mr Weinberger was asked how long it was going to be before work on SDI 'bumped up against' the ABM Treaty. His reply was clear. 'I really don't know,' he said. 'It depends on how rapidly we progress, how much success we have, how soon we are able to find paths that offer the greatest promise . . .' In other words, Weinberger was saying that it is inevitable that, as long as work progresses on SDI, then a point will be reached when the ABM Treaty will have to be swept aside or radically altered.

To many people, the ABM Treaty is one of the most important agreements signed by the two superpowers.[1] Many who hold that opinion attack the concept of SDI simply because it will destroy the treaty. It should be remembered that, if the United States abrogates the ABM Treaty, then so will the Soviet Union. If nothing else, we shall then see a further channel in the superpower arms race and this will lead to instability. Yet this should not be seen as the only, certainly not the main, reason for criticising the SDI programme.

It started as a vision pronounced by President Reagan and based on research technology that had been going on since the 1960s. According to the March 23 speech the noble ideal was to make nuclear weapons (not just intercontinental ballistic weapons) *impotent and obsolete* (the President's words). Within a year, that concept had been laid aside. By 1984 the SDI programme was no longer geared to provide a complete shield against a nuclear attack.

The President's vision, always somewhat blurred technically, was reduced to seeing a project that would possibly be capable of protecting major military systems. Furthermore, the concept of being able to destroy, deflect or degrade an incoming ballistic missile was slowly being tempered by the understanding that the problem was greater than first imagined. The six shooter may get the first six marauders, but a whole tribe of ballistic savages coming at all angles and moments will soon overwhelm the stockade unless something more comprehensive is deployed against them.

The problem with the SDI programme, of course, is that the

[1] See Chapters 12 & 13.

technology is far away and the counter-measures to it are closer. However, two aspects remain and should not be discarded: however fanciful the President's vision, however difficult the problems of SDI, it is inevitable that the technology in some form will emerge. There is enough science and engineering to prove that SDI could work in some *limited* form. By the end of this decade (barring international catastrophe) the world should know where the United States has reached with its programme. By then, the research phase should be sufficiently advanced to see if it is worthwhile developing the idea any further.

The key to SDI will be America's ability to develop the advanced computer technology needed to control the sophisticated sensors, trackers and targeting systems in space. A major factor in the advanced thinking necessary in this military development will be the building of permanently manned space stations – and this, for both the Americans and the Russians, is not a dream. It is crucial to the military development of space beyond the basic SDI programme.

Chapter 9

Space Station

There is nothing new in the idea of space stations. They have long been possible and in some form or another visible. The Soviet Salyut series can be described as space stations that have been operating since 1971. On April 19 of that year, the Soviet Union launched its first experimental space station, Salyut 1. Salyut 1 had three sections: one contained the docking area, another the stabilising system, and the main area the living quarters. The whole construction was only fifteen metres long and was described as having as much room as a large bus. Although it was cramped, Salyut 1 did allow some comforts for the cosmonauts. They had radiators, a shower, a cooker and a waste disposal unit that allowed most things to be jettisoned and burned up in the atmosphere. Salyut 1 set the pattern for space stations in as much as it was something that could be 'parked' in space and visited when necessary. This enabled crews to change over or be joined by others. But it was never intended to be anything more than an experimental station and it was short-lived. On October 11, 1971, Salyut 1 re-entered the earth's atmosphere and burned up. It had been the prototype of a series of very successful low-orbiting craft. Its highest point had been 210 kilometres and its lowest 200.

Two years later, during April 1973, the Soviet Union launched its second Salyut station. The orbit was very similar to that of Salyut 1, but there were two important differences. There were no attempts to dock with the station and the data sent back was on military frequencies. Furthermore, instead of staying up for an extended period, as many Western observers believed it would, Salyut 2 burned up by the end of the month. In June 1974, Salyut 3 was launched with slightly different high and low points of orbit. The following month cosmonauts Yuri Artykhin and Pavel Popovich were launched into space in Soyuz 14 and docked with the space station. As a reminder that space travellers are people, not programmed super-beings, both cosmonauts started an intensive programme of monitoring their reactions to flying in space. The Russians were looking even then to long flights for their cosmonauts and they recognised that it was impossible to simulate all the conditions in mock-up space stations on earth. The two men tested the air conditioning, the electronic facilities, and recorded how the different conditions affected their work rates.

That work included close photography of the mother planet; this was something that caused many in Washington to speculate that the Soviet space station could be, or was being, used as a military reconnaissance vehicle. There was one further attempt to put another crew on board, but it failed and in January 1975 Salyut 3 burned up.

The next craft up was Salyut 4. It was this space station that was in orbit at the time when Soviet–American relations were vastly superior to those of the early 1980s. Salyut 4 was launched towards the end of 1974 and, from it, cosmonauts Pyotr Klimuk and Vitali Sevastyanov watched the historic Soyuz-Apollo space docking. Klimuk and Sevastyanov spent a total of sixty-three days in orbit. When a replica of Salyut 4 was put on show by the Russians, it was clear that this endurance record was quite extraordinary. The cramped living and working area of Salyut 4 meant that the endurance wanted by the Soviet authorities would be hard to achieve. Furthermore, it would have a limited value unless it could be added to. The next but one space station, Salyut 6, went some way towards solving a few of these problems. Many of its research instruments were automatic and it had a docking facility at either end. This meant that if one went wrong it would be possible to send up another docking vehicle, and two vehicles could be docked at the same time.

Cosmonauts were now spending up to three months in space and they needed a strict routine to maintain their efficiency. Their day started at five in the morning and was much as it would have been on earth except that meal times were brought forward. After washing and exercises, the cosmonauts were allowed an hour for breakfast. At 6.45 am they started work with the most essential task, that of checking the space craft to make sure that all systems were working. These systems were monitored from the earth, but there was always the possibility that the cosmonauts would spot something that the earth-based housekeeping system had missed, or could not anticipate. Then at 7.45 am they had another breakfast. Lunch was at 9.30 am, supper at 3.00 in the afternoon, and bed at eight. The meal times were quite long; one reason was that the cosmonauts had to prepare them themselves in weightless slow-motion. When the first cosmonauts went into space, food was prepared in the most elementary way; and what they ate looked rather like toothpaste (normal food particles could in the zero gravity of space find ways into the machinery, with potentially disastrous consequences). It was true also that paste foods were easier to keep, store, prepare, eat and digest. The improvements to the Salyut menu were modest: fruit juice, soup and mini-chunks of sterilised food which at least gave the sensation of chewing that many would find satisfying after a hard day's space walk.

At the start of 1978 a new dimension was added to the Soviet space station programme. The Soviet Union launched a space barge.

The barge was Progress 1. It docked with the space station on January 22, two days after its launching. On board were food supplies, air bottles and some more personal goodies for the cosmonauts such as newspapers and letters from home. The Progress programme undoubtedly gave the Soviet space station system the boost it needed. The obvious drawback, however, was the fact that Progress supply barges burned out after departing from the Salyut 6 mother ship. Salyut 6 continued for four and a half years, an impressive enough performance from a near-earth programme sometimes criticised for its lack of sophistication when compared with the technological advances demonstrated by the United States.

Furthermore, while the United States talked about launching a space station, the Soviet Union had one, albeit not yet near the standard which the Soviet space engineers wanted – but that was a common occurrence in any space project. What is more, Salyut 6 was not the end of the Soviet series. It was replaced in 1982 by Salyut 7. This craft, not surprisingly, appeared to have all the modifications expected from the experience derived from the previous programmes and more was to come. In 1983, large extra solar panels to give increased energy were built on by cosmonauts during two space walks. Perhaps the most important development in the Soviet space station was the support craft for Salyut 7. New types of 'space barges', as big as the Salyut 7 station itself, can take supplies into orbit, dock with the station and provide 'on site' accommodation if necessary and then bring back to earth experiments, film and data records. However, the same problems remain for these Kosmos series barges as they did with Progress: they are not re-usable. This problem will be overcome although not as quickly as some have suggested. One solution could be a Soviet version of America's space shuttle. The Russians are developing such a craft at the experimental flight base, Ramenskoye close to Moscow. The U.S.S.R. has built a mini-shuttle with a crew of 2 or 3. This small space plane is not unlike American early designs that were discarded. The Soviet system has, however, been tested. There was natural speculation that the 'mini shuttle' would be the answer to re-usable space barges. It would appear to be too small for such a role and there is a dawning respect for the notion that this vehicle may be more connected to the military programme. It could be used for tactical reconnaissance or developed as a crew transfer bus for the Salyut series.

Meanwhile, the United States is pressing on with plans for its own space station. During President Reagan's State of the Union address in January 1984, he announced that he had directed NASA to start development of a 'permanently manned space station'. Mr Reagan said that he wanted Americans living and working in space, 'permanently, within a decade'.

The initial description that went with the President's announcement was a little short on detail. It described a low-orbiting space complex that included some sections not connected to the main system. The centre hub was seen as providing the docking bay for the space shuttle. There would be pressurised modules attached to the hub. From this part of the complex would come the eventual day-to-day scientific and military activity. The free-floating sections were said to be unmanned and 'able to provide changeable payload accommodation for activities requiring minimum disturbances and protection from base activities'. It should not be thought that these American space stations are seen as space cities or mini-colonies although such thoughts are not far from the space-planning mind. At first, the American scheme imagines crews of six to eight astronauts. Each person could stay up for about six months at a time. (In terms of understanding the effects of such endurance, the Soviet Union is ahead of the United States.)

At the time of President Reagan's announcement much was made of the commercial opportunities. Industrial, especially pharmaceutical, applications have yet to be fully explored but enough research has shown already the advantages of zero-gravity. For example, certain drugs could be produced at a fraction of the earthly cost once the initial outlay has been overcome. Naturally, commercial interest is encouraged to offset the enormous costs to the Federal Government. (This is one advantage of the capitalists' system which the Kremlin could envy.)

The space station might be seen, too, in the same way as the service station was seen by the motorist in the early years of this century. Motoring technology was going ahead as fast as development could cope, what was lacking was the support systems throughout the country; if the motorist broke down (or his car did), help was a long way off and often inexperienced. Today, space vehicles have a relatively sound performance. The space station is the support system. Equipment could be stored on board. Satellite repairs, rescues and modernisation could be carried out from space stations. Mixing the illustrations, the space station is essential as a supporting base, and in mountaineering terms it provides a base camp in the foothills of space exploration, reducing the need to return so often to earth below.

What to the scientist is particularly exciting is that the space station provides an attainable goal necessary to the American space programme, often trampled upon by political and fiscal cold feet. It does not have the uncertainties of the Strategic Defence Initiative, partly because the technology is more easily defined and demonstrated. Nor is it controversial as a military programme, although its connection with SDI and less ambitious projects is quite visible.

The design stage of the space station has long established that the sci-fi wheel-like complex is not going to work in practice. The drawings that have emerged from the various companies interested in building a station all show a complex made up of bolted-together pressurised tanks. This is a very crude description. It is meant to indicate that what is imagined for the 1990s is a cotton-reel and string design more in keeping with those early young men and their flying machines than the smooth cigar and saucer shapes of the star trekkers of science fiction. The pressurised tanks are not unlike the tanks on petrol lorries. These are the modules in which scientists would live and work. The first drawings produced show these tanks with giant 'fly-swats' poking from some central hub (these are the solar panels).

Early estimates in 1984 suggested that each station would have to have a 40,000 square foot-area of solar cells. This would be enough to provide a station with a 65-kilowatt electrical power requirement. But energy supply is just the basic problem once the system is built. For example, unless some way can be found to re-cycle water, it would be necessary to have a special space shuttle whose only job would be to ferry water from earth to the station.

Every effort has been made to present the project as a civilian programme and indeed there is much to support this emphasis. However, it is an obvious fact that NASA believed from the start that, unless the American Defense Department took part, then the project was likely to falter, or even fail. The Pentagon's ambitions for space-based or partly space-based operations make participation almost a foregone conclusion. The department would, for example, find a space station an enormous help in constructing the huge radars, tracking units and beam weapons needed to make some of the proposals for SDI more realistic.

It appears from preliminary designs that the civilian project is very similar to that contemplated by those involved in missile defence. Furthermore there is an increasing body of opinion in Washington (by no means rejected by some in Moscow to whom the author has spoken) that by the end of the century both superpowers will be building space-based command posts. It is not impossible to imagine that, in time of tension, senior commanders-in-chief, perhaps even presidents, will have the option of going into space, to some orbiting command post, in order to take over crisis management (the weakest link in time of tension) from the new high ground of the latter years of the twentieth century. Indeed to demonstrate the way ahead, there has been some thought given to the idea that because near-earth space has become so simple, some president may choose to demonstrate his faith in the technology by 'riding the shuttle' as one Washington expert suggested to the author.

What is certain is that the concentration of the Soviet Salyut programme has reminded both superpowers of the military advantages of near-earth space flight. What is more, a space station could easily become a jumping-off point for literally higher things. It will not be long before either or both superpowers produce a successful conventional take-off space shuttle, as opposed to the rocket-launched version. Combine such a system with a space station and the ease with which man can get about and use this relatively new environment will be enormous. But let us ignore the weapons of the future, even though that future is closer than some may believe. How would the military commanders use their more conventional space systems in time of crisis?

Chapter 10

The Military in Space

In 1982, the United Kingdom went to war with Argentina over the latter's occupation of the Falkland Islands in the South Atlantic. The Soviet Union launched a satellite to spy on the British Forces.

Towards the end of March, it had become clear that the events in the South Atlantic could lead to some show of force by the British although at this stage armed conflict was not in the Government's mind. Indeed the then British Defence Secretary, John Nott, had attended a meeting of NATO's Nuclear Planning Group on March 23 and 24, and had shown little concern for the future of the Falkland Islands. That meeting was in Colorado Springs and Nott and his advisers visited the U.S. Space Center inside Cheyenne Mountain just a few minutes' drive from the city. Apparently, nothing they were told about satellite movements and developments inspired further concern for what was going on in the South Atlantic. They should have been told that, on the day before the visit, the Soviet Union had launched a spy satellite that could monitor the Falklands.

Although some senior chiefs of staff were eager to return to their Whitehall desks, it was decided that the overall Chief of the Defence Staff, Admiral of the Fleet Sir Terence Lewin (now Lord Lewin), should have no worries about going straight from Colorado Springs to New Zealand for a duty visit. This, then, was the measure of concern in the third week in March. Furthermore, although this concern increased enough for the Chief of the Defence Staff to inquire from New Zealand whether or not he should return to London, he was told that there was no need for him to break his tour. Soon, however, the advice was changed and Sir Terence did return to London, to take charge of the military response to the Argentine invasion. The important aspect of all this is that the Soviet Union was somewhat less sanguine than the British about what was going on in the Falkland Islands, and they had the means to demonstrate their interest.

The Soviet Defence Staff ordered the making ready and then the launching of a spy satellite to monitor activity in the United Kingdom. The satellite Kosmos 1347 was launched from Tyuratam on April 2, the same day Argentine forces invaded the islands. By this time it was well known that Britain was preparing a major task force of warships, submarines and support vessels, and that the main elements were being prepared at Devonport and Portsmouth. On its third orbit, Kosmos 1347 passed over Portsmouth shortly after three o'clock in the afternoon of April 2, recording the numbers of ships, types of vessels, dockyard stores and equipment waiting to go on board and the engineering modifications that had started on some vessels.

Two days later, the same satellite orbited over the other main naval base, Devonport, and collected similar information as the Task Force made ready. During the next three days Kosmos 1347 also flew over Faslane, the home of the Royal Navy's fleet of four Polaris nuclear missile-firing submarines and 'conventionally' armed nuclear-powered submarines such as HMS *Conqueror*. The same tracks that passed over Portsmouth and Devonport allowed the satellite to photograph RAF preparations at, for example, Lyneham where transport aircraft were based. Furthermore, it was possible to observe any activity at British Aerospace airfields and smaller establishments (including one near Cambridge) that were preparing for conversion work on aircraft. So, between April 2 and April 7, the Soviet Union had gathered a fairly comprehensive picture of the size and scale of the United Kingdom's military response to the Argentine invasion – which is more than the British public were allowed.

By the end of April, the Soviet Union had a detailed picture of the role of Ascension Island with its Anglo-American support operation for the Task Force. (Soviet Electronic Intelligence had intercepted communications to and from Ascension Island.) There has been speculation that the Soviet Union gave this Intelligence to the Argentine junta. However, as noted earlier, there is no conclusive evidence to support this hypothesis, although there are indications that some information may have reached Argentina through a third country.

Of course, the Soviet Union was not alone in its interest in the early stages of the Falklands War. The United States had its own 'long-life' reconnaissance satellites in orbit. Two American space craft surveyed the Argentine forces *before* the invasion of the Falkland Islands. One of these satellites had been launched two years before the war on February 7, 1980, from the West coast of the United States. The other was launched from the same place on September 3, 1981.

Five days before the invasion, the 1980 satellite overflew the bases at Comodoro Rivadavia and Rio Gallegos. (It is possible, but not confirmed, that the southern naval port of Ushaia was photographed at this time.) On the following day, March 28, the same reconnaissance craft was over the Falklands and on April 2 it observed part of the invasion. The second satellite had monitored Argentine preparations for the attack on March 28 and 29; it was in a position to see forces leaving for the Falklands. Certainly on April 2 it is understood to have monitored the follow-up force. This information was passed to the British authorities. The events of the final days of March 1982 and the weeks that followed demonstrated the value of space to the military and also showed the disadvantages of not having access to this new high-ground of modern warfare.

The need to use the high ground has been understood by every successful commander in history. In modern times, Intelligence requirements have not much altered and the difficulties in analysis are as confusing as ever. In this age, the rapid movement of men, weapons and information makes necessary a swift assessment of the enemy and his territory. It is this need for speedy assessment that has given the military use of space a peacetime urgency in the minds of commanders that they have never before experienced. Only in wartime have there been such urgent calls for innovation, development and production of new systems.

The commander in the 1980s may have the same basic questions for his Intelligence Staffs as did his predecessors down the centuries, but his reasons for wanting that information are obviously more complex. Military objectives remain more or less common to whichever century the general or admiral might find himself. The first objective is to enforce the political will of government when all other means have failed or have proved inconvenient. To do this, the soldier must either gain enemy territory in such a way that he can hold it on his own terms or defend his own territory so that the enemy will give up any ambitions of conquering him. The sailor's job is to avoid large-scale naval engagements – ideally by bottling up the enemy fleets in port or some harmless part of the oceans. For the admiral's ultimate aim is to keep open sea lanes that might be needed to support the land operation. The land operation is, after all, the only one that has a reasonably measured chance of territorial gain or loss and therefore the one which tends to decide which side has 'won' or 'lost' the war. To achieve this, today's military commander has enough firepower to obliterate, or cause the obliteration, of much of the world – and the methodology and arguments are well rehearsed.

This apparently-sophisticated level of arsenal is, according to defence alliances, the minimum needed to prevent war and to be assured of some success should its deterrent value fail. However, this very sophistication has presented chiefs of staff and commanders with a new set of problems.

At the simplest level, an obvious illustration may be found in the concepts of tank warfare as might be practised in Central Europe. In spite of new (or re-styled) doctrines developed by both the Warsaw Pact and the North Atlantic Treaty Organisation, the deployment and movement (either forwards or backwards) remains a clumsy process. Yet the increases in battlefield technology give the defending and attacking forces so many more options that this cumbersome aspect of armoured deployment is highlighted rather than eased. In other words, modern and emerging technologies are often guilty of making the process of managing a battlefield more complex rather than simpler as some proponents of Emerging Technologies (E.T.) claim.

As a consequence of the advances, and especially the complexities, in military science and engineering, commanders need more information about a wider range of elements and they need this data more quickly than ever before. It is also true that, as they demand and receive more at increased speed, then commanders create further problems in the form of *too much* information. It is doubtful, for example, whether the information-handling system at, say, the headquarters of the Supreme Allied Commander Europe, could cope with the ream upon ream of data provided by new systems. Nevertheless, there is no way in which any military manager would be willing to stand aside from new technologies. It follows, therefore, that the military actually encourage the development of technologies that often have doubtful value.

The military's interest, backed by their priority budgets in many economies, not only encourages new development, it provides the backing for systems that might otherwise never get further than the drawing board. Consequently the military often receive equipment and systems that have little to commend them other than their novelty and promises. Industry and national procurement and development agencies understand these drawbacks; they understand, too, the advantages. Many overall programmes could not continue without the weight, both financial and political, of the military's interest in at least some part of that development. If one combines the defence community's various interests – financial and political backing, the real or imagined need for more information and the fear of missing some technological advantage – then the military use of outer space may be easily understood. Certainly the use of space is the best example of what one might call 'military inevitability'; or, perhaps more expressively, 'if it's available, let's buy it!'

By the late 1970s it was reasonably clear that few major military systems could be developed without some reliance on a space-based function of some sort. Consequently, the temptation was to look at space systems and to see how existing, or new, ground-based elements of a battlefield might be developed to take advantage of the emerging area of technology. Today the military operations of the superpowers are almost one hundred per cent dependent on some aspect of space technology, so much so that there is little or no distinction between a contemplated wartime role for space and a peacetime role.

In peace there is war. If we live, say in London, Paris, Chicago, Budapest, Prague or Rome, then, like most of those in our Western or Eastern-bloc alliances, we talk of peace in terms of superpower relations. The Americans have had their involvements in Central America, the Russians in Afghanistan, the British in, say, the Falklands, but generally we are at peace because NATO and Warsaw Pact forces are not at war. Yet the Middle East is in an almost constant state of war or siege; conflict in Africa continues and South East Asia relentlessly adds its own numbers to the long list of casualties suffered while the world is 'at peace'. (Something like 20 to 25 million people have died in armed conflict since the end of the Second World War.) This is not some plea for world peace. It is, however, a reminder that, in times of *European* peace, war is whittling away at the population of a large part of the globe and that, as weapon technology 'improves', then so might there be an increase in the rate of casualties and the risk of war spilling into a neighbouring region or area of superpower interest – which is one reason for superpowers to monitor these regions from the safety of space. Furthermore, both superpowers are very aware that armed conflict between the Warsaw Pact and NATO could well start because of something going on beyond their borders.

Few in Washington and Moscow would be capable of arguing that war between the two power blocs is likely to start because of some urge by either side to move on the other for territorial and ideological gain. That might have been the case in the 1950s, but it is far less likely in the middle of the 1980s.

Both superpowers have enormous interests beyond their borders and sometimes those interests – perhaps diplomatic neuroses would be a better description – are unconnected with coastlines and territories that might even be threatened. These 'interests' are the results of colonial times, regional treaties, a recognition that the front line of a 'threat' may be as far away as the extreme range of a bomber or missile or the assumed need to protect some strategic raw supply whose shortage could disrupt connections and alliances closer to home. Also, an interest may be declared on the basis of misunderstanding the intention of the other superpower in that region.

This *mis*understanding often goes hand in hand with a *lack* of understanding of the region itself. Whatever the reasons for interest, the fundamental concern is expressed in both Washington and Moscow as one of the protection of National Security. And so, even in peacetime, every effort to monitor those national interests and to police them is as important as any that might be envisaged for wartime operations.

It follows, therefore, that when we talk about the military use of outer space we should be careful not to make the mistake of imagining that the sky is full of space craft that would be activated only in time of extreme tension or war itself. Indeed, at the time of writing, every single space-based military system is fully operational: that is, it is being used every day in the same way and for the same purpose as it would be in war – only the scale of use is different. This peacetime activity is not a practice role, it is the intended function of the space craft. So, against a background of world tension and open conflict together with perceived threats to superpower interests, it is possible to act out the role that military satellites do and would play in some imaginary theatre of war.

Every day, satellites orbit over key areas of tension; but suppose the Middle East and the Far East went from simmering to boiling point and that there were what diplomats call 'uncertainties' in Eastern European states? What follows is not intended as the perfect scenario, but it is true that many war-gamers in Washington and Moscow have played out something similar:

The war between Iraq and Iran has dragged on to the point where the Iraqi leadership needs either victory or a negotiated and guaranteed peace settlement if that leadership is to survive. The Iranians have extended their air assaults to threaten the Gulf States, to involve those states and therefore to force them to bring pressure on Iraq to end hostilities. There has been severe damage to an oil installation in Saudi Arabia. The offending aircraft is shot down, apparently by Saudi interceptors, but there is a rumour that an American squadron on an 'exercise and training' mission in Saudi Arabia took out the attacker. The Pentagon has confirmed that an American AWACS (Airborne Warning and Control System) aircraft on loan to the Saudi government directed the retaliation and was flown, although not captained, by an American Air Force crew.

The Soviet Union accuses the United States of inflaming the Iran–Iraq war, and steps up its supplies, ironically, to Iraq. A resupply of spares puts the Iranian Air Force back in the air and, although operations are short-lived, two 'kamikaze' raids on an American aircraft carrier in the Gulf are successful. There is much loss of American life. In Washington there are demands from many in Congress for American withdrawals from the region, questions raised as to how this attack had been allowed to succeed, condemnation by the ill-informed of the imagined part played by the Soviet Union, and an equally vociferous lobby wanting to know how long the President is going to allow this American humiliation (remembering the Iran Hostage Affair, the attack on the marines in Beirut, and the TWA hostages) to go unavenged.

Some Gulf states, fearful of getting involved in the conflict, quietly seek Washington's assurances of protection, while other states do not want that protection for fear of getting involved by having to provide bases. Other Arab states adopt a more aggressive tone, hoping that an American response will once and for all put an end to the Islamic Revolution in Iran, which directly and indirectly threatens the stability of some Arab governments.

The Soviet Union is equally fearful of conflict in the Middle East. The thought of further disruption in Iran disturbs the Politburo which retains fears of reaction by Azerbaydzhanis in the Iran border area of the Soviet Union and a general suspicion of the growing Islamic influence in the demography of the U.S.S.R. Furthermore, Moscow is deeply concerned that the United States could become a dominant crusader in the Middle East, should Washington order and successfully execute a military action against the Iranians and their brand of Shi'ite revolution.

The Soviet fleet that has been exercising in the Indian Ocean moves towards the Gulf while two of its missile-firing submarines manoevure to within firing range of the large American bomber and submarine base on the British-owned Indian Ocean island of Diego Garcia. The Soviet Mediterranean squadrons are reinforced from the Black Sea and gather in the Eastern Mediterranean.

The tension increases when the American Defense Department announces that the Rapid Deployment Force including the 82nd Airborne Division, backed by the U.S. Air Force, is proceeding to the area for joint exercises with Egypt and Gulf States. The Soviet Union once again describes the American action as provocative. This Soviet fear is endorsed by some NATO countries, an endorsement which adds to American concerns. There are those in the Defence and Foreign ministries in Moscow who are satisfied by this not-unexpected attitude shown by, perhaps, Denmark, the Netherlands, West Germany and a Labour-led British government. The Kremlin imagines that this lack of cohesion in the Western Alliance could be exploited and may prove to be of some military significance as the crisis develops.

In Eastern Europe, however, there is similar caution, together with friction within two Warsaw Pact states. The Romanians refuse Soviet requests to mount 'mobilisation' exercises and the Romanian leader does not attend an emergency summit meeting in the Soviet capital. At that meeting, the Secretary of the Polish Communist Party is asked to give a reassurance that renewed demonstrations by the Polish trade unionist movement, Solidarity, are 'controllable'.

Far from Europe and the Middle East, there are increased worries for both superpowers.

In the Philippines, a newly installed coalition government, to replace the ousted Ferdinand Marcos, has decided that the two strategically important American bases must close down. Subic Bay and Clarke Air Force Base have supported U.S. Naval and Air operations for decades. However, American attempts to keep in power President Marcos and a suggestion by the American President that the new government represents a communist threat to the Far East and American interests in the region lead the Filipino Administration to demand a U.S. withdrawal by the end of the year.

The Pentagon requests the U.S. Navy commander in the area to supply a readiness report to support any American move against eviction. The reply suggests that the major systems of the U.S. fleet are over-reliant on nuclear weapons and that conventional action could not be sustained for more than five days. This report is leaked after it finds its way into the hands of the Director of the Center for Defense Information in Washington. The Director, a former naval commander in the region, says that the report is likely to be accurate.

Further north, a Soviet submarine sinks after it is in collision with an American carrier. The U.S. government accuses the Soviet Union of attempting to provoke an incident. While this protest is lodged, an American electronic Intelligence aircraft flying from Atsugi close to Yokohama disappears from all contact. It was last heard when flying a few miles from Kamtchatka in the region where a Korean Airlines plane was brought down in September 1983. The American National Security Agency headquarters in Japan, at Camp Fuchimobe, reports the missing aircraft. Within twenty minutes of that report, an automatic signals tracker shows that a Soviet combat air patrol had diverted towards the Electronic Intelligence aircraft's flight pattern. A re-run of the tracker tapes offers conclusive evidence that the plane has been shot down.

In Northern Norway and in Washington, reports show that Soviet Intercontinental Ballistic Missile firing submarines have left their bases in the Kola inlet and have gone 'to ground' in the Barents Sea. A Northern Fleet carrier group is heading in the same direction. It is presumed by the Intelligence analysts in Washington that the carrier group is taking up its station as the centre for surface ships and attack submarines posted as 'minders' for the missile submarines.

Electronic Monitoring notes that the spring change-over of Soviet army conscripts has been cancelled and that no troops are being released from conscription.

The Soviet Ambassador is recalled from Washington to Moscow.

NATO ambassadors hold an emergency meeting in Brussels, but no conclusion is reached.

As the tension grows in the Middle East, the United States warns the Iranian government that it should halt its aggression, otherwise Washington will be forced to consider action to protect its interests and those of its friends in the region.

For the first time since the opening of the new Hot Line between Moscow and Washington, American and Soviet officials pass messages that test to the full both sides' ability to manage a crisis. The Washington officials ask the Soviet Union to put on the line a facsimile of their ground and air force deployments and promise that they, the Americans, will in return supply similar information about NATO forces. Washington says that this information will help to ease tension. The Soviet Union does not reply.

At an emergency meeting of the United Nations Security Council, the American representative produces what is said to be positive information that Soviet land, air and rocket forces have been strengthened and brought to a higher state of readiness in Central Europe, Soviet Central Asia and the Far East. A leaked report in Washington by an unnamed 'usually reliable source' claims that a Soviet Naval force has been located in the Atlantic apparently on course for Cuba. A further report from Singapore suggests that Soviet ships have left Cam Ran Bay in Viet-Nam and are heading for the Indian Ocean.

A monitoring group at Kettering Grammar School in England announces that five low-orbiting satellites have been launched by the Soviet Union during the past four days. None of these satellites has been reported to the United Nations in accordance with common procedure.

A further claim by the U.S. representative at the U.N. states that the reinforcement of Soviet troops and equipment close to the narrow border with Norway must be seen as a provocative action. In London, Defence Ministry officials refuse to comment on rumours that RAF Phantoms of III squadron have been flying round-the-clock missions to intercept Soviet bombers probing British air space.

On the same day, the Home Office refuses to comment on reports that members of the United Kingdom Warning and Monitoring Organisation (UKWMO) have been called in for an indefinite period and that Royal Observer Corps men and women are at 870 nuclear explosion monitoring posts for the first time outside an exercise period.

In spite of broadcasts by European radio and television stations advising calm, some one and a quarter million people have left their homes near the inner German border and are heading westwards.

In Australia there is reported sabotage at a complex described as a 'communications base' not far from Alice Springs.

In the River Thames, a Soviet freighter has gone aground blocking a channel into Chatham which has been re-activated by the Royal Navy following its closure in 1983.

An explosion aboard a Soviet fishing vessel in Plymouth is investigated by both military and civilian agencies.

In Singapore, two British dry cargo ships bound for the U.K. are visited by a Royal Naval NCS (Naval Control of Shipping) officer, who asks both masters to avoid the Suez Canal and be prepared to put into a South African port.

All outward-bound commercial flights and sailing from the U.K. are cancelled.

In Japan, there are reports of increased Soviet Naval activity from the Far East HQ's base of Vladivostock. Demonstrators clash with police at the Japanese port of Kobe where an American ship is taking on new stores. The demonstrators claim that the ship is armed with nuclear weapons.

The Warsaw Pact authorities announce that the corridor between West Germany and Berlin is closed. Protests are lodged by Allied representatives in the city and the small Allied Berlin garrison is raised to Full Alert.

Armed police arrest four long-distance lorry drivers at Ostend. In a similar operation at Antwerp three policemen are killed and two lorry drivers escape. Both the two lorries in Ostend and the one in Antwerp are registered in Bulgaria. No explanation for the attempted arrests is given by the authorities. A commentator on Dutch radio reports that the six men were believed to be Russian members of the Soviet Special Forces known as Spetsnaz.

In the Eastern Mediterranean, an American submarine is badly damaged with few of its crew surviving. No details of how the boat was damaged are given by the Defense Department in Washington.

The President of South Korea is assassinated. A crisis meeting of the Administration of Seoul declares a state of emergency and accuses North Korea of having had a part in the assassination.

American troops in South Korea are in a high state of alert and requests are made to the Japanese government to allow more U.S. Air Force planes to use Japanese bases. This follows a further declaration by the Philippines government that, although the end-of-the-year evacuation deadline remains, this only applies to personnel and their dependants. All U.S. aircraft must leave Clarke Field immediately and no U.S. ships or submarines shall be allowed to stay in Subic Bay for more than twenty-four hours at a time.

In Washington, the President is advised that he should ignore this order. He says that the United States will resist all pressures to desert the people of the Philippines.

China, which has remained silent during the growing tension, announces that it has evidence that the Soviet Union is planning to infringe its territory. A statement in Peking warns Moscow that China has the means to counter Soviet violations and is prepared to use the most extreme measures. Three Soviet soldiers on the Sino-Soviet border are killed.

Three American F-15s specially converted to carry anti-satellite missiles fly into the British-owned Ascension Island in the Atlantic. Twenty-four hours later another flight lands at Diego Garcia in the Indian Ocean, a third lands in Western Australia under an agreement recently signed with the new government in Canberra, and a fourth touches down in the Falkland Islands.

A French television crew in Afghanistan claim that the deputy commander of the Soviet forces in Kabul has been murdered.

Six days later, a commentator in London says that it is known that the Soviet general was killed along with three of his staff some ten days earlier. The same commentator, quoting 'diplomatic sources', says that, as there have been no claims by the Afghan rebels that they murdered the deputy commander and because there have been no reports of Soviet reprisals, nor any mention in Moscow of a senior officer having died on 'active duty', then rumours of a mutiny by Soviet conscripts in Afghanistan may have some truth in them.

Western diplomatic sources, quoted by a Scandinavian newspaper in Stockholm, say that the Soviet military exercises in the Western military districts of the U.S.S.R., including the Baltic, have been brought forward. However, unlike previous exercises in the Zapad series, there has been no official announcement of the manoeuvres and there has not been the traditional communiqué by Tass, the Soviet news agency, that Defence Ministers of the Warsaw Treaty States have gathered to observe exercises in the region.

A report in the British political weekly, the *New Statesman*, claims that underground government 'bunker' has been activated in Wiltshire and that all traffic has been stopped from entering the area, near the village of Corsham. A Wiltshire police spokesman says that the road blocks have been set up as part of a series of regular Home Office exercises.

An American transport aircraft on orders to defy the Berlin corridor blockage ignores Soviet commands to land and is shot down. Two women outside the American airbase at RAF Mildenhall in Suffolk are shot dead by American military police when a crowd of about 2,000 women break through civilian police barriers.

A plane carrying the U.N. Secretary General is turned back as it approaches Soviet air space. The Secretary General had announced that he was flying to Moscow for 'urgent consultations'.

Three Libyan fighters are shot down by American carrier aircraft as the Arab planes approach transports flying men of the U.S. 82nd Airborne Division into Cairo.

NORAD in Cheyenne Mountain reports a triple Soviet ballistic missile launch. The report is not confirmed by the early warning radars at Thule in Greenland, at RAF Fylingdales in Yorkshire nor by the early warning satellite. Seventy seconds after the report, NORAD cancels the warning and says that there has been a computer malfunction.

National Security Agency signals monitoring reports to the National Command Center in Washington, that heavy jamming in and around Moscow makes it impossible to confirm its earlier report that all fourteen members of the Politburo have, after an emergency meeting, left the Kremlin, destination unknown.

The United States President leaves the Oval Office and walks towards his helicopter that is waiting to take him to Andrews Air Force Base just outside Washington. The President stumbles and then falls to the White House lawn: a simple heart attack brought on by sleepless nights and enormous tension. He was seventy-six.

Now, all of this is pure imagination. But it is the very stuff of which NATO and Warsaw Pact war-gamers dream. Certainly there are those in the West who have to play through such games in such widespread detail because gone are the days when a simple one-line scenario was thought good enough to spark an East–West confrontation. It is not so many years ago that the war-gamers imagined that Soviet troops would go into Yugoslavia on the death of Marshal Tito and that the West would respond with force. It was always an unlikely scenario, but it was dropped long before the Yugoslav leader's death.

By the late 1970s it was clear that a more realistic war-game had to recognise that, if there were ever to be such a conflict, then it would have more to do with a series of apparently unrelated incidents, tensions and commitments *throughout* the world.

Glance through any good foreign news coverage by, say, *The Times* or the *International Herald Tribune* or listen to a single B.B.C. Radio (especially World Service) news bulletin, and that will be sufficient for most to recognise that the outline of world tension sketched above has a very strong thread of possibility running right through. What is more, the picture could have been more elaborate and still it would have retained a strong element of credibility. Each of these tensions and conflicts must be monitored. Keeping an eye on such events is part of Indicators and Warnings (I&W), a branch of Intelligence analysis that has gained increasing importance during the past five years or so.

It is the need to persevere with monitoring Indicators and Warnings of conflict and tensions which provides a great portion of the illustration of how military and political satellites are used in peacetime. When that peace has broken down, then the same satellites are used in the same way – but then in the conduct of war rather than the maintenance of peace.

The greatest threat to peace is not the 50,000 or so nuclear weapons in the world, nor the billions upon billions of dollars, roubles, pounds, francs or whatever, spent on arms *per se*. Weapons, however terrible, cannot be said to threaten us with war, nor destruction. The real threat to peace is the difficult craft of crisis management. The ideal, and most obvious, way of managing a crisis (apart from building a perfect world) is to identify it in its embryonic form and then take discreet action. The most difficult period of crisis management is when the main problem is in flames and may even be threatening surrounding events. The simplest period is war, because by that stage it is quite possible that events, even those engineered by the crisis manager – may run themselves and present few opportunities of management, only reaction. When both stages of crisis are running at once, then the vulnerability of crisis management is most apparent.

The ambitions of, say, a Hitler were relatively simple to manage compared with the more widespread problems facing world leaders in the 1980s. Ideologies are more powerfully expressed, and political and military ambitions are stronger. The world has to cope with two superpowers, a strongly developing Middle East, an emerging China, a politically up-ended Far East and a diverting Central America. The world is further complicated by an astonishing network of communications that record and transmit political, economic and military drama at such speeds that there is an almost continuous demand for instant reaction and decision-taking: in all, an added complication for crisis management. So, more and more, the managers must turn to space to find out not just what is going on, but what might happen next.

In days of relative peace, satellite gleaning is a less urgent process in the Intelligence War. Yet for the Indicators and Warning analysts information is as essential as it may be for, say, the naval commander in wartime. The peacetime analyst will take his raw Intelligence from space craft other than from those with a purely military mission. For example, an orbiting space station may provide the Soviet Defence Ministry with photographs of the new constructions and installations on Ascension Island. A civilian land satellite will show construction work in the Soviet Union which Intelligence officers identify as an accelerator system to test beam weapons. An American satellite with a main function of enhancing geological surveys may show up excavation work in, say, Soviet Russia which in turn ties with other Intelligence reports of a new Soviet missile complex.

Both superpowers regularly photograph the other's defence installations, and those of their allies. They both use photographic reconnaissance and electronic Intelligence space craft to monitor crisis areas, looking for military and strategic information as well as any signs of how the other is behaving in the so-called out-of-area regions. Moscow and Washington keep a regular watch in the Middle East, although some of that monitoring is carried out by conventional spy planes, such as the improved U-2s that fly from the British base at Cyprus or from ground electronic Intelligence stations. However, even in the latter case, much of that material is relayed to Moscow or Washington via satellite. More than 60 per cent of diplomatic and military signals traffic now goes via satellite, and so one can see that, in our imaginary scenario of tension, satellites would be humming with diplomatic and military information as tension in one part of the world became a crisis or a crisis in another degenerates into a war.

When matters were to become so bad that the superpowers felt a need for urgent bi-lateral consultations, then they would use the Hot Line, which relies on satellite communications. Both capitals would be getting constant updates from photographic satellites, electronic satellites listening to either's communications, and signal from embassies, military posts and National Security Agency and C.I.A. outposts as well as from allies, for instance Britain's G.C.H.Q. Submarines would be reporting their movements and those of the surface targets they were following. Those reports would be sent by satellites. Troop formations, especially reinforcements, would be subject to satellite monitoring; and, finally, Presidential Press Conferences, reports of crisis meetings of the U.N. Security Council, reactions in the world capitals and calls for constraint as well as accusations and counter-accusations would be beamed round the global network of television and radio stations via satellite. And, if all reason and diplomatic effort failed, then the military commanders would be astoundingly reliant on satellites.

Yet it would be pointless for the modern military to have all the so-called advantages of the most sophisticated hardware available unless it can be used when, where and how the commander wishes. To attempt to have complete command, then modern generals must rely on C³I – Command, Control, Communication and Intelligence. If we look at the reasons behind this need, it might be seen that the order of importance displayed by C³I might well be reversed with Intelligence being the first need, Communications the second and Command and Control more or less equal third. Given this juxtaposition of the commander's needs we might reasonably outline his Intelligence brief should there be an international failure to manage a crisis and a move by the two superpowers towards a state of open hostilities.

The commander, be he a Soviet marshal or an American four-star general, must have a detailed picture of the enemy's own forces; and this is far more than the detailed information that he would normally have in peacetime on what is called the other side's ORBAT – the Order of Battle. The commander must know where the enemy has his military units. Have they been moved from the peacetime areas? How many men, vehicles and weapon systems are in those units? For example, an armoured division in peacetime often does not have the same number of troops as it would in time of war or during the period leading to war. Soviet divisions are kept in three states of readiness. A satellite reconnaissance may give the American commander an idea of how many, and what, divisions have been reinforced to bring them from perhaps a B category level of readiness to an A category.

There must be an analysis of support equipment for a division: whether or not engine spares for tanks, tank repair vehicles, armoured mine clearance vehicles, fuel bowsers, medical units, extra helicopters, bridge-laying equipment and personnel for all this military hardware are available. Has the railway network been cleared of normal civilian timetables? Are there unusual numbers of flat-bed rolling stock on the feeder lines to what could be a theatre of war? Are there signs of ammunition trains? It will be important to know something of personalities. Have senior generals taken up field positions? Have mobile headquarters started to move from their conventional peacetime areas? And what about aircraft? Is there more than usual activity from the transport fleets? Have interceptor squadrons been enlarged? Have some aircraft, particularly tactical bombers used for attacking an enemy's front lines and main operating bases, been dispersed to other airfields (hopefully to avoid being destroyed on the ground in a pre-target action)?

The naval staffs will be looking for reports of all the major fleet units. Are ships putting to sea in particularly large numbers? Are some ships moving away from normal patrol lanes to Out-of-Area (O.O.A.) operations? Have dockyard repair teams continued to work beyond normal shifts to prepare ships alongside for sea? Have submarines left their normal ports and anchorages? Are extra numbers of stores ships loading and leaving ports, especially at odd hours of the day? Have aircraft carriers put to sea to be joined shortly by extra aircraft (both fixed wing and helicopters)? Are ferries staying in harbour rather than keeping to their schedules? Are merchant ships alongside and being fitted with helicopter platforms?

Further analysis would possibly include information about civilian activity. For example, are certain towns being evacuated and are Civil Defence procedures being observed at key factories? Both these could be weighed as indicators that the other side is expecting enemy action, perhaps air raids.

The need for information is not confined to knowledge of the enemy. As we have seen, large armies, navies and air forces present their own management problems – especially if they are multi-national in structure. Taking NATO as the example, the Supreme Allied commander Europe (SACEUR) will know the general dispositions of his troops and those forces of the other NATO commanders, particularly the Supreme Allied Commander Atlantic and the Commander Eastern Channel. Yet, SACEUR will need to know how *his* reinforcement programme is going. Have ammunition supplies and logistics caught up with units? Have reserve forces moved from, say, their U.S. base at Fort Hood in Texas? When are they due in Europe? And, in the U.S.A., the commanders will want to know if the way is clear for further reinforcements. The information will be sent in from every continent and from every form of monitoring system. This will include reports from on-the-spot agents and remote sensors such as satellites.

The Soviet system has similar alert procedures. Intelligence gathering ships, 'sleepers' (agents put into Western countries to be 'woken up' during a crisis), electronic Intelligence units throughout the network of embassies, aircraft and even merchant ships and fishing boats will all be feeding raw Intelligence (Intelligence that has yet to be analysed) to the Soviet Union. Much of that information will be sent via satellite; the analysis that follows may be transmitted by satellite.

It can be seen clearly that the reliance on space systems holds true for both superpowers although there is some evidence to suggest that the Western system places a greater burden on its systems than does the Eastern bloc. However, this is not to say that the Soviet Union, in spite of her often sharp criticisms of American military involvement in space has not displayed an advanced need to match many new military systems to every aspect of its considerable space programme.

Chapter 11

Soviet Space

It is often imagined that it is almost impossible to produce a satisfactory analysis of the superpower military involvement in space. The main criticism appears to be, that because there is so little reliable information about the Soviet programme, it is difficult to produce an objective analysis. Certainly, a series of Western reports and papers has been quite disappointing in this respect. Often those in official or semi-official positions in, say, Washington have been reluctant to do anything more than quote previously and publicly presented statistics and assessments. This attitude is likely to continue until two unlikely events occur: the Soviet Union opens its 'space books' to expert scrutiny, and/or Western government sources change their attitudes about saying little in order to prevent the Soviet Union from knowing officially how much Washington knows and, equally important, how Washington *got* to know.

Yet there should not remain an impression that, with the exception of the launch details presented to the United Nations or on the Tass news agency printers, little is known about the Soviet programme. As we have seen in earlier chapters, it is possible to build a reasonable picture of Soviet space activity. Furthermore, quite a lot can be gleaned from political priorities within Moscow's space programme and the surely identifiable facilities and resources devoted to that programme.

So, it is worth looking more closely at the Soviet system. By doing this we may more easily draw our own impressions of, and conclusions as to, the importance attached by the Soviet leadership to the new high ground so easily identifiable *but so costly to reach*. For it is the effort, in terms of money and political prestige, that is an indication of a government's commitment.

The most obvious starting point in any analysis of the Soviet space programme is to point out that it is, and always has been, organised in a wholly military manner. This statement could easily be dismissed as nothing more than an attempt to pin the military label on what is usually presented as a civilian programme. Yet it might be argued that, in many organisations, a military structure and ethic is little more than the most obvious organisation of resources which owe more to the defence community than to anything else. In this, there is nothing sinister, it is simply a fact that many national projects work better if organised along the clearly stated lines followed by military systems.

Certainly it is doubtful that the Soviet space programme could have come this far so successfully had it not been for the military connection. It must be remembered that, in the U.S.S.R., few, if any, organisations are better structured than the military. No other organisation has the financial resources and hardware needed by the space engineers and scientists. The Soviet Union was never in a position to do anything but use military rocketry to boost its payloads into space. Also it is doubtful that any other body would have the influence to demand and get resources needed for this most expensive of scientific ventures. And with this military guidance and influence came the standard of organisational efficiency so often missing in purely civilian departments in the Soviet Union. At the same time it would be wrong to make too much of this involvement and that of the higher reaches of the political apparatus. It has been pointed out elsewhere that the 'top level commitment to space activities is underlined by the personal involvement of the Soviet leadership in space decision-making. Ultimate responsibility for the programme has rested with the nation's ruling Politburo.'[1]

One assumption drawn from this report is: 'A number of reasons may be surmised for the interest of Soviet leaders in space. They clearly recognise the military benefits and applications of space research. Undoubtedly, they are aware of scientific technological pay-offs in other areas. But they also seem to recognise and seek to exploit the political benefits derived from the space programme.'

[1] U.S. Senate Report of Soviet Space Programmes, December 1982.

All this may be true; but again this should not be seen as anything causing enormous surprise. Any major space programme and its related costs must necessarily have the highest political approval whether in the U.S.S.R. or the U.S.A. In the Soviet Union it is a fact of the political system that even low-key programmes must have the stamp of the Politburo, the U.S.S.R.'s innermost 'Cabinet' of political leadership. Equally, and not unnaturally, no chance is lost to take political advantage of the space programme. One example of this is the way in which other socialist countries have been encouraged to send astronauts into space with Soviet crews. This has provided immense satisfaction for those in Moscow whose role it is to impress upon others the advantages of the Soviet system. It was the late Leonid Brezhnev who emphasised this when he said, in a speech to the 26th Soviet C.P. Congress in February 1981, 'the cosmonauts of the fraternal countries are working not only for science and for the national economy; they are also carrying out a political mission of immense importance'.

To the Soviet leaders, 'carrying out a political mission' *is* of immense importance. For them the thoughts of Lenin remain essential to the survival of the Party and those thoughts are the political guidelines to which the U.S.S.R. is committed. Consequently, if space is seen as a political element in the overall Soviet plan, this may signify its importance, but it is also a justification for the huge resources it consumes while other projects flounder and founder for lack of funds and technology.

Yet, in spite of the political and scientific kudos to be gained from the many space programmes, they are certainly, in Western terms, shrouded in secrecy. Secrecy is very much part of the Moscow character. Soviet secrecy is a special brand which respects the need for silence if only to cover incompetence and the enormous inferiority complex that hides behind the Kremlin walls, the curtains of a Zil limousine or the high green corrugated fences of the élite's dachas. When this is added to the obvious need for security, then the darkness surrounding the reasoning behind the Soviet Union's space policy is the more understandable and sometimes impenetrable.

A dominant power in this policy is the Defence Minister. It is his ministry that provides much of the support facilities as well as the political enthusiasms and justifications. Furthermore, his Strategic Rocket Forces and the Air Forces play important roles.

The Strategic Rocket Forces, which control the Intercontinental Ballistic Missiles, are responsible for all space rocket launches. (There is an obvious connection between the two functions.) The training of Soviet cosmonauts comes under the Air Force at the specialist training camp Zveozydgrad, near Moscow.

Exactly who, or which body, has overall day-to-day control is difficult to say. Some have suggested that this might be a branch of the Soviet Academy of Sciences. The Academy is a wide reaching organisation, although one section is often equated with the American National Aeronautics and Space Administration, NASA. However, the Soviet organisation has a much wider role than does NASA. The Academy is a multi-disciplined research centre with branches throughout the Soviet Union. At the same time, national and international discussion on space matters takes place usually with senior members of the Academy, whose policy body, the Academy Praesidium, reflects the opinions, policies and directives of the Soviet Politburo. Although there may be doubts about its present-day importance (by no means substantiated doubts), there is sufficient evidence to suggest that it has had great power. Also, any statement on space policy that is made by the Academy must be taken as a reflection of official Soviet policy. This is an important consideration for those who would wish to consider further the direction and function of space in Soviet thinking. Perhaps when more is known of the shadowy department known in Moscow as YKOS (pronounced OO-KOS) which appears to have the most power, then more will be understood about the motives of the Soviet space programme and its relationship with the military.

Day-to-day running of the programme is directed by a committee which includes the military and technology ministries, department of planning and resources and, of course, a representative from the military office of the Main Political Directorate. This committee, or 'Commission', would not unnaturally include the head of the design team. For many years, until 1966, that was Sergei Korolev's famous role. At the time of writing it would appear that Vladimir Chelomei may have the overall job as Chief Designer with Valentin Glushko as his chief rocket engine designer. The importance of these men is such that in the past they have had the ear of each Soviet leader. Korolev, for example, could and did bypass the State Commission and confer directly with Krushchev. Korolev did not always get his own way, but his access was a further indicator of the importance of senior space men and therefore the programme itself. Things have changed since the special relationship between Korolev and Krushchev. Today, the space programme occupies a more formal place in the Kremlin's list of priorities. Nevertheless, there is every reason to suppose that this formalisation has helped to enhance, rather than reduce, the programme's importance.

Naturally, and especially in Soviet terms, formalisation quickly becomes akin to something like institutionalism. Consequently, the space programme is safer than some imagine; certainly it is safer than it was in the 1960s when it needed all the support it could muster. There were enormous pressures towards the end of the 1960s to conserve resources and materials. It should be remembered that, because of ideological differences, it was difficult if not sometimes impossible for the Soviet Union to share in technologies being developed in the West that would have relieved the load of the space programmes. Furthermore, there did not appear a sound enough technology base within the Soviet Union to which some crucial Western technologies could apply.

A final and continuing difficulty had much to do with the Soviet Union's lack of a convertible currency. Therefore, with limited access to 'hard' currencies, in particular dollars, space technocrats had to make out their cases against opposition from those in the military who wanted money for conventional weaponry, industry, resource engineering, etcetera. None of these was an insurmountable problem but put together they made life difficult for a programme that was enormously costly. Hungry for material and technology research, hugely demanding in political and social priorities and, therefore, constantly in need of success, how that success was measured – apart from obvious international triumphs over the American space effort – is difficult to understand apart from acknowledging that the Soviet involvement in space continued at a somewhat Russian, methodical rate.

Just as we find it difficult to get an accurate technological picture of the Soviet space programme, so the details of financial and political resources are obscure. Ever since the Soviet Union established its formal Secrecy List in 1926 (the fruits of the Revolution were somewhat sour and had not been as abundant as advertised), the amount of information about any project has been scant. The 1926 dictat was emphasised in 1956 and became the basis of the U.S.S.R.'s equivalent to any country's Official Secrets Act – a catch-all piece of legislation in many states. Add the 1956 decree to the instinctive Russian trait of secretiveness, self-delusion and recognised deception and the result is that the space programme remains at arm's length from Western eyes and at the same distance from many in Moscow who might wish seriously to question its function and value.

It could be argued that none of this matters because, whatever the stresses in the programme and no matter how many internal arguments, the results are for all to see in orbit every day of our modern lives. Yet an understanding of the priorities and motives of a programme such as space, or rocketry or nuclear systems allows us some insight into the priorities of the state itself and indirectly something of its motives. Such an understanding may have considerable influence on the control of superpower relations and the approaches to arms control.

One way of questioning priorities is by assessing how much money is spent on a project compared to other areas in the economy. The Central Intelligence Agency in one of its overt studies has suggested that the Soviet Union is spending between one and two per cent of its Gross National Product on space. As a comparison, it is thought that the Kremlin authorises about 12 per cent of GNP on an overall defence budget. The difficulty with these figures is that much of the space programme is part of the military programme and so there is understandable confusion. What is more, some of the space budget may have been contained in the science budget.

There have been periods when the science budget has reflected intense activity in the Soviet space effort. For example, there was a 500 per cent increase in the budget during the 1955–65 concentrated flight preparation programmes.[1] After this period, some if not all of the main projects may have been absorbed into defence. The science budget took on a new format including its responsibility to areas of higher education, thus making it even more difficult to guestimate where the money was being spent.

Exactly who was responsible for spending that money was obscure. This last point was particularly annoying for analysts

[1] State Budget Statistical Digest, 1966.

in the West. To be able to identify the responsible ministry could have shown which Politburo member had influence on the space programmes. The identity of the member would have indicated the importance of the programmes. And so speculation continued that the military had the largest say and therefore perhaps the largest slice of the space budget.

It is possible in the United States to assess the importance if not the exact dollar contribution of the American military to space development. Analysing the Soviet space effort has not been so easy for the Americans.

As early as the mid-1970s, the 'Congressional Sub-Committee on Allocations and Resources in the Soviet Union and China' received a report suggesting a strong if not majority military influence: 'We doubt that they [the Soviet Union] have a program that splits the military and civilian. Most of the activities that we know appear to be carried out at military facilities . . .'

At the time of that Congressional report, there was – and there still is – a tendency to want to believe that the military dominated the space programme. But, although the evidence that 'most of their activities appear to be carried out at military facilities' was and is true, it should be recognised that, while a lot of money was being channelled into launch site construction, a great many of the launches were civilian based – not unlike the U.S. programme. The American analyses may be criticised as being less than sound for it has been said that the methodology is open to serious questioning. For example, at least one method used by the United States Intelligence community for working out Soviet defence spending has doubtful credentials. The Americans add up the Soviet arsenals and orders of battle, then work out how much it would cost in America to have the same: the result is presented as the Soviet Defence Budget. The weaknesses in this system of calculation are too obvious to debate. But those weaknesses do present themselves as reminders that it is dangerous to read too much into Western analysis of the importance of the Soviet space programme as suggested by expenditure. Even so, as indicated earlier, the space programme has achieved its own, almost indestructible, status. The political capital invested has become as important as the financial, indeed the latter could not have been sustained without the former. And it is true that, in spite of its failures and limitations, the Soviet space programme has recorded enormous success. Those successes have been applauded at home and abroad and they have been understandably exploited to prove to the Kremlin's satisfaction at least the Soviet Union's parity with the other superpower. To give this up would make little political and diplomatic sense, never mind the obvious military disadvantages abandonment would bring about.

Furthermore, enough has been written in the Soviet Union itself to suggest that, where doubts about financial priorities do exist, they cannot overcome the by-now established place of space programming within the Soviet system. As if to emphasise this, a strongly defined justification for the space programme was made in 1977, on the occasion of the 20th anniversary of Sputnik 1. In an article, Soviet scientists made the common assumption that space flight was to the advantage of all mankind and those on earth should not begrudge the resources devoted to this new frontier:

'It would be wrong to set up an opposition between activity in space and on Earth or to absolutise the importance of one of them to the detriment of the other because achievements in space development have a beneficial effect on the economic development of the nation, while the march of social progress on Earth creates new potential for the further cognition of near-terrestrial space. Man's penetration into the Universe, his study and conquest of it are not a manifestation of his inability to cope with terrestrial problems, not a flight from them but a qualitatively new, often unique, means of resolving many of the pressing tasks of developing science, technology and economics. The development of space research in the U.S.S.R. clearly and patently shows the prospect of using cosmonautics for the benefit of man that is revealed under socialism.'

To some extent this was the Soviet equivalent of the American proposition that without space exploration we would not have non-stick frying pans; it was perhaps received with as much interest.

Yet there is clearly a major difference in the programmes when rehearsed under two such widely differing systems. The Western capitalist system can reasonably show that some parts of society survive because of NASA. Large corporations, small sub-contractors, whole communities, even the souvenir business make a profit from space; consequently there is a tangible contribution to the economy. It might be argued that some parts of industry are so skilled at profit-taking, that the American space programme costs more than it reasonably should. The Soviet system, however, does not provide for the same scale of exploitation and opportunity. It does, as noted earlier, have impressive political credentials. The same article quoted above is quite clear on this:

'Cosmonautics *is becoming*[1] an important branch of the national economy. It is for good reason that the country's latest five-year economic development plans include extensive programmes for activity in space, the application of space technology in the interests of Soviet society.'

And, to justify this, the article goes on, 'Many discoveries and inventions made in the course of space research have now been introduced into non-cosmic spheres of technology and production and are being utilised in agriculture, in the organisation and management of the national economy, and in everyday life.'

There are many such references and claims in Soviet official literature. While it is obvious that such questions are raised although inadequately answered, it is a reminder that, contrary to what many in the West believe, the Soviet authorities often feel that they too have to justify the huge expenditure on space programmes while more Earthly demands go unsatisfied. This is not to claim that the Politburo in Moscow is subject to the wishes of the Soviet Union's 270-million population. However, it has been noticed that, in addition to the political advantages of trumpeting Soviet space achievements, the authorities do see the advantages of justifying the investment at a time when many in the Soviet Union are openly cynical about the claims made for other major capital expenditure projects – and agriculture, mentioned in the above article, is an obvious example.

The matter of resource allocations covers more than financial backing. True, there has to be dollar–rouble investment to produce the equipment and facilities necessary to maintain the varying space studies and to expand them. Equally, and as a consequence of this allocation, other areas suffer. It has, for example, been noted that in the United Kingdom the effort and resources put into defence-based research has meant that other

[1] 'Is becoming' – not 'has become'.

areas of industry have suffered considerably. The same is true in the Soviet Union. This problem is magnified by the limited resources available in the first place and so we might refer to the earlier thoughts on a technical wizardry that cannot satisfy its basic needs in some areas.

An American official assessment is that the Soviet economy is 'large enough and strong enough, despite shortages, that it can support what is now the world's largest space programme, with no sign that this level of effort cannot be sustained indefinitely'.

Again, resource allocation is not simply a matter of priorities as it is in any form of economy stretching from Wall Street to the humblest housewife feeding and running a home. In the Soviet system it would appear to be a more obvious extension of the criticism levelled at the British defence industry. The defence and space industry in the Soviet Union gives the impression of having first call on modern technology that might otherwise improve the overall economy. As one talks to many who have had close contact with the Soviet space programme, it appears that it is absorbing not just the better brains and technology, but elements of both that are on a par with the people and equipment in the American programme. This would appear particularly so at the top end of the scale of excellence.

It would therefore seem rather obvious to conclude that the Soviet Union will continue to devote huge technical and financial efforts to developing its space research. Such a statement is as predictable as saying that the Soviet Union will continue to build up its armed forces, or – and going back eighty years – having developed a motor car the United States would not opt out of automobile engineering. For straightforward reasons of technical achievement and research, the Soviet Union appears to have a clearly mapped out research, development and production programme; perhaps only some catastrophe such as an accident in space (especially with the SALYUT series of space stations) would make the programme falter, but not halt. It certainly shows no sign of suffering the political uncertainty of the American programmes during the past thirty years. Furthermore, because the Soviet space system is irrevocably tied to the military needs of the U.S.S.R., it will remain in that area of the establishment charged with the most important of all ambitions in the Soviet Union – the protection and maintenance of the Party. From this it may be seen that, where at one point the space programme needed the support of the military, today the Soviet military needs the support of its space programmes.

Equally, the American programme is tied to the needs of the Pentagon. And so we have established that space is the environment of the two major military powers in this world. Those powers have the capability, although not necessarily the desire, to destroy this world. The systems with which they maintain this balance of fear are largely either space-based or rely on systems in space. The connection between the two military environments is simple: just as the major weapon systems have become subject to bi-lateral legislation, so the space systems find themselves pencilled in the margins of draft arms control treaties. However, space technology has advanced at a faster rate than any other military engineering during the past ten years or so; consequently it is more difficult to conveniently slot it into existing legislation.

It is by no means certain that modern arms control procedures are able to cope with existing space systems and those imagined for the coming century. Part of the problem is that space is too often seen as a separate subject from earthbound weaponry, but as we have seen the two are very much elements of the same military force structures of the superpowers and the emerging space powers. The international military uses of space are likely to cause a 'space proliferation' problem as sensitive as that described for the spread of nuclear weapons. Before we are able to slot space systems into the present arms control process we must first examine that procedure and wonder if indeed, it is capable of dealing with the problems about to be launched upon it.

Chapter 12

Arms Control

Arms control is close to being an obsolescent concept. It is very difficult to make a convincing case for arms control, as we understand it, as the deciding factor in limiting growth and deployment of what are generally termed weapons of mass destruction and introducing international stability. Restrictions on development processes are probably the only respectable results of what might be held as examples of diplomatic sham and dull scholarship. Certainly the euphoria of the heady days of the 1970s and so-called détente were part of an illusion. Nothing that was signed during the 1970s led to a decrease in the numbers of nuclear weapons. There are more nuclear weapons and warheads in the world a full decade after the promises and solemn signatures of the leaders of the two superpowers. The United States and the Soviet Union have greater destructive power after two strategic arms treaties promised to curb that power. Instead, legislation allowed weapons to be researched, developed and deployed in such a manner that norms for nuclear deterrence were established which suggested that any future treaty, negotiated under present guidelines, would be little more than a paper illusion.

It can be shown that both superpowers negotiated agreements under SALT I and SALT II which actually *encouraged* new weapon systems. During this same period we have seen the full development of the multiple warhead missile capable of discharging up to 14 nuclear warheads each one of which can seek out its own target. This system is arguably the single most destabilising influence on the East–West military balance. Yet it has been built by both superpowers at a time of great trust in the arms control process.

The trust is partly established about the fable that the two superpowers are determined to rid the world of nuclear weapons. Indeed, at the start of 1985, the Soviet Union and the United States issued a joint statement expressing this ambition in the clearest of terms. The statements came at the end of the two-day meeting in Geneva between the then Soviet Foreign Minister Andrei Gromyko and his American counterpart, George Shultz. The meeting laid the way for the new series of arms control talks between the superpowers. Paragraph Five of the Shultz–Gromyko communiqué emphasised the aims claimed by both Moscow and Washington: 'The sides *believe* that ultimately the forthcoming negotiations, just as efforts in general to limit and reduce arms, should lead to the *complete elimination* of nuclear arms everywhere' [author's itals].

Now this statement was clearly untrue. Indeed, most in Washington and Moscow believed that the 'elimination of nuclear arms everywhere' was utterly impossible and, furthermore, totally undesirable. An often-expressed opinion might be summarised as follows: no President of the United States and no Secretary of the Communist Party of the Soviet Union would ever commit his nation to the dismantling of nuclear weapons and the military nakedness that it would imply; no Congress nor any Politburo would ever endorse such a commitment; neither superpower would ever believe that other powers such as China, Israel and even an erratic Arab state would unequivocally follow such an agreement; both superpowers believe still that, with the elimination of *all* nuclear weapons, conventional war would become not necessarily acceptable but more probable; no satisfactory way could be found to verify such an agreement.

The cynicism behind these views was, and is, largely justified on strict military grounds and when the record of arms control is examined in any depth; this is not the place to make such an examination[1] although a few basic points might be made.

The idea of removing all European or Intermediate Range Nuclear Missiles (SS-20s, Pershing II and Cruise), as laid out in President Reagan's Zero Option, had far more to do with the internal politics of Washington than with realistic hopes that the offer would be taken up by the Soviet Union. At the early stage

[1] For more on this subject, see bibliography on page 235.

of the Reagan Administration the so-called Zero Option formula was the result of a bitter fight between the State Department, the Defense Department and the then ineffectual National Security Council. The concept of Zero Option as seen in the Defense Department was based on the hypothesis that the Soviet Union would never agree to it, therefore no East–West agreement would be forthcoming. In other words, the most influential sector of the Reagan Administration was attempting to prevent the White House from reaching any agreement on Arms Control with the Soviet Union.

Also, the basic concepts of parity in the nuclear balance have very little to do with making the world a safer place in which to live. Often-expressed definitions of nuclear parity do not line up with reasonable definitions of stability. A very good example is to be found in the numbers game involved in counting missiles or, more realistically, warheads. In theory, and largely in practice, it is suggested that both superpowers should be allowed to have the same number of nuclear warheads. For the moment it is convenient to ignore the obvious complications such as, what is a nuclear warhead? Is it one carried by a missile? A ground-launched missile? Is a plane capable of carrying an intermediate range missile, but based in America, to be included in intermediate range talks on the basis that it would be moved forward to threaten the Soviet Union? What about submarines? Are submarines to be included in strategic or intermediate range talks? Or, because they are obviously mobile, in both? Or, should there be separate agreements covering submarines? And, what about the British and French nuclear systems? Why should they not be included in the final totals agreed? All these are practical complications that have to be resolved before any such talks may get under way. However, there is an even more basic argument, which brings us back to the so-called numbers game.

There does not seem to be any major reason why any one side should have the same number of nuclear warheads as the other. There is no reason for, say, the Soviet Union to have the same number of bombers, submarines and missiles as the United States. The argument of nuclear deterrence should be a little more sophisticated – leaving aside the debate about the morality, even the desirability, of anybody at all having nuclear weapons. The key to the more sophisticated debate is what used to be called military sufficiency. As the term suggests, military sufficiency is about having sufficient nuclear weapons in the right 'mix' to be able to threaten the other side so dramatically that it would not believe it worth going to war. In the crudest terms, one side with hundreds of thousands could achieve this absolute deterrence. In more modest terms, it would be necessary only to hold the minimum number of warheads over and above those that may be lost in a surprise attack to take out previously determined targets.

At this point, we arrive at one of the complexities of arms negotiations: how to reassure the country's leadership that 'survivable' systems are truly 'survivable'; and, secondly, how to reassure the leadership that the figure arrived at will impress the other side sufficiently to make sure that they never launch that surprise attack.

However, the basic hypothesis may still be proved: that the real necessary level of any country's nuclear arsenal is the figure and mixture of weapons that may be maintained and modernised in such a way that the potential enemy remains impressed and convinced of the futility of a premeditated attack. This equation, that sufficient weaponry equals deterrence, is not necessarily the same as equal weaponry equals deterrence. To arrive at the smaller figure, it may be necessary for any treaty to spend less time on balancing numbers and more time on making sure that limits, or even bans, are put on technological development that may allow one side to surprise the other with innovations and counter-measures that would weaken the efficiency of the minimum deterrence.

The importance of this argument may be imagined when it is laid alongside the SDI debate. As we have seen, SDI will not mean the removal of nuclear missiles, but it could result in military sufficiency rather than the existing system – military overkill.

The complement to a more stable form of arms control procedure has very little to do with the discussions that have taken place traditionally at Geneva. The necessary hope of arms control has been that it would make the world a safer place in which to live. The Geneva process has not achieved this. The reason for the preservation of nuclear peace has only something to do with those dreadful consequences imagined by the superpowers should war break out. It could just as easily be argued that there has never been a real reason for the Western and Eastern bloc to go to war during the past forty years or so.

Arms control has not, therefore, been responsible for preserving peace. Taken a stage further, it should be remembered that arms control negotiations and even agreements do not decide the states of relationship between the superpowers. Negotiations and treaties do nothing more than reflect the relationship. Treaties are signed only when the two sides have established a working relationship that for the moment suits both of them. A treaty then becomes only a badge of that relationship and the chances are that very little put into such agreements will in practice guarantee that peaceful arrangement. Therefore the complement to Geneva and to the real maintenance of a stable relationship is far more likely to be the sort of discussions that have taken place in Stockholm, where 35 states including the superpowers have attempted to produce a set of guidelines designed to make war by miscalculation and misunderstanding less likely.

As mentioned above, this is not the place for a detailed argument on the rights, wrongs and future of arms control. Yet the fundamental arguments and suspicions have to be rehearsed because every form of arms control is practised in Geneva, and attempts at establishing greater confidence between the superpowers' blocs as debated in Stockholm, must eventually include discussions and clauses on space-based systems.

The issues of Geneva and Stockholm cannot be simplified without accord on the issues discussed elsewhere in this book. Yet these issues are more complicated than ever. They may be placed in the broad groupings: Strategic Defence Initiative (SDI), Anti-Satellite (ASAT) systems, Verification, and what might be called the Third Force. This latest grouping does not figure in general discussion, nor does it find itself on the Geneva agenda. However, the Third Force in space, although studiously avoided by both Moscow and Washington – partly because they see it as a threat to their absolute dominance in space – will become a major issue (and one to be discussed later).

The general issue of space and a limited number of systems have always had a place in the drafting of arms control treaties. In theory, reconnaissance satellites (known to those whose job it is to agree the jargon of treaties as 'national technical means') have been protected as being a way to check if the agreed treaty is being observed. This legitimate form of overflying was for some time the most jealously guarded system of verification. However, when the two sides met for the talks that were to lead to the 1985 Geneva discussion, the space issue had been broadened. The six-paragraph joint Soviet–American communiqué at the conclusion of the preliminary meeting, the Shultz–Gromyko talks-about-talks, emphasised the subject of space, but left vague the detail of its place in the forthcoming negotiations. Paragraph Three of the communiqué outlined the subject for negotiation:

'The sides agree that the subject of the negotiations will be a complex of questions concerning space and nuclear arms – both strategic and intermediate range – with all these questions considered and resolved in their interrelationships.'

Immediately there was uncertainty. Did this mean that there could only be an overall agreement when there was agreement in all three subjects, or could disagreement on one hold up a treaty in the other two? It should have been normal to dismiss these queries as acceptable vagueness in any first round of what was to be a long session of negotiations. Yet, for the Soviet Union, space was clearly the major issue and one from which it believed maximum anti-American propaganda might be derived. The subject and attention of space had already managed to show up the United States as the villain of the piece.

This was partly due to the fact that President Reagan's Strategic Defence Initiative had been handled badly as a publicity exercise. Few had known about the March 23, 1983 speech until it was made. Therefore the American information system was not ready to handle the questions that followed, nor to counter the speculation as to its real significance. In Europe, people who were expected to know about the subject were not really as informed as they might have been had there been earlier consultations.

The pundit industry of academics and strategists was immediately called upon to take positions on a matter over which the Reagan Administration itself was vague. European leaders and ministers found that they were not as briefed as they should be. This was partly because senior officials, who should have been up to speed on the technology and strategy behind the SDI speech, were not as informed as they made out. Consequently, the advice given to governments was often unspecific and incomplete. Furthermore, pundits – both official and otherwise – found themselves being forced into positions on SDI from which they could not pull back once they did become better informed. Through all this, the Soviet Union, about to go through yet another leadership change, saw an opportunity to exploit the inevitable differences between the United States and her European allies.

Soviet officials with whom the author has spoken rarely missed a chance to exploit these differences and to emphasise the Soviet case for further control of space systems. Many of those officials were openly curious about the apparent lack of knowledge in Europe of the American position. This period, between September 1984 and the summer of the following year, was marked by a stream of American officials, including General Abrahamson and George Keyworth, President Reagan's Chief Scientific Advisor, visiting Europe to explain the American point of view. Yet even this attempt to catch up on the consultative process seemed badly organised.

Two examples are outstanding. A senior White House adviser (one whose technical and scientific credentials were outstanding) held a series of talks in Europe during February 1985. These talks included a visit to London. However, nobody in Washington, nor in London, had bothered to fix a meeting between the White House aide and one of, if not *the*, most influential Whitehall mandarin when it came to SDI. This man, John Weston of the Foreign Office, was known to be highly sceptical of the American project and especially of the way it was being handled. He was known at the time to be against any general Europe commitment to SDI. Yet the White House official and his staff had never heard of John Weston. They were about to.

The following month, the British Foreign Secretary, Sir Geoffrey Howe, made a comprehensive assault on the long-term thinking of SDI during a speech to the Royal United Services Institute for Defence Studies in London. It was a speech that suggested, to the rest of Europe and to Washington, that the Western Alliance should tread warily before lending support to anything but the idea of research into SDI. In Washington there was absolute fury. The Pentagon's Richard Perle, also in London for a different conference, publicly took Sir Geoffrey to task in a very undiplomatic manner. Soviet officials were gleeful. Americans appeared either angry or perplexed or both. They certainly should not have been surprised. For, according to the Foreign Secretary's staff, the man who wrote the speech was John Weston. (Now serving in the British Embassy in Paris.)

It was said in Downing Street that on two occasions there had been attempts to get the Prime Minister, Margaret Thatcher, to make a similar speech, but she had refused. Mrs Thatcher preferred to restrict her comments to the conversation that she had had a few months earlier with President Reagan. (Following that meeting, Mrs Thatcher and President Reagan had issued a four-point statement which, in summary, declared that while it would be prudent to go ahead with research into SDI, any plans to deploy weapons should be subject to treaty.) So, Sir Geoffrey was given the speech to read. According to some in Whitehall, in spite of the strong terms and warnings of the address, the feeling inside the Foreign Office was far stronger than even the speech suggested, verging on outright opposition to the Reagan concept.

The second example of the failure of America's 'Buy SDI' campaign at that point of the arms control preliminaries concerned European visits by the head of the American Arms Control and Disarmament Agency, Kenneth Adelman. He had spoken to many officials and had sat in conference with senior advisers, ministers and experts. However, a general opinion of many who met him during these talks was that Mr Adelman may have been well informed on policy and the basics of SDI but he appeared not to have at his fingertips much of the detail that the Europeans were starting to question.

As head of ACDA, and with a competent and well-informed staff about him, Mr Adelman appeared as a less than ideal SDI salesman and one who was not much given to detail and analysis. One impression from a Dutch observer was that it was not only Europe that had been caught by surprise; it was apparent that '70 per cent' of Washington was finding it difficult to understand exactly where space fitted into arms control policy. The Soviet Union had no such difficulties.

Critics of Soviet proposals to curb space weapons suggest that Moscow's enthusiasm for international legislation dates from moments when the Soviet Union believed that it had a lead in this field. According to many, once the Soviet tests on ASAT were complete then the Kremlin proposed a ban on such weapons. The suggestion is that the Soviet reasoning was simple:

having developed the system it would be easy to 'cold store' it for eventual use. But a Treaty would prevent American development which the Soviets knew was about to start. The matter was complicated by the announcement of the American SDI programme which involved anti-satellite technology. To understand better the Soviet and American attitudes to space and arms control, it is worth going over a few pointers to the American rationale for SDI as seen by Washington and Moscow. Again, talking to Soviet experts, it is clear that the Soviet Union often has a deeper understanding of American reasoning than is sometimes imagined.

The publicly presented image is that Soviet objections and concerns sprang from President Reagan's so-called Star Wars speech. Certainly the Soviet Union does not date the Reagan Administration's space policy – as opposed to the U.S. general policy in space – from that moment. Often, officials will point to a lesser-known Presidential decision made the previous summer, in July 1982.

In August 1981, the then new President of the United States, was persuaded to set up a study of all the space programmes run by various agencies with a claim on Federal funding. The study was complicated by interagency rivalries and duplications. There had, for some time, been a series of differences in priorities among, say, the defence and civilian programmes. The different factions had, as might be expected, split into mini-factions. Therefore, instead of learning from the experiences of those early days of space exploration when similar conflicts probably played a major part in America running second to the Soviet Union, the various agencies remained rivals.

Furthermore, there were understandable differences in priorities and objectives that no study would find it easy to resolve. One example was the Space Shuttle. Space Shuttle was always seen as a civilian project with NASA as the programme leader. Naturally it was scheduled to handle defence experiments; NASA recognised that without Defense Department funding and regular use for satellite launching, such as the Top Secret Aquacade programme, the shuttle could run out of money. Also, if the Defense Department abandoned the Shuttle programme, then commercial companies might lose confidence in its efficiency. As well as the very visible programmes such as Shuttle and plans for a space station, the American space programme was supporting a massive infrastructure industry and a connected research programme.

As might be imagined, a considerable problem for the study was that many of these programmes, projects and industries were unco-ordinated. The fear was that the study would produce nothing more than a statement of general policy. By 1982, work was finished and those with connections to that study recognised its shortcomings. However, the way was open for a national policy statement. For those watching which way America intended to go in space, that policy document was essential reading. In Moscow not long after the document appeared, it was clear that this interest had spread to some of the most influential people in the Soviet Union – including the military and those concerned with arms control.

On July 4, 1982, President Reagan endorsed the guidelines of America's space policy: there were six basic 'goals' – two of them directly involved defence. The first goal was perfectly clear on this point.

'Strengthen the security of the United States.' This was the prime aim of American policy. Gone were the early declarations about the benefits to mankind; the giant leaps for the future of all peoples. The number one issue was the defence of the United States. The last of the goals remembered the original ideals, but even then there was a direct indication of the methods of their achievement: 'Co-operate with other nations in maintaining the freedom of space for activities which *enhance the security* and welfare of mankind.' And later, in a White House document, there was a further and unambiguous indication of the dominant part in space of the defence community. Referring to exploration, the document stated that the United States is committed to the explorations and use of space by all nations for peaceful purposes . . . 'Peaceful purposes' allow activities in pursuit of national security goals. A further paragraph encouraged 'domestic commercial exploitation of space . . .' but the next line pointed out that, 'these activities must be consistent with *national security concerns* . . .'

The references to Shuttle were again unambiguous. 'The United States Space Transportation System (STS) is the primary space launch system for both *national security* and civil government missions . . .' The following paragraph was equally emphatic: '. . . the United States will pursue activities in space in support of its right of self-defence . . .' And then: 'the United States will continue to study *space arms control options*. The United States will consider verifiable and equitable arms control measures that would ban or otherwise limit testing and deployment of specific weapon systems, *should those measures be compatible with United States national security . . .'*

The author has added emphasis to the document, in part to show the manner in which many in Moscow were reading this document especially as it applied to the future of arms control. Until the Reagan Star Wars speech, the July 4 statement was the most interesting set before the Russians by the United States since President Carter's PD 59 in 1979, outlining changes in strategic policy.

When the March 1983 speech did arrive, the Soviet Union appeared to be just as much in the dark as anybody. As we have seen earlier, the speech itself was vague and deliberately so. Arms control experts in Europe, including those in the Eastern bloc, were at a loss to assess the significance of the Strategic Defence Initiative. Few even knew who was behind the President's speech. It was assumed that Mr Reagan, not known for his grasp of strategic issues, must have been influenced by a very small group with access to the White House. The general impression at the time was that, as there had been no warning of the significance of that part of the speech dealing with space, then the numbers of people involved in its writing were few. For the arms controllers, it was important to know exactly who was backing the idea. The Russians had long been expert in detailed political assessments of Washington. They had, in the earliest days of the Administration, picked out the hawks from the minor hawks (in the Soviet view, there were no doves in Reagan's Washington). For example, Richard Perle of the Defense Department was identified very quickly as the intellectual stamina behind moves to make almost impossible demands on any East–West arms control negotiations. Consequently the diplomatic ears of the Soviet Union were to the ground, listening for scraps of evidence that might indicate the strength of the SDI speech and the brains behind it.

They had very quickly spotted the influential figure of Edward Teller. Some had selected Lieutenant General Daniel Graham as the man of influence. This was an incorrect assessment and abandoned. There were reports of Edward Teller having given

President Reagan an impromptu briefing on the possibilities of space-based systems providing an effective anti-ballistic missile defence. In fact, Teller had briefed the President in September 1982 on the possibilities of a new system, much to the annoyance of some of the most senior defence officials – both uniformed and flannel-suited – in Washington.

It is said in Washington that, shortly after the meeting in the White House between the President and Edward Teller, the cause of ballistic missile defence was picked up by the deputy National Security Adviser, Robert 'Bud' McFarlane. At that time McFarlane's boss, William Clark was thought to be against the project; within twelve months of supporting the principle behind Teller's argument, McFarlane has taken over from Clark, but in the autumn of 1982 he did not have the political sway in the court of Ronald Reagan. By some careful diplomatic tiptoeing, McFarlane managed to get the Chiefs of Staff, especially the Chief of Naval Operations, to accept that research work on an advanced ballistic missile defence (BMD) system was worthwhile. The Air Force, in particular, was not slow to realise that such a system would fall into its command and that such research would guarantee further development on anti-satellite techniques, because the initial research of both BMD and ASAT overlapped.

In February 1983, the Chiefs of Staff voiced their support for the concept at a meeting attended by their Commander in Chief, the President. Robert McFarlane, still subordinate to William Clark, played no more than a nudging role, deliberately letting the military put forward the proposals that he guessed the President would find attractive. President Reagan did 'buy' SDI there and then and hurried to a study of its possibilities. The result was the March 23, 1983 speech and the possibility of a major change in American strategic thinking. The most important factor was that it had President Reagan's backing and his absolute enthusiasm. When the Soviet diplomatic assessments were made, the most obvious and first conclusion was that the man with the most influence over the SDI programme was not necessarily Robert McFarlane, nor the Defense Secretary Casper Weinberger, but the President himself.

The Russians recognised that the Presidential backing for what was officially nothing more than a notion – the White House liked the term vision – was in fact greater than people imagined.

It had been recognised for some time that the weakness in American space research and especially the so-called defence-related areas was caused by the lack of co-ordination and the uncertainty over future funding. Like so many programmes in the United States, the laboratories relied on survival appropriations. As there were few visible results coming from the fragmented programmes there was always the danger that funding would cease. Presidential backing meant that funding would be lobbied for at the highest level. Necessarily, of course, it would also be scrutinised at a higher level, especially as the budget, instead of being a series of often obscure mini-allocations to various projects, would be in one large block of publicly accountable billions.

It was also guessed, at the time, that the emphasis on other space programmes would be supported if those programmes could be seen to have a benefit to SDI. One such project was ASAT, again because the initial stages of SDI research were expected to produce, as a bi-product, anti-satellite technology.

For the arms control community this meant three things, or so they thought. Firstly, there could not be an American agreement to sign an ASAT treaty as proposed by the Soviet Union. Secondly, it would appear inevitable that the 1972 Anti-Ballistic Missile (ABM) Treaty would be violated once research into SDI developed into a deployable system. Thirdly, given the certainty of these three aspects of the SDI programme, together with the likelihood that it would institute a change in America's strategic policy, then space was about to become the most important issue in arms control.

By the summer, the Soviet Union had drafted yet another set of proposals banning ASAT weapons. An earlier set offered by Moscow to the United Nations appeared reasonable but was not, for a number of reasons. The most obvious objection for the United States was that the Russians had such weapons and the Americans did not. The general objection was aimed at the rather ingenious wording which, to the ill-informed, appeared perfectly reasonable. (It is still sometimes quoted as an example of the Soviet Union's willingness to lead the way in banning ASAT weapons.) In précis, the Soviet Union proposed that all anti-ballistic weapons in space should be banned. That indeed sounded reasonable to many at the United Nations. However, there was no point in America agreeing to the Soviet proposal to ban such weapons in space. The Soviet ASAT system was not in space. It was on the ground. The SS-9 rockets waited in their launching sites with the hunter-killer satellites on top. Under the Soviet treaty, their ASATs would not have been banned. The treaty would have been as effectual as the discredited U.N. Chemical Weapons Protocol, which allows countries to have chemical weapons but not to use them. In wartime, most arms control bets are off.

By the end of 1983, the Geneva arms talks on Strategic (START) and Intermediate (INF) nuclear weapons were off also. A leadership change was on the way in Moscow and President Reagan was heading for his election year and, according to most observers, another four years in Washington. 1984 looked like being a fallow year for arms control.

In April 1984, the Russians had a further indication that President Reagan had little intention of putting space in the arms control melting pot. There were few doubts about the American position and those might have been removed with a Presidential report that went to Congress the day after All Fools Day. The report quoted the July 1982 policy statement on space, emphasising that the United States would look at arms control in space systems as long as those 'measures be compatible with United States National Security . . .' In general terms, the statement declared that the Administration had spent some time looking at the possibilities of arms control talks with the Soviet Union. However, the reports cooled any hopes for arms controllers with a stark rejection of the suggestion that negotiations would be worthwhile in Washington's view: '. . . no arrangements or agreements beyond those already governing military activities in outer space have been found to date that are judged to be in the overall interests of the United States and its allies . . .'

The American position was that the existing agreements to which the statement referred were adequate and that Americans could see no reason to negotiate separate and new treaties. The existing agreements were indeed wide-ranging. Bi-lateral, multi-lateral and general annexes to associated treaties included a 'ban on testing', orbiting, or stationing of nuclear or other weapons of mass destruction in space; a ban on development, testing and deployment of space-based anti-ballistic missile systems or their components; and a requirement for international consultations before conducting any activity or experiment that would cause potentially harmful interference with other countries' peaceful space activities. However, treaties could never be regarded in general terms and, from the American and Soviet point of view, many of the clauses in existing legislation were woolly.

Definitions were sometimes less than clear and areas that were banned for the deployment of systems often allowed sufficient research and development to introduce an atmosphere of instability. Therefore, in spite of Soviet calls for direct bans on weapons, they knew full well that some of the American doubts aired in the report to Congress would be Soviet concerns once the fine print was debated at any negotiations. Simple problems might need enormously complicated solutions. One example that would inevitably lead to long negotiations without any assurance of agreement would be the immediate question: what is an anti-satellite weapon? Without absolute agreement on that definition, an ASAT treaty would be worthless if not impossible to construct.

At this point in the spring of 1983, both the Russians and the Americans recognised that it would be enough to say that an ASAT weapon was one capable of destroying and degrading a satellite. Certainly some systems were simple to identify. The Soviet SS-9-based co-orbital interceptor was designed to knock out satellites. The American system based on the F-15 aircraft was declared as an ASAT weapon. But what about weapons that had other roles, but which could be quickly re-tasked by basic modifications to their guidance logic? Once this complication was taken into account, a treaty seemed further away. Apparently both the superpowers had recognised that a Soviet SS-18 missile, for example, or an American Minuteman could be 're-worked' to act as an anti-satellite weapon. As one U.S. Presidential Adviser put it, 'I assure you, an SS-18 is one terrific ASAT weapon if that's the mission it's programmed to carry out, including in fact, with modest modifications, attacks on geostationary orbiting satellites . . .' This kind of thinking complicated even further the debate which until that stage had generally believed that the essential communication and early warning systems (high orbiting satellites) were out of reach and therefore only on the very edge of the ASAT question.

Soon, other objections surfaced. How could there be acceptable legislation against directed energy weapons such as lasers and particle beams with sufficient power to damage satellites or their sensors? How could either side be sure that a laser system was below the power-line necessary for it to be a weapon? What was to be done about electronic signals that could jam satellites? How much legislation and inspection would be needed to cope with Shuttle flights, which were perfectly innocent until tasked to intercept, even hi-jack (space-jack?) a satellite? This led to the concern that some commercial systems could 'have characteristics which would make it difficult to frame a definition to distinguish them from weapon systems. An effective space arms control measure should take into account weapon capabilities beyond those of specialised ASAT systems, and at the same time it must not unduly constrain the legitimate functions of non-weapon systems . . .' These words in the Presidential report to Congress laid out the basic difficulties, and more importantly from the Soviet view, signalled that no draft proposals would face anything but a rigorous examination intended to shred the Russian case before their very eyes. It was clear that the Americans were returning to the more fundamental objections to the Soviet proposals – the fact that the Soviet Union had an ASAT system and that they, the Americans, had not.

In 1983, it was emerging also that the military concern in both Washington and Moscow had more to do with what were called targeting satellites rather than with the more conventional systems. Satellite technology had by the early 1980s become sophisticated enough for space craft to perform more than one function. The Soviet and American satellites had been developed so that they had the ability to act as 'spotters'. They were indeed the modern version of the scout hidden on a mountain top or in a tree, directing the raiders to unsuspecting wagon trains. Again, both sides recognised that there would be a case for opening up the space debate to include these systems. The Americans claimed, and do still claim, that the link between targeting satellites and an ASAT capability was fundamental to any American position. Furthermore, the Reagan principle which applied to all his dealings with the Soviet Union was being maintained: any arms control negotiations process could only be approached when America was in a position to argue from the strength of having at least the same force levels and capabilities as the Russians. From the President's point of view, this was becoming an issue of similar importance to strategic weapons – the long-range nuclear missiles and warheads.

The Pentagon, the C.I.A. and the National Security Council were united on this matter. They were concerned with Soviet ocean reconnaissance satellites which used radar and electronic Intelligence systems to give Soviet commanders the data they needed to attack American and Allied surface fleets. The sentiment was carried by the White House in what became its rejection of Soviet proposals for a conference to ban ASAT systems. According to another Presidential report '. . . a comprehensive ASAT ban would afford a sanctuary to existing Soviet satellites designed to target U.S. Naval and land conventional forces. The absence of a U.S. ASAT capability to prevent Soviet targeting aided by satellites could be seen by the Soviet as a substantial factor in their ability to attack U.S. and Allied naval warfare capabilities. Uncertainty over their ability to employ satellites to target Naval forces would decrease the Soviet perception of their chance for success, thereby adding to deterrence and stability. A U.S. ASAT capability would contribute to deterrence of conventional conflict . . .'

Yet if the ASAT weapon was really to contribute to deterrence then, first and foremost, the system under development had to be deployed. The plan at that time (1983) envisaged an ASAT base on the East Coast and another on the West Coast, together with a back-up and logistical system that would allow the F-15s with their Miniature Homing Vehicle missiles to be scattered throughout the world in a crisis.

But, in 1983, there were no official plans for the United States to develop an ASAT system to take on the high altitude satellites. Although there were cases to be made for having, say, a capability to attack GSO satellites (geo-stationary orbiting), the real and immediate threat was lower down the orbital scale. However, the new enthusiasm for SDI produced a number of possibilities for alternatives to the F-15-based system. With the excitement of technological improvements and possibilities, little political pressure at home and negligible Allied pressure abroad, together with the Administration's belief that it had to 'catch up', an ASAT treaty was not an urgent problem.

The Soviet Union believed that the time was right to launch an offensive, and wanted a treaty. By the summer of 1983, another set of proposals had been drafted in Moscow. These once again suggested that all ASAT systems should be banned. This universal clause took care of the previous objection that any earth-based system could outwit the treaty. The Russians believed also that all systems that could attack earth from space should be banned. To a general public, that might have seemed a reasonable suggestion; after all, with talk of futuristic beam weapons it would be better to ban them now.

For the Americans, the Soviet proposals were predictable. They believed that the Soviet tactic was to stop the test programme and development of the Miniature Vehicle, the F-15-based system. Banning such a system then would leave the Americans without the confidence of having tested the technology which they might in the future wish to deploy. The Russians, however, could easily put their tried and tested system into store; to some extent its rather primitive technology would be protected by such a treaty. As for the idea of banning weapons in space that could destroy targets on earth, the Americans almost 'laughed out loud'. The thinking on SDI included the possibility of beam weapons that would either be based in space or would use space systems and be capable of attacking ballistic missiles in their first stage of flight. There was no way in which the Americans were going to go along with a treaty that banned the basis of SDI which was, it should be remembered, not simply a weapon system, but the embryo of a complete rethink of American strategic philosophy – and it had the enthusiastic support of the President. The 1983 Soviet proposals for an Anti-Satellite Treaty were an attempt to scupper SDI. It failed; it was bound to. In fact doubts among the Reagan Administration's own ranks were more likely to curb SDI than Soviet attempts at diplomatic deviousness.

There was at the time another reason for there being few chances of getting a comprehensive space weapons treaty. The Soviet space programme was in full swing and, unless the Americans believed that some treaty would curb the Soviet programme to America's advantage, then a treaty conference was almost pointless. Moreover, neither the Russians nor the Americans thought that a treaty as then envisaged could survive the biggest test: that of verification. The difficulty of proving the motives of research programmes and test projects had become more pronounced in recent years. For example, laboratory work on energy sources could have industrial as well as military use;

more to the point, unless there were an open door policy in the Soviet Union, the Americans would be hard to convince that such facilities in the Soviet Union were not bending, even defying, any treaty. An obvious example was Soviet work on energy weapons. The Soviet Union was testing primitive beam systems; the Americans believed that some of those tests had been carried out against American space craft, although they could not prove this.

Recently, although hardly mentioned in public, American space officials have been convinced that Soviet tests of beam weapons have been carried out against American satellites. The suspicion is that Soviet lasers have been tried out against U.S. polar orbiting satellites, 'blinding' them at crucial stages of their orbits. Some in Washington have suggested that, far from this being a reason to negotiate a treaty banning such systems, agreements should be avoided because, as we have seen, they would be so difficult, if not impossible to verify. Furthermore, say some experts, the Soviet laser experiments act as a reminder that the directed-energy research programme in the U.S.S.R. is far advanced and represents yet another incentive for American dollar-technology to catch up and overtake the Russians. The alleged Soviet tests were for some Americans further indications that the Soviet Union was not particularly interested in a workable space treaty, although the evidence offered to support this assumption has not been convincing. Those same critics have often believed that the Soviet leadership is not interested in arms control for its own sake. Instead they have accused the Russians of opting for arms control at moments when they, the Russians, need to freeze certain areas of strategic or intermediate range weapons 'advances', thereby curbing American developments especially those which appear to be on their way to eroding a Soviet lead. It is an attitude that has some justification, yet necessarily prevents real development in arms control processes that would get away from the traditional weakness of the numbers game discussed earlier in this chapter.

The Soviets refused to be put off by American reservations. In the early summer of 1984, the Soviet Union proposed a meeting in Vienna to start talks 'preventing the militarisation of outer space'. Much to the Soviet Union's surprise, the United States accepted. There was some confusion in Washington about the American acceptance. There had been diplomatic soundings in

Washington by the staff of the then Soviety envoy to the American capital, Ambassador Dobrynin; the Ambassador himself was said to be wary of American motives but suspected that a space conference in Vienna might be acceptable to the White House. This information was relayed to the Kremlin via Foreign Minister Andrei Gromyko. It does appear that, at one point, the White House would have gone along with a conference devoted solely to space systems. However, the draft response was amended, and the U.S. reply on July 29, 1984 said that, yes, the Americans would be willing to go to Vienna, but the opportunity should be taken to re-open talks on strategic and intermediate weapons. (These latter areas had collapsed the previous December when cruise missiles started to arrive in the United Kingdom.)

The linkage between space and nuclear systems did not at that stage suit the Soviet leadership. It should be remembered that the summer of 1984 saw a Moscow leadership in something of a foreign and domestic difficulty. The attempt to persuade West European governments to reverse the decision to take American cruise and Pershing II missiles had failed. It represented a major foreign policy failure particularly for the then Foreign Minister, Andrei Gromyko; furthermore, it could not be disguised that, should the missile deployment go ahead, then the Soviet Union would walk out of the Geneva talks accusing the Americans and their Allies of wrecking the negotiations. This was not a particularly smart tactic because it depended largely on Moscow's ability to split Europe from America (the so-called decoupling tactic). Clearly, the Dutch and Belgian governments appeared the weak links as far as the U.S.S.R. could predict. But the strength of the Italian and British resolve would be sufficient to encourage the West Germans, the fifth link in the missile deployment chain. Therefore the Soviet approach could not hope to succeed. Worse still for the Kremlin, it was apparent that, if they walked out, they would have to come back, because the U.S.S.R. had too much to lose in abandoning the arms control process altogether. This was especially so, should Moscow wish to concentrate on wrecking America's SDI ambitions.

Arms control was about the only way for the U.S.S.R. to dampen the effects of President Reagan's enthusiasms. An alternative was to hope that Congress would block the funding, which at that stage appeared unlikely. A third, but vague, hope was that the technology of the American laboratories would fail to support some of the Presidential vision. Considering that the Soviet Union believed more heartily in American technology than did the Americans, this too was an unlikely solution to Soviet minds. And, of course, Soviet research into many of the same processes suggested that much of the basic technology was indeed possible; consequently, with Moscow convinced that American dollar technology would deliver Mr Reagan's dreams, by the time that Andrei Gromyko and George Shultz met in Geneva in January 1985, the scene was set for a new Soviet approach to America.

However it appeared that the Russians were insisting that the most important feature should be space and that it should be clearly stated as such. The Americans were determined to emphasise the importance of negotiations on the old problems of strategic and intermediate range weapons. There were at that time suggestions that the U.S. negotiators might be in a position to offer some deal such as a three-year ban on anti-satellite weapon deployment, but only in return for some real concession on Soviet nuclear systems. The difficulty in Moscow and Washington was that the Soviet Union appeared to be nowhere near willing to make major reductions in 'offensive' weapons.

And so, when the talks started in March 1985, there were few optimists in either camp; the problems had been filtered through the mesh of technical and political reservations and, although the issues were clearer, they were no less difficult to resolve. America wanted major concessions on strategic and intermediate range systems. Without those concessions, which had to be almost 'spectacular' as one American Defense Department official thought, the Reagan Administration was unlikely even to offer an agreement to Congress for ratification. The Soviet Union was not inclined to make 'spectacular' concessions, and appeared determined to wring from the talks thorough restrictions on space systems that would upset what to the Russians appeared to be the copper-bottomed research programme backed by President Reagan, and lead to the fading of his SDI vision.

Shortly after the talks started, a close aide of President Reagan explained to the author why the American leader was determined to see SDI research through the stuttering and stumbling that might be thrown in its path by arms control.

He first of all accepted that Mr Reagan was not making out his case from any deep understanding of the enormous technical and scientific problems. (The President was not about to do post-doctorate work at M.I.T., he agreed.) He believed that an eagerness to find an alternative to existing policies of deterrence by the threat of outrageous destruction was at the centre of President Reagan's decision to back SDI research: 'We are not just talking about defence against ballistic missiles – we are talking about an evolving change in our basic military strategy. It's a change that could be first characterised by inclusion of defence against ballistic missiles into options that leaders had. But it would be followed by defence against other delivery systems and ultimately directly linked to strengthening our conventional (i.e. non-nuclear) deterrent, thereby elevating the nuclear threshold by incorporating better technological coverage . . . SDI as imagined is about striking at weapons, not people. The beauty is that nobody gets killed . . .' The impression was that, unless and until all the President's men cried 'impossible!', then this particular White House was not going to let doubtful arms control processes, ones which had been proved futile as means of reducing the risks of nuclear war, get in the way of the vision announced on March 23, 1983.

There are, however, those who have neither the military nor the political motives of Washington and Moscow, and believe that neither the vision of unproven technology nor the deviousness of military insecurity should be allowed to overshadow the need to control the military uses of outer space before they become, like nuclear weapons, uncontrollable.

Chapter 13

The Objectors

There are more peace campaigners than there are nuclear weapons. There are more unions of concerned peoples lobbying for new measures in arms control than there are arms control negotiations. The great advantage held by all these groups is that none of them is faced by the practical problems of the politics of arms control. It is government that has to produce a formula which will look attractive to the other side without the military and politicians at home throwing up their hands in despair and crying, 'Sell out!' Arms control treaties have to offer curbs on systems, a formula by which they are verifiable, an element of stability which will survive reasonably beyond the life of the treaty itself and at the same time be attractive enough to please whatever political faction or emphasis that might succeed those who agreed the terms of the treaty. In other words, peace campaigners have the advantage of not having to deliver the goods to everybody's satisfaction. In this sense, the attempt to control the military use of space is no different.

This cautionary note in no way dismisses the value of those campaigns which seek to make the world a safe place in which to live; nor does it ignore the general criticisms thrown at the worldwide campaigns, many of which often embarrass those political administrations apparently engaged in the arms control process, especially the process to legislate for nuclear weapons – until the announcement of 'Star Wars', the only issue to arouse strong international feelings and organised campaigns. (The campaign against chemical weapons, for example, is not nearly so well organised nor internationally supported.)

Anti-nuclear campaigners are often seen by government as naïve groups ignoring the realities of military deterrence. The often-heard argument from, say, the British government (of both political persuasions) suggests that, as nuclear weapons cannot be disinvented, then there is no practicable chance of banning them; and therefore to suggest that there is such a practicable chance is both naïve and misleading to campaign followers. It is said also in the West that many of the anti-nuclear campaigns have been infiltrated by groups and organisations bent on damaging Western society and those policies which the Soviet Union finds unpleasant.[1] A third criticism is one which is less convincing and one which therefore evokes less debate: there are many in government who say that it is irrelevant to argue that nuclear weapons are amoral systems and to contemplate their use is immoral, because such argument has no realistic point of debate. Indeed, in the 1980s there have been many at the most senior levels of government in Britain who have smiled, almost patronisingly, at this, the most convincing of arguments against nuclear weapons.

The morality would appear reasonable: each society has a duty (a moral obligation) to defend itself against attempts to destroy it. This obligation is based on the utter belief that society's way of life and belief is, in spite of the obvious imperfections, *based* on a moral and ethical code that is beyond reproach. That society, therefore, must be defended to preserve the moral and ethical code. However, if a nuclear war led to the destruction of that society, and of life lived under its moral and ethical code, then a nuclear conflict could not be justified. So runs the argument, which perhaps ignores deeper theological debate. However, what all three (and there are many more cases for and against nuclear weapons) arguments amount to is one obvious question to ask any nuclear power, especially the minor powers such as France, China and the United Kingdom.

If, say, the United Kingdom did not have nuclear weapons, would the Prime Minister of the day be recommending to the Cabinet, Parliament and therefore the electorate that the U.K. went out and bought them? In other words, knowing what we do about the military and political power of nuclear weapons, would Britain (for example) choose to become a nuclear power

[1] For an interesting study of this argument and its wider implications, see *Campaign against Western Defence* by Sir Clive Rose, Macmillan, 1985.

if she were not one already? The question then is: can the same argument be applied to space weapons?

To a great extent, those who have campaigned for absolute control over the military use of space are where the anti-nuclear campaigns would have been in the 1950s, had they had the knowledge and organisation they have today. Organisations such as the British-based Campaign for Nuclear Disarmament may inspire images of left-wing anarchy, bedraggled and back-packed clashes with authority, naïve clergy, feminist vitriol and cries of 'pinko dissenters' from an Establishment which often has failed to examine the issues involved. The more rational and usually better informed members of, say, government and its attendant bureaucracy take a great deal of notice of the protest: firstly, because the political element is too near the surface to be ignored – CND is more likely to influence an electorate than are any of the political parties in Parliament.

Secondly, the days are gone when CND and its like marched open-toed with placards, babies in pushcarts and nothing else. Along with other organisations, it has become a well-informed group which can call on a string of able researchers and scientists so that the anti-nuclear case might be presented in a comprehensive and persuasive manner. Certainly in the United Kingdom, the sound information flow from the protest groups is more revealing than that from government. Furthermore, the organisations supplying information have extended beyond the lobbies. In the United Kingdom, work by, say, the Science Policy Research Unit at Sussex University and the Department of Defence Studies at Aberdeen University has gone further than most to make available sensitive but unclassified information to wider audiences. This information includes the detailed analysis necessary to understand the economics of defence, which in a society struggling to preserve, never mind improve, its social lot, is an increasingly relevant aspect of the protest. (The work done at Aberdeen on the economics of defence is of particular note.) Internationally, the publications of the Stockholm International Peace Research Institute and, in America, the Center for Defense Information, have had an increasing influence on the political debate and the way in which defence analysis is presented. The result is a wider and perhaps more thoughtful debate on issues that have come to worry a bigger section of society than was perturbed in the monochromatic 1950s.

We have seen also the increasing interest of the so-called professional classes in Western society. As a generalisation (with all the implicit doubts aroused by such a term), the protests of the 1950s and 1960s were never able to hold for long the public loyalties of the respectable middle-class groups such as doctors, lawyers and scientists. One reason for this was the reputation with which the campaigns became surrounded. It was not that the issues were impossibly contentious, perhaps the problem had more to do with information and atmosphere. The bearded protest is not a bad vision of what was happening twenty years ago. If that description is granted, then it implies an image that was worthy, yet somehow not quite acceptable, even perhaps a danger to career prospects by association. Consequently, many of the scientific brains, that might have given the protests a greater understanding of the technical issues, drifted away to get on with their careers.

It was true that much of the information needed to maintain interest and upon which campaigns might have been developed was available only to a classified minority. Today, in the 1980s, the formation of more established groups such as might appear under the title of 'Doctors Against Nuclear Weapons' have allowed the professions to join their own 'lodges' of the wider protest without having to be directly associated with the placards and slogans of the still stereotyped CND. Also, the increase in scientifically-based protest has encouraged those in the professions to listen to the overall arguments against government policy, because those arguments have been presented in a scientifically respectable manner. In short, the professions appear at ease with the sources of the debate.

If some of this hypothesis is accepted, then the connection with the superpower debate on space systems and the increasingly detailed non-government campaigns becomes obvious. The anti-nuclear campaign has not withered as many senior government figures – on both sides of the Atlantic – suggested it would after its burst back into the headlines during the early 1980s. That revival was due mainly (if not solely) to the decision to base ground-launched cruise missiles and Pershing II missiles in Western Europe. The decision, taken for political rather than sound military reasons, prompted an extraordinarily intensive Soviet campaign to stop deployment; it was a campaign that was directed at the fears of Western Europeans and the weaknesses in certain political coalitions, particularly in the Netherlands and Belgium. The Western Alliance countered with, among other things, a campaign to show how the West was threatened by Soviet SS-20 missiles and an insincere Soviet approach to arms control. This all took place, as has been noted on other pages, at the time of the first Reagan Administration.

In Europe, President Reagan quickly established a public image as a not very successful movie actor, who knew little nor cared much if anything for foreign relations, strategic studies and Europe. He had the image of a super-hawk who believed all could be achieved by driving a hole through traditional approaches to East–West relations, by making America a super-arsenal, by threatening the Soviet Union with everything from isolation to extinction if need be. The diplomatic tension was maintained by equally hostile attitudes in Moscow and by the United Kingdom's government broadly supporting her traditional ally in its policy towards the Soviet Union. Even the nationalistic revival in Britain encouraged by the Falklands conflict had an adverse element, inasmuch as once the battle was over, the government's victory rejoicing appeared to go beyond the public enthusiasm. The overall result was a sense of fear, which only encouraged the anti-nuclear campaign. And so, not unnaturally, it is possible to make a case that government actions and handling of military and diplomatic affairs helped the cause of the CND and its like.

At the peak of this concern, President Reagan made his 'Star Wars' speech.

For the campaigners, the obvious reaction was to interpret the March 23, 1983 statement as yet another war cry from a hawkish administration. The lack of information, including a sound explanation as to what President Reagan actually meant, only muddied the protest waters. Unable to see what it was that had bitten their protest hook, the campaigners tugged hard and came up with a wriggling, almost uncontrollable specimen of politico-military thinking that left itself wide open to criticism and provided a platform for the growing band of informed scientific and strategic protest.

Therefore, after a long history of doubtful method, the international arms protest lobby probably matured as an informed and organised body at a time when the twenty-one-year-old militarisation of outer space process came of age. The objectors were far beyond the simplicity of ban-it-it's-bad-for-you placards. The people who led the campaign against the military uses of space and then the development of the Strategic Defence Initiative were informed and, in the main, articulate. The people promoting the case for SDI and ASAT (anti-satellite) systems were often just as articulate although this was rarely the case at the political level. Consequently the case for SDI (the focus of the military-space debate) was badly put, especially in Europe. It mattered not that reams of technical information were available for Europeans to learn what was in the SDI programme; the politicians had only a meagre grasp of the subject, therefore their performances were not highly rated and publics listen to politicians (even if they do not believe them) and not to well informed officials.

Against them, the scientific and technical communities were able to produce detailed anti-military literature that was well received and understood. The new lobby had all the advantages of being well informed and expert at putting across its message. The scientists who joined this lobby benefited from the new respectability of the protest movement. They were part of the phenomenon of the early 1980s that caused the public to point an unaccusing finger and remark that, if these people who had scientific and technical backgrounds were against the proposals for the further military use of space, then there had to be something in what they said. This was a much more credible voice than the somewhat predictable tones emanating from the original ban-the-bomb-type groups. It should not be imagined that the world scientific and strategic studies community as a whole was against the proposals coming from Washington and, indirectly, from Moscow. (The real advances in research programmes in the Soviet Union tended to be conveniently ignored in the protest, largely perhaps because the American position was so exposed and simple to debate; and, of course, there was little hard evidence about the state of the Soviet programme.)

However, those groups that did form the nucleus of the protest were very well informed and, in the American case, contained people with experience in government. These people were part of a tribe of out-of-government scientists, lawyers and academics which is a characteristic of the Washington political process. The tribe divided nearly into those who had a great reputation before going into government and those who achieved that standing in office. Whatever their credentials, these people formed an informed colony which, although in political limbo, gained the ear of a communications industry impressed by insiders.

The most telling protest came when political insiders linked arms with the scientific community. Consequently the most impressive response to the SDI and Anti-Satellite plans of the Reagan Administration came from a group calling itself the Union of Concerned Scientists.

The Union of Concerned Scientists has had an influence that would be the justifiable envy of more established groups. It was, and is, American-based. Two months after the Reagan Star Wars speech a panel from the Union made public the result of long and detailed research, not on the Strategic Defence Initiative announced by President Reagan, but on the need for a treaty between the superpowers that would effectively ban anti-satellite weapons. Mention here of this research is a reminder that the concerns of many, other than the Union, predated the March 1983 speech and most certainly go beyond the predictable debate over SDI. The Union's panel was an impressive list of scientists and strategists: Carl Sagan, Herbert Scoville Jr, John Steinbruner, Hans Bethe, Henry W. Kendall, Franklin A. Long, Leonard C. Meeker, Richard L. Garwin, Admiral Noel Gayler and Kurt Gottfried. Each was a respected member of the community of pure and military scientists from institutions such as Cornell, Brookings and Harvard. On May 18, 1983, Gottfried, Gayler and Garwin appeared before the U.S. Senate Foreign Relations Committee. The three men presented a draft Treaty Limiting Anti-Satellite Weapons. The idea was to focus attention on issues that could easily be raised during any negotiations between Moscow and Washington.

During a symposium on ASAT systems later that year in Stockholm, Professor Gottfried outlined that reasoning and features of the Union's proposal: 'it would obligate the signatories not to destroy, damage or change the flight trajectory of any space object, *no matter to whom they may belong*. Fundamentally the draft is a test ban, in that the Parties would not be permitted to test in space, or against space objects, weapons that could destroy, damage or change the flight trajectory of space objects, or space weapons that can damage objects, on the ground or in the atmosphere . . .' Furthermore, the Union's draft contained an obligation on both superpowers to go further than banning testing and deployment. The proposal, if ever adopted, would mean that further negotiations would start once the original treaty were agreed – and those negotiations would ban *possession* of ASAT weapons.

This clause was not as obvious as some might believe. For example, the 1925 Geneva Protocol on Chemical Weapons may have banned their use, but nothing in that agreement banned possession. Considering that treaties may be easily discarded during war, then banning possession, i.e. destruction of existing systems, was an important aspect of future proposals, although enormously difficult to legislate against. So many other systems could be used as ASAT weapons, it would be hard to come up with a fool-proof definition of an ASAT weapon without questioning the functions of even innocent satellites which were capable of being manoeuvred into the path of an enemy's space craft.

The Union, recognising this difficulty, appeared to confine their proposal to what was practicable in terms of unambiguous definition. Indeed, Gottfried said at the time that the focus on a test ban (rather than an all-out ban) and the postponement of negotiations towards prohibiting possession of such systems were motivated by the Union's belief that the present ASAT capabilities did not at that time (1983) present a serious threat to the United States nor to the Soviet Union, by the implications of imminent developments in ASAT technology and by the quite different verification process posed by a ban on ASAT testing as compared to a prohibition on possession.

Here was a much more refined, a more carefully thought out presentation. It was listened to with respect by the Senators and eventually by a more diverse audience. In Europe, the thoughts of the Union and others were considered by senior officials and in some rare cases by politicians. This was no ordinary campaign and had to be treated as such. However, the debate at this stage centred on ASAT systems although much of the detail reflected the growing awareness of and wariness towards SDI. Not surprisingly, the most real objections and, for that matter, the most widely circulated support, tended to come from individuals.

Single papers of protest were published based on technical objections as well as on strategic grounds. In Europe those written (not always in total condemnation) by, for example, Professor Lawrence Freedman of London University, Michael

Guionnet of the Centre National d'Etudes Spatiales in Paris, Dr Bhupendra Jasani of the Stockholm International Peace Research Institute and J. W. Scheffers in the Netherlands, demonstrated that the subject of outer space could be approached from more than one direction. And these directions did not arrive at the same conclusion – that the military should not be in space. Instead of the knee-jerk of protest groups tending to condemn because it was military and therefore suspect, these and a handful of other experts made important contributions of alternative views to a subject that was increasingly becoming subject to black and white interpretation. Many of these protests were from groups and individuals catching up to the space debate as if they had but recently seen the bandwagon pass by; but in the United States, as in certain circles in Europe, the published concerns of scientists in particular pre-dated the Presidential speech of March 1983.

In March 1968, Richard L. Garwin (now adjunct Professor of Physics at Columbia University) had hinted of things to come in a paper called 'Anti-Ballistic Missile Systems'. In 1981, Garwin's paper published in the *Bulletin of Atomic Scientists* was entitled 'Are we on the Verge of the Arms Race in Space?' This theme had appeared earlier in a number of books, monographs and papers including Dr Bhupendra Jasani's *Outer Space – Battlefield of the Future* in 1978, the writings of John Pike of the Federation of American Scientists, Dr Albert Carnesale, Professor Kurt Gottfried of Cornell University and Kosta Tsipis of M.I.T. (This is but a short list of those writing on the future of space as a military environment and it is meant as nothing more than an illustration of the diverse backgrounds of the space lobby.) Much of the writing had concentrated on the military and technical aspects of the subject. The next move against anti-satellite systems and the Strategic Defence Initiative came from another quarter – the legal consideration.

It may seem inevitable that once an argument is in full swing then the lawyers will appear. Indeed one of the best papers on ASAT Treaties came from the Washington lawyer Walter Slocombe, a former Assistant Secretary of Defense and one deeply concerned with arms control as a Strategic Arms negotiator during the Carter Administration. The lawyers, of course, were not in this debate for fat fees, although there was potential political kudos to be gained. The main thrust was to question the legal issues behind the military's plans for space and, more importantly, the preservation of existing agreements.

There are five treaties dating from 1963 which have some clauses concerning arms control in space. The 1963 Test Ban Treaty prevents nuclear weapons testing in space as well as in the atmosphere and under water. The 1967 Outer Space Treaty puts restrictions on the exploitation of space, the moon and other celestial bodies. The 1972 Anti-Ballistic Missile (ABM) Treaty limits such systems and their research and development. The 1972 Strategic Arms Treaty protects satellites. The 1979 Moon and Celestial Body Treaty restricts activities to peaceful purposes. Of all these agreements, the concern of scientists, strategists and lawyers centred on the 1972 ABM Treaty.

In Washington, a lobby group was set up called the National Campaign to Save the ABM Treaty. It had all the verve of the type of campaign normally associated with Saving the Whale, or some similarly emotive subject. And the list of names sponsoring the Campaign was particularly impressive if not obviously bi-partisan. It included McGeorge Bundy the former Presidential National Security Adviser, two ex-directors of the C.I.A., William Colby and Stansfield Turner, Dean Rusk and Cyrus Vance, both former Secretaries of State, an ex-Secretary of Defense, Robert McNamara (the man most associated with the introduction of the Mutual Assured Destruction (MAD) philosophy), Admiral Noel Gayler, the one-time head of the National Security Agency, and Ronald Reagan's predecessor at the White House, Jimmy Carter.

There were many more names in the original list of politicians, scientists, military men, diplomats and academics. Some of those on that list could have been termed 'peaceniks', in other words committed more than most to zealous forms of disarmament processes in order to rid the world – in their terms – of the dangers of nuclear and space warfare systems. They were the people who appeared at major gatherings where the basis for the debate was so 'liberal' that it could have been confused with unilateralism. But such a wide grouping of backgrounds suggested that, for the first time, people of considerable standing were coming together not under one of the traditional protest banners, but beneath something that had a single aim: to protect the cherished ABM Treaty.

The ABM Treaty was signed in 1972, but as an idea it went

back to the era of President Johnson. Had there not been an invasion by the Soviet Union of Czechoslovakia in 1968, then so many aspects of nuclear weaponry and arms control might have been different. There had been plans for both superpowers to work out ways of limiting the strategic forces – the long-range ballistic nuclear missiles and nuclear bombers. The question of defences against those systems would probably have been considered although such a U.S. suggestion had been coolly received by the Soviet Union in 1967. Instead, the events in Eastern Europe in 1968 delayed the start of those talks for more than a year. This was enough time for the almost revolutionary process of multi-target missiles to begin to take shape and for the concurrent delay on restricting the ways in which a state might defend itself.

When the subject was discussed in the 1960s, the argument centred on the proposition that, by limiting the means of defending themselves against an attack, then both superpowers would come to realise that nuclear war meant widespread death and destruction; it would be impossible to hide from a counter-attack. The conclusion drawn was that this was the obvious banker in what was to become known as the MAD (Mutual Assured Destruction) doctrine. Both superpowers would be naked should there be a nuclear war and therefore the incentive to start one was reduced. Prior to the 1968 invasion, the Americans had thought that the limitation on defences against ballistic missile attacks was so important that it should be discussed before anything else with the Soviet Union. This would allow both sides to come to a more realistic conclusion at a later date when they negotiated offensive (missile and bomber) reductions.

By the time Moscow and Washington had gone through the almost statutory twelve months of diplomatic mourning that follows the absolute collapse of a fundamental principle in their relationship (in this case the invasion of Czechoslovakia) the emphasis appeared to have changed. The case put forward by President Nixon's arms controllers set aside the priority of the Johnson White House, which was to begin by placing severe limits on defence systems. However, the concept was by no means rejected. Instead, the new Administration decided that there should be some agreement that would give equal importance to a search for controls on offensive and defensive systems – i.e. the long-range nuclear warhead carrying missiles and bombers (offensive systems) and the shorter range anti-missile missiles (defensive systems).

The temptation was gradually to give the technologies involved in both systems equal importance and therefore to believe that somehow they were connected sufficiently to be included in the same arms control discussions. The obvious difficulties embraced the fact that, at that point, the science and engineering were not available to cope with incoming missiles. To set up a feasible, and even reasonably leak-proof, umbrella against missile attacks was impossible. It would always be so easy to modify attacking missiles to counter the defensive technology then available. Even by doing nothing more than putting extra missiles into the attack, the defences would be overwhelmed.

There was a further problem. It was not enough to say that anti-ballistic missile defences were beyond technology as it then existed. What would happen if technology improved sufficiently in, say, the coming decade, to make an anti-ballistic missile defence a reasonable if not wholly effective proposition? This was not an idle question considering the advances that were envisaged as a consequence of wider use of micro and computer technology, including data handling.

Furthermore, what would happen if either or both superpowers ignored the technical limitations and went ahead with a comprehensive and widespread ABM system, perhaps through fear that the other might do so, or because of a belief that science would soon make the system feasible? The short answer to both questions of the same problem was that, while building defences, both sides would embark upon a furious offensive ballistic nuclear missile programme to make sure that the envisaged defensive umbrella could be penetrated. As a consequence, the general conclusion was that a workable ballistic missile defence system would not work because the technology was not available to counter the simple modifications to existing enemy missiles and certainly not to cope with the enemy's accelerated missile building programme that would follow. (Hardly surprisingly, these are arguments applied still to the basis of many cases against America's Strategic Defence Initiative.)

The superpowers, having returned from a cheerless period of diplomatic relations following the Soviet adventure in Czechoslovakia, started negotiations to limit strategic missiles and to look at ways of introducing a form of stability by guaranteeing that both sides would remain vulnerable to attack by these missiles. The result, in 1972, was the first Strategic Arms Limitation Treaty, SALT I, together with the Anti-Ballistic Missile (ABM) Treaty.

The ABM Treaty was later amended (in 1974) and may be interpreted as limiting both superpowers to just one ABM site (the original Treaty allowed two sites). That site was restricted to one of two locations: the single ABM system could be either around the national capital or around an ICBM (Intercontinental Ballistic Missile) site. Furthermore there was a limit placed on the numbers and locations of ABM radars and limitations on development and testing of new systems. The ABM systems had to be contained within a radius of 150 kilometres and there could be no more than 100 launchers. There were to be restrictions in future development.

Test and development were always an important part of any arms control treaty; limitations on research and development make an important contribution to strategic stability because they tend to offer both sides some guarantees that neither of them will easily break out from the agreement to gain a surprise advantage. It is true, for example, that there is no point in banning one missile without banning development of another which will replace it, probably with an improved range and destructive power. The ABM Treaty recognised this in the original document and in a series of amendments during the 1970s. Article 5, for example, covered the weakness in Article 3 which stated simply that no more than 100 missiles and launchers should be deployed in the defence zone. The Article 5 restriction made it illegal to develop and test ABM launchers that could launch more than one intercept missile at a time. And, to safeguard against either side getting around the Treaty by using research and development work, carried out elsewhere in the defence industry, all multi-launch systems were banned. There was even a ban on automatic launchers that would allow ABM teams to reload rapidly – in theory this would put some restriction on both sides bringing in extra missiles from outside the 150 kilometre zone to beef up the ABM defences.

The same Article put a further restriction on development, which was to have particular relevance to the research behind President Reagan's Star Wars speech. There was a ban on the development, testing and deployment of ABM systems or *components* which were sea-based, mobile land-based or *space based*.

Article 6 stated that only ABM missiles, launchers and radars should have the capabilities to counter strategic ballistic missiles in flight. And the final Article recognised the need to provide both sides with an assurance that the Treaty would be honoured. Both superpowers said that they would be monitoring the other and agreed not to 'interfere with the national technical means of verification of the other party . . .' In other words, both promised not to destroy or degrade each other's reconnaissance satellites. At first sighting the Treaty appeared to be a comprehensive way of preserving the vulnerability and therefore that concept of stability. However it was clear that some parts would need clarification as new approaches and technologies were applied to strategic defence and offence.

What, for example, would be the procedures for altering or updating systems? What would happen if one side decided to move its ABM system from one missile field to another? Would it have to dismantle the first before erecting the new one? If so, it would be vulnerable during that period. When, in 1974, the agreement was reached to set up but one ABM site each, then provision had also to be made for a change of mind about locations. Again, what would happen if the Russians wanted to move their defences (at the moment set up around Moscow) to one of their strategic missile sites along the Trans-Siberian Railway? These and other problems were discussed and to some extent resolved in the S.C.C. (Standing Consultative Commission). The S.C.C. was set up after the SALT I ABM agreements to sort out such difficulties arising from a set of Treaties which were far from perfect, which were the result of the two sides negotiating what were after all relatively new concepts in arms control and which were bound to produce afterthoughts either by recognising weak points in the documents or by technological innovation. The S.C.C. would provide also a point of contact that could offer continuing opportunities for clearing up misunderstandings and the chance to prevent miscalculations on both sides at time of superpower tensions.

The complications are mentioned here to show that a considerable amount of effort had been made to protect the letter and the spirit of the ABM Treaty and to give some idea of the obvious difficulties in the drafting, negotiating and successful conclusion of a space treaty; in all, a reminder to the campaign groups that it is not enough to say, 'Ban it!' Treaties, if they are to work, must be unambiguous, with clear definitions and a reliable follow-up process, which is why the S.C.C. was so important. The type of treaty often proposed by campaigners against the military uses of space would probably include a re-write of the ABM Treaty. This would provide the protection that those campaigners seek for some, but hardly all, elements in space and it would retain the theory of paradoxical stability as provided by the ABM agreement.

But why should it be necessary to re-write a treaty that in theory provides the protection for so long advocated by both superpowers? It can be that treaties become diplomatically and legally rusty. They are, however, prone to another form of corrosion: interpretation. This is hardly surprising; after all, what are called 'definitional issues' have been around for some time. (Thou shalt not kill is probably the longest-standing and most often abused pact accepted by man. As a bald statement, it would appear to have taken into consideration most safeguards and fears. Yet 'definitional issues' could point to, for example, 'an eye for an eye . . .' and immediately present an argument of interpretation more associated with modern agreements.)

Above all, uncertainties about what is and what is not allowed under the ABM Treaty stem from the ways in which it is possible to interpret the language used in the document, even in its revised form.

One obvious example of ambiguous interpretation is the word 'develop'. To anybody outside the world of watertight negotiations, to say that there should be, for example, no development of more than one rocket would appear to be an unambiguous statement. In the West, there is an industrial process of research and development. To some extent the development proceeds from a full research programme. Once research shows that a project is feasible, then it goes into its development stage which would possibly lead to a prototype being built – the stage before production. Therefore, if a treaty states that a rocket may not be developed, then the programme should not proceed beyond the research phase. But what happens if the development of the rocket is part of the research phase, or can be shown to be? It is possible for example to produce a guidance system in the research stage which has to be tested in perhaps an existing missile system. By carrying out such tests, a new system could be said to be in development.

Then there is a problem with translation as well as interpretation. The English language text in the ABM Treaty uses the word 'develop' (Article 5, para 2: 'Each party undertakes not to *develop*, test or deploy ABM launchers for launching more than one ABM interceptor . . . nor to *develop*, test, or deploy automatic or semi-automatic or other similar systems . . .') The Western interpretation of the word develop could be conveniently ambiguous. The further complication comes when the Soviet Union is asked for its interpretation of the same verb. The Soviet negotiators chose to use a verb which they believed to be less open to misunderstanding in their language; the verb 'sozdavat' might be translated: to frame, to make or even to create. The Soviet definition suggests that research work cannot go very far before it becomes part of, if not entirely, a creative programme – which could be interpreted as violating the Treaty. However, let us suppose the American verb, to develop, is the correct one. In Russian, the verb 'razvivat' is also used to mean to develop, and to evolve. At what point could it be possible to say that a pure research project has 'evolved' into a development programme?

The ABM Treaty negotiations went some way towards resolving these difficulties. The Americans accepted that development should be understood as the stage following research. The Russians apparently spent time examining the programme of development to show that there were numerous examples where research, development and testing merged. To the Soviet mind, the definition was blurred and so they believed that the restriction should apply to a system or a *component* once it was clearly identifiable as part of a Ballistic Missile Defence programme.

But what is a *component*? Is it an essential part of a system – one without which the system is rendered useless; one which is peculiar to that system? Or is it something as common as a switch, which could be tested and developed in some other research and development programme? Therefore should the Treaty declare that component development anywhere is banned if that component could be fitted to the offending weapon, thus making it a breach of some agreement?

The American position at the time of the negotiations and follow-up meetings between the superpowers was that 'in the obligation not to develop such systems, devices, or warheads would be applicable only to that stage of development which follows laboratory development and testing . . . the prohibition on "development" applies to activities involved after a component moves from the *laboratory* [author's itals] development and testing stage to the field testing stage, wherever performed . . .'[1]

Critics of American approaches to the ABM Treaty have seized on Ambassador Smith's testimony as evidence that '. . . current plans of the Administration for the Strategic Defence Initiative, if carried through during the 1988–1993 time period, would be inconsistent with the Limits of Article 5 of the Treaty . . .' The 1984–88 Five Year Defence Guidance, signed by Secretary of Defense Caspar Weinberger, states the U.S. plans to initiate 'the prototype development of space-based weapons systems . . . so that we will be prepared to deploy fully developed and operationally ready systems . . .'[2]

And so it was interesting that, when the director of the SDI programme, General James Abrahamson, testified to the Armed Service Committee of the House of Representatives in Washington early in 1985, he suggested that at some point the SDI programme would have to depart from the ABM Treaty. Later, in April of that year, the General appeared before the Senate Appropriations Sub-Committee on Defense. General Abrahamson was careful to stress that 'all the *research* in SDI will be carried out in strict compliance with our obligations within the ABM Treaty . . .' The emphasis was on the research programme; clearly there can be no guarantees that protect the ABM Treaty from SDI development. But then does it matter? Could it be that the concerns expressed by the SDI objectors cover only the Treaty as some cherished expression of superpower agreement. Groups such as the National Campaign to Save the ABM Treaty see more sinister problems arising.

Indeed, the National Campaign believes that, if President Reagan's SDI proposals set aside the ABM Treaty, then the competition that would follow to build ABM systems would lead to an uncontrolled build-up in offensive nuclear forces, i.e. more

[1] Evidence of Gerard Smith who was Chief American ABM Treaty negotiator, to Senate Armed Services Committee in 1972.

[2] 'The Impact of US and Soviet Ballistic Missile Defence Programmes on the ABM Treaty', Thomas K. Longstreth, John E. Pike and John B. Rhinelander.

intercontinental rockets and perhaps bombers. The argument against this might be that a return to twin-track negotiations and a successful outcome of such talks would remove these concerns. Some Americans and Russians are convinced that the technology of anti-ballistic missiles will inevitably have greater influence in both capitals than political and diplomatic reasoning. Consequently, there is a feeling that twin-track negotiation will have to produce a formula which would allay the fears expressed above: that if SDI (including the Soviet system) results in the ABM Treaty being set aside, then there will be a massive increase in the missile race between the superpowers in order to penetrate the future defensive umbrellas.

Twin-track talking at Geneva would, in theory, renegotiate the ABM document to allow more ABM systems, but a renegotiated Treaty would only be signed and ratified if another treaty at the same signing limited the numbers of offensive missiles and future research and development programmes. Therefore in theory, at least, twin-track treaties could prevent any increase in offensive systems.

The objectors, however, believe that other treaties, agreements and understandings are in jeopardy. For example, as mentioned elsewhere, the research programmes in the United States and the Soviet Union would appear to include the development of the nuclear-pumped X-ray laser. There are many who believe that the enhanced X-ray is not a feasible form of directed weapon. It is said to have a very limited application. However, research continues and it includes the use of nuclear power as the energy source for the system. The basic concept is that a small nuclear explosion would be used to transmit energy through laser rods to produce the X-radiation that some scientists believe could be part of the SDI arsenal in outer space. Such a beam would be directed at a missile, not in its important boost stage, but in the phase beyond the atmosphere. It would perhaps be seen as a back-up for the front-line part of the system which would concentrate on destroying the missile moments after lift-off.

The objectors aim their criticisms at the X-ray laser's energy source – the explosion. It is imagined that the small nuclear explosion would have to take place in space. This would appear to contravene the 1963 Limited Test Ban Treaty. The Treaty which was negotiated by the then three nuclear powers, the United States, the Soviet Union and the United Kingdom, banned nuclear explosions in the atmosphere, underwater and in outer space. Such a system, sometimes envisaged for the X-ray laser, would, if space-based, breach also the 1967 Outer Space Treaty. This treaty attempted to maintain space as a strictly peaceful environment. Article IV of the 1967 Treaty banned all signatories from placing in orbit 'any objects carrying nuclear weapons or any other such kinds of weapons of mass destruction, install such weapons on celestial bodies, or station such weapons in outer-space in any other manner . . .'

It could be suggested that the weaknesses in some of these arguments hinges on the point at which these weapons were deployed – assuming that they were ever built. It may be possible to base a weapon on earth and send its beam to the target in space; it would then be difficult to make a case that the 1967 Outer Space Treaty and the 1963 Limited Test Ban Treaty were really being violated. Here would be a point when the international lawyers might wrangle over the definitional detail involved in basing a system in earth that in time of war would be extended into space. (From this point of the argument, it might even be said that all nuclear-tipped intercontinental missiles are illegal under the 1967 Outer Space Treaty. An ICBM would fly through space carrying with it its nuclear warhead – sometimes as many as 14. The ICBM could be said to violate the 1967 Treaty's Article IV because it is carrying a nuclear weapon into orbit or partial orbit.)

However, by the time it was a matter of debate, then a war would be on and who might tell what happens to agreements and treaties in war in this nuclear weapons age? The concern of many is for existing treaties and for the processes of negotiation. There is a group which contends that the American SDI programme, and eventually its Soviet equivalent, may rupture also the process for resolving the difficulties of interpretation as set out by the ABM process. The S.C.C. (Standing Consultative Commission) had attempted the enormous task of dealing with questions as and when they occurred, and in private. There had been a series of successes for the S.C.C. mentioned earlier. The argument used against the Reagan Administration was that the President chose to debate in public those matters that could be sorted out in private, within the S.C.C. The criticism claimed that he had needed to attack the Soviet Union in public over apparent violations of the ABM Treaty, in order to help maintain the credibility of his ambitions for SDI, in particular the reasoning that would lead perhaps to the United States 'bumping' into the Treaty.

The example of this departure from the usual channels used to clear up misunderstandings was the American allegation that the Soviet Union had breached the ABM Treaty by building a large radar in a remote area north of the city of Krasnoyarsk in Siberia. This radar was described by Washington as an early warning system and therefore infringed Article 6 which outlawed early warning radars unless they were along the periphery of the territory pointing outwards. The contention was that the new radar added protection to the Soviet Union by providing extra coverage, especially against a possible attack from a submarine-launched ballistic missile.

This possible form of protection may seem to be a perfectly reasonable form of self-defence and nobody in Washington denied that, as a system, the Krasnoyarsk radar made sound sense and was an admirable addition to the Soviet Union's protective umbrella. The objection from the Americans was that, however sane the construction of the radar, it nevertheless breached an existing treaty and therefore was a violation that should be made public. There were those in the Pentagon who took every opportunity to cite this apparent violation in order to allow the U.S.A. to breach the agreement on a tit-for-tat basis and to demonstrate to Administration critics that any form of arms control with the Soviet Union was a doubtful exercise.

The Soviet Union, not surprisingly, has a possible reason for the radar. Moscow denied that the Treaty had been breached because the Siberian system was a space-tracking radar – not an early warning system and therefore not an infringement of the Treaty. It matters not, said the objectors, who was right and who was wrong. The procedure for settling the dispute in private, the S.C.C., had been abandoned. The S.C.C. may have been abandoned on this point, but the U.S. Administration claimed that it had done so only when the S.C.C. failed to resolve the dispute.

As we saw earlier, the S.C.C. had been successful in answering questions raised on matters of definition and, more importantly, in amending the existing agreement. Indeed the very issue of radars and their functions had been discussed, apparently amicably, in the same forum. (The Soviet Union had queried

American constructions in 1975 and in 1978.) By abandoning the Special Consultative Commission before it could do more than hold preliminary discussions on the Krasnoyarsk radar, the Reagan Administration had, at the very least, proved itself to be impatient with the trusted procedures.

A group of influential legal men, Lawyers' Alliance for Nuclear Arms Control Inc, went further. In a 1984 study, the group stated that 'it will now be more difficult to arrive at a satisfactory resolution of this serious issue since the Soviets may view a decision to cease construction of the radar as public acknowledgement that they were cheating and cannot be trusted . . . the net result, whether or not intended, is to reduce the effectiveness of one of the most precious assets in nuclear arms control – the Standing Consultative Commission. If a nation wished to prepare a foundation for abrogation of the ABM Treaty, the route of publicly accusing the other side of violating the Treaty could be an effective one . . . there are substantial arms controls costs associated with the Strategic Defence Initiative – in particular the almost certain destruction of the ABM Treaty, the undermining of other nuclear arms agreements, the poisoning of prospects for future agreements, and the weakening of a valuable procedural mechanism for resolving disputes in an orderly way . . .

'The ABM Treaty has worked up to this point because both sides wanted it to work. Of equal significance, it is in the fundamental self-interest of both the United States and the Soviet Union to stop an arms race in outer space before it starts in earnest . . .'

These are creditable sentiments: but how might the superpowers go about legislating against an arms race in space? Could it even be too late, because the race is on 'in earnest'?

Chapter 14

Review

This last chapter offers a summary of the military uses of outer space together with some thoughts on the implications for arms control and, therefore, for the future of our society.

The history of this form of military engineering is romantic as must be all forms of exploration. It started in the nineteenth century with serious attempts to design rockets that would fly beyond the ranges that might be needed to bombard an enemy. The temptation was to reach for the moon. It was not until October 4, 1957 that the general public believed that this might be possible. With the launching of that first Sputnik, even the most closed military minds recognised that the arms race had burst into space – the new high ground. Today, both the superpowers have space-based systems allied to every form of warfare: early warning, reconnaissance, electronic eavesdropping, communications, navigation, weather forecasting and reporting, nuclear missile flight correction and, now, the crude outline of beam weapons in space. The fantasies of the nineteenth century have come true, most of them during the past 25 years. Here is a reminder of what those systems can do.

Early Warning: The Americans have a series of satellites under the general heading of D.S.P. (Defense Support Programme) in geo-stationary orbits. They watch Soviet missile silos and the ocean areas from which the Americans suspect a Soviet submarine-based missile might be launched. The efficiency of the system is not quite clear. The satellite is capable of providing a 30-minute warning, but may have to be modified in order that it can guarantee to distinguish between an empty silo and one with a missile inside. The Russians have a constellation of nine early warning satellites in highly elliptical orbits spaced out in

40° sections around the equator. The Soviet system does not appear to be as stable as the American one according to independent analysis (not the author's).

Photo-Reconnaissance: Both superpowers have satellites, usually orbiting at less than 200 miles of altitude, that can photograph objects on the ground in such detail that items no more than 30 cm wide have been identified clearly. (Stories that newspaper headlines can be read from 240 kilometres are somewhat suspect.) About four out of every ten satellites are used for photo-reconnaissance. The Soviet Union launches more than the United States but that is mainly because the Russian craft have shorter life cycles. Photo coverage is about equal. The Chinese have apparently launched some of these types of space craft; the first one was probably in September 1982. France has the technical capability to operate photo-reconnaissance systems. A programme of regional reconnaissance independent of the United States could well involve French technology. There have been suggestions in Japan that that country could build such satellites, perhaps encouraged by the need passively to reinforce its defensive systems and to join a regional monitoring programme.

Electronic Intelligence (ELINT): If photo-reconnaissance is the eye, then ELINT is the ear of the military commander. These satellites seek and monitor signals from each other's military communications, ground to air communications, air defence frequencies, radars and missile test signals. Long operating experience has given both superpowers the capability of identifying functions and habits of key signals and stations. This experience makes the work of the space ferrets that much easier and it helps to identify departures from routines – an important element in early warning and alert procedures.

Ocean Surveillance: This is a sometimes inexact form of Intelligence gathering and occasionally controversial (e.g. some satellites have on board nuclear reactors and there have been occasions when these have fallen back to earth rather than being boosted into a high graveyard orbit). The satellites are known as RORSAT (Radar Ocean Reconnaissance Satellite), EORSAT (Electronic Intelligence Ocean Reconnaissance Satellite) and NOSS (Naval Ocean Surveillance Satellite – an American system). The function is to track surface ships and relay numbers, courses and speeds. Limitations include distortion in particularly rough seas. Some Intelligence analysts have said that sea-states caused by little more than Force 7 winds may be enough to prevent accurate radar satellite coverage. EORSATs rely on picking up ships' transmissions. Therefore a flotilla commander can evade detection by switching off radars and signals during the period of the satellite's coverage.

Communications (COMSAT or SATCOM): The vast majority of Soviet and American military communications relies somewhere on a satellite link. Improvements to satellite links, the ability to bounce signals from one satellite to another and the miniaturisation of receiver units mean that everybody who needs it will soon have the option of linking to satcom (satellite communication). Perhaps as much as 80 per cent of American military signalling goes via satellite; the Soviet military is not so reliant on satcom. Satellites are able to act as space-based answering machines (known as store dumping) so that messages may be left on the satellite for operational commanders to pick up when convenient. Typical orbits: Soviet Molniya communications satellite has maximum height of 29,840 km (apogee) and minimum altitude (perigee) of 506 km. Weighs 1,000 kg. Soviet Raduga 10 (launched October 9, 1981) had circular orbit of about 35,800 km. Latest communication satellites (both American and Russian) allow commanders to hold four-way 'conversation' with ground, air, surface-ship and submarine forces.

Meteorological (METSAT): Useful for weather forecasting and essential for reading weather situations in parts of a war theatre where forces are about to operate. Accuracy achieved would have to be good enough to allow missile commanders to correct rocket flight trajectories to compensate for wind and water vapour during a flight.

Navigational (NAVSAT): Both superpowers have established constellations of NAVSATs and are updating them. These are able to fix positions to within 20 metres. New systems allow soldiers to know exactly where they are and, at the other extreme, for submariners to feed into missile computers exact starting points of flights to target. The navigational systems have, or will have, secondary functions such as nuclear explosion detection and maybe the ability to provide data for damage assessment following a nuclear attack.

Anti-Satellite (ASAT): ASAT systems are operational in the Soviet Union and in the final development stages in the United States.

The Soviet system is based on the SS-9 rocket (in its ASAT role known as SL-11) which would launch a 'hunter-killer' satellite into orbit. The satellite would meet the enemy satellite and either hit it or explode in its path. The American system has been tested extensively; it is a combination of aircraft and 'hittile'. A converted F-15 jet would carry a missile to a high altitude. The missile would seek out the satellite and hit it (hence hittile) with a non-nuclear warhead. Neither the Soviet nor the American system has to be able to destroy the satellite. The only object is to stop it functioning and to prevent it from being repaired by remote control. So far, both superpowers have systems that could attack low orbiting satellites (reconnaissance and ocean surveillance, for example). High orbiting (communications, navigational craft, etc.) are safe from the existing ASATs. However, it is argued that the technology is available to devise systems to attack even geo-stationary craft. It would be possible to send up 'space mines', satellites that would be activated only in wartime, that could then be directed to destroy the high orbiting system. It is said that these space mines could not hide because occasional signals would be transmitted to and from the craft for routine 'housekeeping' work. However, there are few technical reasons why they should not be deployed; a space mine could be disguised as a malfunctioning satellite, or have no official description. There is nothing in international law which insists that an artificial earth satellite's function and role has to be declared. Or it could be blatantly deployed as a 'mine'. Another area of ASAT is emerging from technology associated with Strategic Defence Initiative (SDI) research. Many of the basic systems under examination, including ground-based lasers, could be used as ASATs. There is some evidence to suggest that the Soviet Union has used lasers to interfere with American military satellites in polar orbit.

Strategic Defence Initiative (SDI): An American term, sometimes called Star Wars, for a U.S. research programme that is looking at the possibility that advanced weapons might destroy enemy ballistic missiles. The Soviet Union has been working on a similar project for some years. Both superpowers appear to be working along the same lines to produce a combination of directed energy beams, e.g. lasers, and advanced information-handling processes that would allow weapons to be produced that could identify, track and attack missiles in their earliest stages of flight.

Ideally, say the engineers, the attack should take place shortly after lift-off, the so-called boost phase of the missile. There are few ways of knowing exactly how much effort the Russians are putting into their programme. The dollar technology of the Americans would be expected to put them ahead in this particular space race. However, there have been occasions when the same advantages have been wasted.

*

The United States were beaten into space by the Russians. Many of the spectacular 'firsts' went to the Soviet Union, partly because the Americans suffered greatly from over-confidence, inter-Service rivalries, political indecision and duplicated effort. The history of space invasion since October 1957 has been one of anticipation, enormous technological advances and huge bills. It has, too, been one of nervousness on the part of those who watched space being used as an experimental environment in the arms race. There appeared to be easy ways in which international agreements and protocols would protect that environment. Some legislation did put a brake on space-based development, although the economic and scientific constraints were equally protective. Furthermore, without the technological proof, few could make out impressive cases for providing extra restrictions which might apply only to systems that were yet to be developed.

Society in normal times expresses its greatest satisfaction when its members stick to widely accepted norms of behavioural constraints. Even successful revolution against the consequences of those constraints has to replace them with others – in some instances, more draconian. The paradox of a 'free' society is that it is maintained only by enormous bolts of legislation. Therefore society, once faced with a real or imagined threat to its stability, turns to the statute book for protection. The complication arises when the threat is man-made and has to be maintained. It is at this point when, in theory at least, societies' trust in the legislative process is most vulnerable.

The history of superpower arms control shows few if any examples when anything other than political and military values played an effective part in the decision to discuss specific issues and even fewer examples of public opinion influencing the outcome of those decisions. This may have a lot to do – perhaps almost everything to do – with the fact that arms control is very much the domain of the United States and the Soviet Union. Even on those occasions when other countries have been involved, the agreements of Moscow and Washington had decided the outcome of the most multilateral discussions.

One obvious illustration is to be found in the Stockholm Conference on Security Co-operation and Disarmament in Europe. The Conference was tasked to find ways in which so-called confidence building measures could be established and existing ones improved between the superpower blocs. For example, by having an improved 'Hot Line' between Washington and Moscow and regular inspections by military observers of manoeuvres, the chances of misunderstandings might be reduced and therefore war by miscalculation become less likely. Every state in Europe other than that of Albania went to the Conference. Each state recognised that in a nuclear weapons age (more particularly, in an age of possible nuclear fall-out) no country can expect to be protected by its political neutrality and non-alignment. Therefore, each state had the right to make major contributions to the outcome of the talks. Yet in practice, unless the two superpowers were *inclined* towards any agreement, the views of the 33 other states, although considered, would not prevail. There can be no agreement without the nod of approval from Washington and Moscow – that is what being a superpower is about.

From these difficulties and anomalies, we can deduce some of the enormous problems facing those who would wish to have strict international control on the further development of space as a vast adventure playground for the military:

- there is little or no public and, in some cases, government understanding of the issues.
- there is little widespread public perception and debate of any need for international constraints.
- there is nothing to 'touch' in the world of space militarisation, therefore without a 'Greenham Common' of space systems the protest theatre cannot be played out to illustrate opposition and to attract the attention of others.
- smaller countries are as yet unclear about the significance of space systems in general and so have not joined any enquiry into the effects on themselves and their futures.
- the concerns that are voiced tend to focus on the American

SDI programme which in fact gets in the way of the wider issues.
- the major space systems are in the hands of the superpowers and therefore they must necessarily control the language and conditions for agreements.

It could be argued that this superpower control makes the possibility of new arms control measures easier to come by and old ones more likely to be observed. In a two-horse race the emphasis on limiting legislation has its attractions if it can protect both against huge advances over the other. However, as with nuclear weapons, there is emerging a two-tier level of proliferation in space systems – horizontal and vertical proliferation.

In the jargon of nuclear weapons strategy, proliferation means the increase in the numbers of those weapons. Vertical proliferation is the increase in warheads owned by the established nuclear powers, the U.S.A., the U.S.S.R.. the U.K., France and China. Horizontal proliferation is the spread, or possible spread, of nuclear weapons to other countries, e.g. Israel, South Africa, India, Pakistan, Argentina and Brazil. Military space systems are subject to the same degree of proliferation. The superpowers are busy adding to their capabilities, thus fuelling vertical proliferation through, for example, increased Anti-Satellite (ASAT) systems and whatever becomes of both Soviet and American research into beam weapons. The spread of technology is adding to the horizontal proliferation. China, Japan, France and India are four countries quite capable of developing reconnaissance satellites and ASAT weapons. This proliferation is to be the Third Force in space.

It might be possible to show that, by developing, say, independent reconnaissance satellites those countries, the Third Force, would in time of tension or war find those systems threatened and even attacked by superpowers nervous of the information available to third parties and the all-possible transfer of that information to either Moscow or Washington. This may be stretching the argument against independent space development, yet it has real significance when the option and hopes for peaceful uses of this spreading technology are considered.

It would be too easy to call for a ban on all space systems with some military use and it would be wrong to do so. Many military systems have peaceful uses and, in some ways, preserve peace

– or so it may be argued. Navigational satellites developed by and for the armed services may be used by commercial shipping and airlines. Ocean surveillance from space can be used to track drug- and gun-runners or to help in search and rescue operations. Technical advances in military communications may be passed on to civilian users. Even spy satellites have enormous value because they can, and are, used to check that existing arms control agreements are being honoured. And all the time the superpowers maintain sophisticated orbiting early warning systems, then the less likely one or other of them would be tempted to launch a surprise attack.

Given that some military systems have peaceful purposes, one way of safeguarding confidence in that peace may be to draw up legislation that would protect, rather than ban, military satellites. Another way would be to spread the safeguards to countries other than the superpowers, to the Third Force countries.

There are some who would have a treaty protecting satellites because of their frequent desire to ban new kinds of weaponry. An ASAT treaty in its most comprehensive form would ban any weapons or systems that damage, degrade or destroy a satellite. This is one more simple-sounding proposal that is full of difficulties on close examination. If we take the two Anti-Satellite weapons declared by the Soviet Union and the United States and ban them and their like then that would seem to be the end of the matter. How simple to produce a document which declares: 'No state can have anti-satellite weapons. Sign here!' The problems start to show themselves with the age-old confusion over definitions. What is an ASAT weapon? The Soviet SS-9-mounted hunter-killer satellite and the American F-15 flown missile are easily labelled. But what about weapons or even other satellites that could do as much damage if they were so programmed even though their normal functions have nothing to do with ASAT systems? In theory, and as we have seen in earlier pages, once the technique of space docking was perfected, then the ability to manoeuvre close enough to another craft went some way towards developing an ASAT weapon. Of course, the hunted satellite can be manoeuvred out of harm's way but the hunter may get close enough to degrade the systems on board. Also, a reconnaissance satellite that is being manoeuvred to avoid attack has to have a very comprehensive and resource-consuming group of ground monitors that can track all potential attackers.

Yet another problem is that a manoeuvring satellite has difficulty in performing its set tasks and it must be remembered that the hunter may have no other instructions than to degrade the hunted's operational ability rather than destroy. It could be even undesirable to destroy a satellite in a period of rising tension. This could lead to war, whereas the task of harassment may be nothing more than a way of making it difficult for an enemy to track ground movements or sea deployments that are preparations for defence rather than a signal for attack.

Taken two stages further, the problem of definition is increased. It has been shown that some early work on SDI overlaps with ASAT technology. The direct energy programmes in both the Soviet Union and the United States are a clear example of ASAT weapons research being in its infancy. By the end of this century, probably by 1995, present ASAT techniques will seem as appropriate as the steam-driven car – workable, but well below the state of modern technology. The June 1985 laser experiment using a reflector window in space shuttle was one example of what the Americans call the state of the art catching and almost overtaking existing conventional research. The laser was a simple test, the ability to use computers to adjust it was the important aspect. Although the U.S. laser experiment was not directly connected with ASAT research there was a clear indication that it could be adapted quite easily once the computer technology was resolved.

Here again is a case of some draft treaty having to consider research in other areas.

Considering all these problems a number of obvious questions arise. Is it necessary to have an anti-satellite treaty? Could not existing international agreements do the same job? Could any future treaty be verified – especially as research programmes are impossible to verify to the satisfaction of everybody? Would an ASAT treaty be anything more than a declaration of intent rather than an effectual ban on potentially destabilising systems?

It would seem essential to produce an anti-satellite treaty as soon as possible. The major purpose of such an agreement would not, as many have campaigned for, be a means to protect space from the military, it would be to act as a means of preventing war and, if it failed to help do that, then to reduce the possibilities of a conventional conflict running to a nuclear war.

In time of superpower tension, the essential functions of communications and Intelligence-gathering would be an enormous contribution to maintaining whatever stability remained in the world and perhaps improving on it. We have seen how important are photo and electronic reconnaissance satellites and the upmost reliance placed on satellites for command, control and communications. At this point we depart from the usual considerations of using these space craft in a war-fighting role. In a crisis that has not broken into military conflict, these same satellites would be used to assess the situation, deployment and readiness state of the forces of the potential enemy. Those assessments may be translated into an analysis of the other side's intentions, or, more accurately, his military options. The communications systems keep everybody informed, thus adding to confidence rather than inducing uncertainty and misunderstanding.

The military commander, while recognising the value of his reconnaissance and communications satellites as a means of maintaining stability, would understand that the other side's systems posed a military threat. The balance between threat and stabilising factor would have to be considered carefully, yet it is very possible that, given the ASAT technology held by both sides, a pre-emptive attack on the satellites would be militarily tempting – and relatively simple.

It could be argued that such a strike would demonstrate a degree of resolve that would deter the other side from going to war. As no troops would be killed, no territory lost and perhaps no immediate public awareness of what had happened, then there is a grain of reason in this suggestion.

Equally, it is difficult to imagine that an attack on a satellite should go unanswered by a retaliatory attack. There are few who would be willing to guarantee that the conflict would end at that point. Indeed, the very argument that no territory nor lives would be lost, therefore escalation is unlikely, looks very weak, particularly because the idea of losing territory and people is the more acceptable concept of deterrence.

A further, and extraordinarily important, point of danger is that an ASAT attack would be so tempting for the reasons already stated, that the tried although strained processes of diplomacy may easily be usurped. Again it may be said that an attack that sheds no blood might be used as a demonstration of resolve in support of diplomatic efforts to resolve the crisis. Few would expect the outcome to be anything other than escalation to war on earth. It is very difficult to disregard the chain of events that would follow and very possibly, perhaps probably, lead to nuclear exchange.

Consequently, the thought must remain that, of the military scenarios for the start of a nuclear war, an Anti-Satellite attack would appear to be high on the list of serious possibilities.

It could be said that the essential satellites are protected. The ABM Treaty and the Strategic Arms Limitation Treaties agreements state that neither side shall interfere with 'national technical means of verification'. These are considered to be the very Intelligence-gathering satellites that are used to check that both sides are observing arms control treaties. Those same satellites have a support function for military commanders as well as a verification role. However, these satellites are not as protected by the existing treaties as some have argued. The satellites would appear to be protected only in their role as part of the verification process. In time of tension, the space craft would be seen to have a purely military function. Furthermore, treaties containing those protection clauses have limited life spans and may be ignored (the ABM Treaty is such an example). When the treaties go, so does the satellite protection. Here, then, seems to be further reason for an anti-satellite treaty.

One of the constant objections put forward by the United States is that of verification. It is often said that a small element of cheating in a strategic agreement makes little difference to the overall stability that such a treaty might inspire. However, an anti-satellite force would not have to be very large. The numbers of targets are limited and once open conflict started then launch bases would be obvious targets for more conventional forms of weapons; and the chances would be that most if not all agreements could easily be forgotten. Therefore, to verify a treaty that would cover a small number of systems would be even more demanding than trying to safeguard a more complicated agreement. It has to be remembered that an anti-satellite system could easily be disguised as, or incorporated into, another weapons programme. Given the degree of openness in the United States, it is probable that the Soviet Union could be more easily satisfied that the agreement was being observed, than would the United States about Soviet compliance; yet this is always likely to be the problem between the superpowers and cannot forever be used as a reason for not reaching agreements.

Making an enormous assumption that both sides would accept verification norms that would, ironically, include a clause protecting satellites, what ways are there of producing an anti-satellite treaty?

The most obvious answer would be an immediate ban on testing weapons and the eventual dismantling of existing systems, the support and bureaucratic programmes that go with them, a ban on testing of ASAT technology itself and the introduction of data exchanges that would allow all parties to a treaty a degree of certainty that the agreement was observed. There are, as has been shown on other pages, enormous loopholes to be found in such simplicity. The problems of definitions and the confusion between ASAT and other forms of space technology are but two areas for disagreement. The added problem is that a great deal of the SDI programme and its Soviet equivalent would be curbed by such an agreement.

These problems point to difficulties in achieving an agreement, they do not however rule out such an agreement. Indeed it must be recognised that even a limited protocol with all the imperfections that might be imagined should be high on the agenda of international arms control. Intelligence-gathering and communications satellites are here to stay. There is too much commitment simply to declare that, instead of banning ASAT weapons, why not ban satellites? Apart from the reality of the situation, military satellites do have an important role to play in international stability. It is this international interest that leads to the next two stages of discussion in an ASAT treaty: who should negotiate such an agreement and who should be involved in the verification process?

It is always assumed that the superpowers are the two countries to decide the terms of an ASAT Treaty. It is said that the United States and the Soviet Union have the technology and the hardware, therefore they occupy the seats at the negotiating table. Why should this continue to be so?

Just as even the smallest states cannot be protected by their neutrality and non-alignment from a nuclear war started by 'conventional' means, so they cannot be protected from one started by 'unconventional' means, i.e. anti-satellite weapons. Moreover, the spread of space technology is faster than the spread of nuclear weapons power. There are many countries other than the United States and the Soviet Union in space. More are on the way to becoming 'space nations' – the Third Force in the debate. Some countries may feel it in their national interests to develop Intelligence-gathering satellites and anti-satellite weapons, both relatively simple projects; France, China and Japan are examples of such countries. Equally important, the list of satellite owners and co-owners is so enormous that it would be difficult to find many countries in the industrial and semi-industrial world without some link to space.

So, apart from the overall threat posed by an anti-satellite system, many countries may feel that their interests are sufficiently in need of some protection to put their pens to an ASAT agreement – which would mean perhaps a seat at the negotiating table.

If an ASAT negotiation were to take in other countries, then a model for that discussion might be found in Stockholm, where the Conference on Security, Co-operation and Disarmament in Europe is due to end in the summer of 1986. That meeting of 35 nations, including the superpowers, was established with the modest aims of establishing confidence between the two superpower blocs so that war by misunderstanding and miscalculation might be avoided. It would appear that this same sentiment would apply to the protection of satellites. It would make a deal of sense to widen the scope of international discussion to take in confidence-building measures that might lead to more exchanges of observers, technical and military data and general explanation in areas where lack of certainty could be added to suspicion elsewhere and lead to incorrect assumptions and therefore war. There can be few serious objections to space systems being included in this wider gathering of confidence-building measures.

There is a point of further consideration that could force the superpowers to give way on a wider discussion of an ASAT agreement. The most logical progression of the peaceful uses of Intelligence satellites is, as we have seen, for countries other than the U.S.A. and the U.S.S.R. to launch them. If, or more likely when, other countries get their own Intelligence-gathering satellites then there will be a more international rather than a superpower need for legislation to protect them.

But is it possible that such craft would be launched only by a handful of states who have some independent security concerns? It is possible to imagine South Africa, Israel, India and perhaps Japan wishing to keep their own eyes on adjacent states; but there are not many other countries that could consider the cost worthwhile. An added problem is that, although the technology to build a satellite is relatively easy to come by, no Intelligence satellite is truly independent unless the country has its own means of launching. A satellite is one thing, a launch system is very much another. However, there is an area for further consideration: multi-national co-operation that excludes the superpowers.

The idea of countries coming together to use satellites for monitoring was considered during the late 1970s. It is time that a more sophisticated and detailed examination of the problems, but above all of the advantages of joint satellite observations, was undertaken. Such an examination might well take in some of the following issues.

The superpowers keep a constant watch on each other for military and commercial reasons, in fact the two are bound. A detailed assessment by satellite of Soviet harvests or industrial construction and infrastructure including road and rail links, and fuel stocks, allows the United States to judge more accurately how Soviet resources are being used. This in turn can, and should, be used in an overall assessment of the Soviet Union's ambitions and what is being done to achieve them. Consequently, a more detailed assessment of priorities allows one country to be a little more sophisticated about its perception of the most difficult area of all strategic Intelligence analysis: a potential enemy's intentions. The priority of superpower satellite monitoring remains, however, with military information. The satellite does not 'shut its eyes' when it passes states other than the other superpower. Many more nations are under surveillance than is realised; from such satellite monitoring Intelligence reports are produced; including classified American reports on some of her allies. The same is true of the Soviet Union's observations of her friends.

All this is possible because the superpowers have a monopoly of satellite monitoring that has the high definition instruments needed for detailed Intelligence-gathering. Even though they scan other countries, both superpowers object strongly to third countries developing the capability of looking down on America and the Soviet Union. Yet those third countries could be playing a valuable role in world stability were they to have the satellite capability.

They could, for example, monitor arms control agreements and provide an independent system of verification. But, because no single country could afford to build, maintain and expand its own space Intelligence system, the way forward, or indeed upward, should be on a regional basis. The emphasis should be on regions in the broadest meaning of the term. It would not be a good idea to have, say, a European consortium of NATO states. The credibility of the result of their analysis would be suspect; such a system could lead to unnecessary transAtlantic friction.

The basic needs of such an organisation are self-evident. A group of countries which includes representatives of neutral and non-aligned states should be invited to establish a Regional Observation Group, which we might call R.O.G., something along the lines once suggested by the French government. It should be independent of existing power-bloc organisations although, realistically, the technically advanced states within the group would inevitably be members or associated with blocs.

The Regional Observation Group would be responsible for monitoring military developments within the region. At the lower end of the scale, this would be done by feeding, into a central secretariat, reports from embassies, electronic listening agencies and general overtly gathered Intelligence reports – this is the kind of operation in which most if not all states indulge as a matter of course. It is at the most sophisticated level, where there should be set up a satellite monitoring system. To do this, as we have seen, the R.O.G. would need three facilities: satellite technology, independent launching systems and an analysis centre and distribution unit.

The satellite technology exists. The capability to build a near-earth orbiting satellite able to photograph broad land areas has been operational in Europe and the Far East for some time. France could easily be the European leader in this area; Japan in the Far East. The more sophisticated sensors needed to gather positive military Intelligence would be simple to develop given the enormous resources available in Europe and Asia. In Europe, for example, there is an organisation called the Independent European Programme Group (I.E.P.G.). Its function is to develop ways in which European states can have military equipment at more reasonable prices by industrial and political co-operation. It is identified with the North Atlantic Treaty Organisation but there is little reason why it should not be expanded or used as a model for the sort of commercial and political consortium necessary to produce the technology for an independent Regional Observation Group.

As to a launch facility, that too exists. The French have developed what appears to be a reliable launching system and France would wish to have it available for an R.O.G. which would be involved with the future financing. Oddly, the biggest problem of the three facilities would not be the huge scientific and technical adventure of building the satellites and launching them; it would be the ground base for the gathering and analysis of the information.

A ground base would need to be in a country that was non-aligned, or as near non-aligned as can be imagined in this time of blurred political understandings. Location would be a very political decision as would be the use of the information. Some countries might believe that the raw Intelligence should be given to individual members of the R.O.G. and that it would be up to them to publicise it or not. Others would think that, for the organisation to be effective, then the results of the satellite observations should be presented as a joint analysis.

Let us imagine how a problem might arise: a R.O.G. Satellite report suggests that the Soviet Union has violated an existing arms control treaty; some non-aligned countries may not wish to jeopardise their reputation for neutrality by being involved in the implied criticism. Similarly, supposing a R.O.G. satellite contradicts claims made by the U.S.A. that the U.S.S.R. has violated a treaty; a traditional ally of Washington may not wish that information to be broadcast. Furthermore, political persuasions of a R.O.G. member may change enough for a newly elected government to have reservations about information distribution.

A further point of consideration would be the auspices of the organisation and therefore its data distribution. At first glance, it would be sensible to set up an R.O.G. within the framework of the United Nations. But both superpowers would veto its establishment. Moreover, the lacklustre bureaucratic system associated with the U.N. would in some ways detract from the operational efficiency of the R.O.G. Yet it would be wrong not to think of it as a multi-regional system. A European R.O.G. (E.R.O.G.) could be linked to an Asian Regional Observer Group (A.R.O.G.). Remembering that the satellite monitoring would be supported by more basic Intelligence-gathering, then membership could be widespread. Satellite ownership would not be the only passport to a R.O.G.

Undoubtedly, the greatest contribution of a system such as R.O.G. would be to international stability via what are commonly called C.B.M.s, Confidence Building Measures. Suspicion *between* the superpowers is not an unreasonable instinct. Suspicion *of* the superpowers is an equally reasonable instinct to be found in most other nations – including the closest allies of America and the Soviet Union. A system of independent monitoring headed by a satellite monitoring network would in the long term provide an important way of looking at suspicions and perhaps curbing some of the more adventuresome actions that encourage those suspicions.

If some of this reads too much like an ideal without a chance of practical application, then that is understandable. There has been a justifiable cynicism abroad that the superpowers will go their own ways whatever others think and would wish. Perhaps, though, the technology that has helped the powers to acquire the super prefix is spreading beyond their control to the Third Force in space development. Economic, political and even social pressures might be reaching a point when the thinking is right for such ideas as a Regional Observation Group to make practical sense, rather than for it to be a grand scheme with few takers, other than those with the most to gain. The truth is that every country would have something to gain.

The militarisation of space has produced enormous potential advances in stability, but with the one weakness that both sides see a need to be able to destroy those very systems that can help guarantee that stability in time of tension. The spread of nuclear weaponry to every system from long-range rockets to small battlefield artillery pieces is directly linked to the consequences of protecting space-based systems.

There is no magic wand that can obliterate the technical memory that builds nuclear weapons. There is no way in which the technology of space systems and advance weaponry that will be used directly or indirectly in space can be effectively shelved in the long term. Consequently, there is an urgent need to put sensible controls on the use of that technology. A comprehensive treaty to protect satellites is essential. It has to be constructed in such a way that it would apply in times of crisis and, equally, in time of war. It may be said that, in war, all treaties are swept aside. This is no reason to ignore the problem and no reason to believe that effective legislation on the deployment of anti-satellite technology cannot be found. Technology has advanced space science too far for a fool-proof treaty to be found. There is, however, much to be said for getting the best legislation possible, which in itself may introduce the element of stability missing today, and which would in some way compensate for the loopholes most surely to be found.

It might be argued that the biggest danger of nuclear war between now and the end of the twentieth century is to be found in two areas. The spread of nuclear weapons beyond the existing five nuclear powers may so easily lead to conflict inspired by irrational reason with no regard for the consequences. The caution of the super nuclear powers may not be copied by the soon-to-be nuclear powers. Secondly, such a conflict – either an East–West confrontation or a regional war – could so easily begin by misunderstanding and miscalculation. The ability of almost any country to manage a crisis is perhaps the weakest element in strategic, political and military planning. And we have seen how military and political management is more than ever reliant on space systems.

It is no longer acceptable that the need to safeguard those systems should be so dependent on the attitude and political differences within and between the two superpowers. There is room to improve existing legislation and to provide new norms of agreement. If no pressures are applied for the necessary safeguards, then the consequences will truly rain down on those who did not concern themselves.

Glossary

The following glossary covers terms, systems and organizations found in this book. In addition other acronyms and abbreviations have been included for those who are less than familiar with the general jargon of strategic affairs.

ABM	Anti Ballistic Missile
ACDA	Arms Control & Disarmament Agency
ADC	Air Defence Command (old title)
AEC	Atomic Energy Commission
AEW	Airborne Early Warning
AFB	Air Force Base
ALBM	Air Launched Ballistic Missile
ALCM	Air Launched Cruise Missile
ARPA	Advanced Research Projects Agency (old title)
ASAT	Anti-satellite
ASW	Anti Submarine Warfare
AWACS	Airborne Warning & Control Systems
BAMBI	Ballistic Missile Boost Intercept
BMD	Ballistic Missile Defence
BMEWS	Ballistic Missile Early Warning System
CEP	Circular Error Probable
C^3I	Command, Control, Communications and Intelligence (pron. C-cubed I)
CIA	Central Intelligence Agency
CinC	Commander in Chief
CSCE	Conference on Security and Co-operation in Europe
CSOC	Consolidated Space Operations Centre
CTB	Comprehensive Test Ban
DARPA	Defense Advanced Research Projects Agency
DEW	Directed Energy Weapon
DIA	Defense Intelligence Agency
ECM	Electronic Counter Measures
EHF	Extremely High Frequency

ELF	Extremely Low Frequency
ELINT	Electronic Intelligence
EORSAT	Electronic Ocean Reconnaissance Satellite
FEBA	Forward Edge of the Battle Area
FOBS	Fractional Orbital Bombardment System
GEODSS	Ground-based Electro-Optical Deep Space Surveillance
GLCM	Ground Launched Cruise Missile
ICBM	Intercontinental Ballistic Missile
IISS	International Institute for Strategic Studies
INF	Intermediate (range) Nuclear Forces
INTELSA	International Telecommunications Satellite
IRBM	Intermediate Range Ballistic Missile
ITV	Instrumented Test Vehicle
KH	Keyhole (satellites)
KT	Kiloton
MAD	Mutually Assured Destruction
MBFR	Mutual and Balanced Force Reductions
MHV	Miniature Homing Vehicle
MIDAS	Missile Defense Alarm System
MIRV	Multiple Independently Targeted Reentry Vehicle
MOL	Manned Orbital Laboratory
MX	Missile Experimental (officially called Peacemaker, although more commonly, MX)
NASA	National Aeronautics and Space Administration.
NATO	North Atlantic Treaty Organization
NORAD	North American Air Defense Command
NPG	Nuclear Planning Group (NATO)
NPT	Non Proliferation Treaty
NRL	Naval Research Laboratory
NRO	National Reconnaissance Office
NSA	National Security Agency

NSAM	National Security Action Memorandum
NSC	National Security Council
NSDD	National Security Decision Directive
OSS	Office of Strategic Services
PBW	Particle Beam Weapon
PD	Presidential Directive
PVO	Protivozdushnaya Oborona (Soviet Air Defence)
R&D	Research and Development
RORSAT	Radar Ocean Reconnaissance Satellite
SAC	Strategic Air Command
SAINT	Satellite Inspector
SALT	Strategic Arms Limitation Treaty
SAM	Surface to Air Missile
SAMOS	Satellite and Missile Observation System
SDI	Strategic Defense Initiative
SIGINT	Signals Intelligence
SIOP	Single Integrated Operational Plan
SIPRI	Stockholm International Peace Research Institute
SLBM	Submarine or Sea-Launched Ballistic Missile
SSBN	Ballistic Nuclear Missile Submarine
SSN	Nuclear Powered Submarine (SS = sub surface)
STS	Space Transportation System (Shuttle)
START	Strategic Arms Reduction Talks
TTBT	Threshold Test Ban Treaty
UHF	Ultra High Frequency
ULF	Ultra Low Frequency
VHF	Very High Frequency
VLF	Very Low Frequency
WTO	Warsaw Treaty Organization

Short Bibliography

The Royal Aircraft Establishment Table of Earth Satellites, D. G. King-Hele, J. A. Pilkington, D. M. C. Walker, H. Hiller & A. N. Winterbottom, Macmillan, London, 1983.

Outer Space – a New Dimension of the Arms Race, Ed. Bhupendra Jasani, SIPRI, Taylor & Francis, London, 1982.

Space Weapons and U.S. Strategy, Paul B. Stares, Croom Helm, London, 1985.

The Viking Rocket Story, Milton W. Rosen, Faber, London, 1956.

The Memoirs of Richard Nixon, Richard Nixon, Sidgwick & Jackson, London, 1978.

Deadly Gambits, Strobe Talbott, Knopf, New York, 1984.

The New High Ground, Thomas Karas, Simon & Schuster, New York, 1983.

Russian Space Exploration – the first 21 years, Julian Popescu, Gothard House, Henley-on-Thames, 1979.

The Puzzle Palace, James Bamford, Houghton Mifflin, Boston, 1982.

Jane's Spaceflight Directory, Ed. Reginald Turnill, Jane's, London, 1984.

Space Exploration, Salamander, London, 1983.

U.S. Intelligence and the Soviet Strategic Threat, Lawrence Freedman, Macmillan, London, 1977.

The Right Stuff, Tom Wolfe, Bantam, New York, 1980.

The Center, Stewart Alsop, Hodder & Stoughton, London, 1968.

Index